D1430883

PRAISE FOR
On Parole

"A small, stark novel full of tiny, careful details—an ink-brush portrait painted in infinite shades of gray...Seamlessly translated...This is an austerely graceful book, one which should help cement Yoshimura's reputation here and bring over more of his 20 bestselling novels in its wake."
—*The Washington Post Book World*

"A finely calibrated portrait of a taciturn man whose emotional life has been blighted by his imprisonment...Yoshimura's evocations of Japan's cities, jails, and workplaces are precise, and his spare, sensual prose has all of the intensity of poetry....A vivid psychological portrait...of a man no longer able to express his own will."
—*Publishers Weekly* (starred)

"Akira Yoshimura, who is a bestseller, a prizewinner and a literary doyen in his native Japan, has his readers off balance right from the start in this neat, bleak novel....The abrupt and shocking end is a large part of what gives Yoshimura's book its energy....It's a measure of Yoshimura's mastery that we're disturbed and fascinated....The more Yoshimura writes about, say, railway timetables, the more we're transfixed by what the man on the train might do next."
—Michael Pye, *The New York Times Book Review*

On Parole

Also by Akira Yoshimura

SHIPWRECKS

ONE MAN'S JUSTICE

AKIRA YOSHIMURA

On Parole

Translated from the Japanese
by Stephen Snyder

A Harvest Book
HARCOURT, INC.
San Diego   New York   London

Kari-Shakuhō by Akira Yoshimura
© 1988 by Akira Yoshimura
Original Japanese edition published by Shincho-Sha Co., Ltd.
English translation rights arranged with Akira Yoshimura
through Writers House, Inc/Japan Foreign-Rights Centre
English translation copyright © 1999 by Harcourt, Inc.

Library of Congress Cataloging-in-Publication Data
Yoshimura, Akira, 1927–
[Kari–shakuhō. English]
On parole/Akira Yoshimura; translated from the Japanese by Stephen Snyder.
p.   cm.
ISBN 0-15-100270-3   ISBN 0-15-601147-6 (pbk.)
I. Title.
PL865.O72K3713   2000
895.6'35—DC21   99-25991

Text set in Goudy
Designed by Linda Lockowitz
Printed in the United States of America
First Harvest edition 2000
A C E G H F D B

On Parole

The air on his skin was unfamiliar and left him strangely agitated. Though the shutters and the glass door to the hallway were closed, drafts seemed to swirl about the room. It had been a long time since he had slept in a futon laid out on tatami mats, and the musty smell of the straw was pleasant, but at the same time the mats seemed insubstantial beneath him, as if a wind were blowing under the floor.

The room he had occupied until that morning measured less than seventy square feet: concrete walls on three sides and chipped, gray iron bars facing the corridor. What air there was should have come in that way, but none did, as if a thick plastic panel had been placed over the bars. The air was utterly still, stirring slightly only when he moved. Nevertheless, over the course of the long months and years he spent there, almost without realizing it, Shiro Kikutani came to feel a kind of peace. It was peace he felt when he lined up with the others to go to the workshop, or went out to the exercise yard to stand in the sun, or scrubbed himself in the showers; for in those places too he was shut off from the world, surrounded by the same high concrete walls.

For some time now he had felt the need to urinate, but he did not get up. Until last night he would have hopped out of bed and gone in the can in the corner of his cell. But now he was daunted at the thought of walking down the hall to a room marked by a wooden sign bearing the letters WC. The realization that he could open the door of his own free will and walk to the toilet without being watched by a guard filled him with something approaching terror.

The blackness he felt pressing in around him made him anxious as well. In fact it was not particularly dark, with light from the hallway coming in through the frosted-glass door, but to Kikutani the darkness seemed thick and inky. The cell he'd lived in until the night before was always bright, lit by a line of fluorescent lights in the corridor that cast the shadow of the bars on his bed. No doubt the light was meant for the guards who paced up and down the corridor keeping a close eye on the prisoners, but to Kikutani it brought a sense of security that helped him sleep. Tonight, however, though he was exhausted and almost feverish, he could not sleep. The darkness seemed to strangle him, and he found himself turning, mothlike, to look at the dim glow coming through the smoky glass.

He could hear a woman laughing somewhere. He listened more intently. She must be walking along the street in front of the building. She sounded drunk, laughing and screaming at someone. He realized now that a jumble of noises had been coming to him out of the darkness since he shut off the light: cars passing, people talking, a bell ringing on a train platform in the distance. The only sound that had reached him in his cell was the echoing of the boots of the guards on patrol. The noises outside now washed over him like a flood.

He turned over, and a pain shot through his abdomen; he would have to urinate soon. "You must learn to blend into society as quickly as possible." The admonition from his parole officer, Kiyoura, came back to him, and he realized how stupid he was to be lying there in pain. He was free to do as he liked now, and he didn't need to ask anyone's permission when he wanted to go to the toilet. Getting out of bed, he crossed the tatami and opened the glass panel. The guards had always opened the door of his cell, and he nearly panicked now as he did it himself. Once he was through the door, he steadied himself and set off down the hall. Faint breathing could be heard from the men sleeping behind the doors on either side.

He reached the wooden door, opened it, and stood before the toilet. As the urine gushed out, the ache in his bladder subsided, and he found himself staring at red and blue neon smudged on the tiny frosted window in front of him. Though it was quite late, the town seemed to be going about its noisy business. Nothing to be afraid of, he told himself as he studied the window.

He'd had a presentiment. For two years he thought of little else, trying to read the faces of the guards and the other people who worked in the prison, looking for clues as to when it might come.

According to the twenty-eighth article of the penal

code, once a prisoner served a third of his sentence, preparations for his parole would begin, though he was unlikely to be released until two-thirds of the sentence was served. For indefinite sentences such as Kikutani's—they were not unusual—once a prisoner served twelve or thirteen years, he would become eligible for parole. Everything depended, of course, on a clean record and good behavior.

Kikutani spent the first years of his sentence reliving his crime, the police investigation, the trial. He had received an indefinite sentence, but believed there had been a certain inevitability to his actions and felt no remorse. On the contrary, it seemed unfair to him that he should have to spend his days locked away in prison, and at times he nearly despaired. But when he reached the eighth year of his sentence, his attitude changed. He thought that he had grown accustomed to his surroundings—settled in, as it were—yet he would find himself losing his composure when he saw the joy in the face of a prisoner being released after serving only part of a long sentence. As he made his way to and from the workshop or stood in the exercise yard soaking up the sun, he would eye the high walls, knowing that beyond them people were living free lives. And when he saw planes taking off or landing at the airport nearby, he was painfully conscious that they carried people who were free to travel wherever they wished.

"Indefinite incarceration," his sentence had read, and the words seemed oppressive, but indefinite did not necessarily mean forever, and he clung to the hope that his time would be cut short by parole. A fly that had found its way into his cell landed on his foot, and as he stared at it, he felt a pang of envy for the freedom of this tiny insect.

Some prisoners with indefinite sentences became eligible for parole after fifteen years, and some had to wait as long as twenty. When the record was good, the prison officers in charge would send a report to the warden, who would file a petition with the provincial parole board. At some point, Kikutani learned about these procedures, and he set about trying to make a good impression on the guards, following every rule to the letter whenever they were watching.

Having taught Japanese at a high school, he was assigned to the print-shop section of the prison workhouse and put in charge of proofreading. The shop employed prisoners who, before their convictions, had been printers; there were also former government officials, businessmen, an electronics manufacturer, and a publisher. All these inmates, Kikutani included, were given ranks according to the privileges they had earned; with good behavior, they could work their way up from fourth to first rank. The first rank, which Kikutani reached in time, meant a private cell and permission to continue working after dinner. Kikutani would sit far into the night hunched over his papers, his pencil racing across the page.

In the autumn of his twelfth year in prison, an official came to the print shop and led him to a room in the prison office, where Kikutani found a short, older man in a dark-blue suit sitting behind a desk. When the official identified the man as the investigating officer for the parole board, Kikutani could feel himself flush. A visit from the parole board's investigative branch meant that the warden had petitioned the board on Kikutani's behalf and that the board had agreed to consider the case. This interview was the beginning of the procedure.

"My records indicate that you've been a model prisoner, but I'm curious to know how you've found prison life." The man's tone was almost respectful.

"Yes, sir," Kikutani managed, but that was all. His whole body had gone rigid.

"Your younger brother has come to see you a number of times, hasn't he? What do you talk about?"

"Different things," said Kikutani. He wanted to say more, but his mouth clenched shut. The man in the suit made no effort to draw Kikutani out. After a short silence, he rose from his chair.

"Take care of yourself, then," he said and, bowing slightly at the prison official, gathered up his black briefcase and left the room.

Back in the print shop, Kikutani was filled with regret that he hadn't been able to manage better answers to the man's questions. It was crucial to make a good impression on the investigating officer, and yet Kikutani had said nothing, made no impression at all.

In the fall of the following year, he was interviewed again. This time he had prepared something to say, but one look from the man and Kikutani was petrified, reduced again to monosyllables. Then, too, the questions themselves were pointless, trivial—Is your appetite good? Do you find the work interesting?—and no mention was made of parole. After that, there were no more visits from the investigating officer, and Kikutani began to wonder whether the process leading to his parole had stalled for some reason or perhaps been stopped altogether. Those days were anxious ones, as he lived with an unbearable mixture of hope and fear.

Two more years passed, and then last year, just as the summer heat was beginning, a parole officer in his forties named Kiyoura came to interview him. Kikutani was elated; in preparation for Kikutani's parole, the warden had sent a prisoner report to the head of the parole board's investigative branch, which appointed a parole officer to look into such matters as a guarantor for the prisoner and to see to his placement after his release. That this parole officer was now paying Kikutani a visit was evidence that the process was in motion.

Kiyoura announced that he was a Buddhist priest, but he hardly looked the part, wearing a good suit and having a full head of hair. Unlike the investigating officer's, his eyes were kind and his manner of speaking open and candid.

"Your brother is a good person, isn't he?" he asked, as if to weigh Kikutani's response.

"Yes," said Kikutani, realizing that Kiyoura must have gone to see his brother.

Half a dozen times a year Kiyoura came to visit Kikutani, bringing him books, clothes, and the like, and each time, when the interview was over, he would invariably say good-bye with a mournful look on his face.

He would motion for Kikutani to have a seat, but before Kikutani could sit, his eyes swung automatically to the guard for permission.

"Sit," said the guard, and Kikutani, with a bow to Kiyoura, sat. The parole officer would ask him a variety of questions: How was his health? What kind of work was he doing? What sorts of things gave him pleasure and what did he dislike? What did he think of the athletic meet they held in the prison each spring? As Kikutani answered briefly, Kiyoura would nod and smile. After twenty minutes or so, the interview came to an end.

"Make sure you get plenty of exercise and keep yourself healthy. I understand you'll be turning fifty in less than a month. I'll come again," said Kiyoura. Kikutani stood, bowed politely, and left with the guard. Back in the print shop, he forced himself to look at the galley proofs spread out on his desk, but his eyes were not following the words. Kiyoura's questions had been casual, and he'd said nothing to lead Kikutani to believe that he would be paroled soon. Perhaps Kiyoura was not allowed to drop any hints. Perhaps, even if Kikutani was to be paroled, it was still a long way off. Nevertheless, the fact that Kiyoura had contacted Kikutani's brother indicated that progress was being made, however slow the pace. It occurred to Kikutani that he should talk to his brother about this, so that night he wrote a short note on a postcard asking his brother to come to the prison. He gave it to a guard to mail.

The visit took place two weeks later. As he entered the room for the meeting, Kikutani was flustered to find Kiyoura standing behind his brother. The parole officer had instructed Kikutani's brother to report the contents of any letter he might receive from him, so no doubt Kiyoura knew about the postcard. His stern expression, so different from the one he'd worn at their previous meeting, worried Kikutani, but his brother behaved as if this were any other interview, asking first about his health before launching into a report on the family. The family was just Kikutani's brother and his brother's wife and their two daughters, since Kikutani's father had died before the "incident" occurred and

Kikutani's mother two years later. The elder of his nieces, he learned, had graduated from junior college in the spring and found work in a department store in a city an hour away by train. According to his brother, she was adapting to her new job quite nicely.

At this point, however, the conversation ended, and both brothers fell silent. When the time allotted for the interview had passed, Kikutani stood and, with a bow to Kiyoura, left the room. That night in bed, he kicked himself. He knew that the parole process was a slow one. The law required deliberation. He also assumed that they would be careful not to give a prisoner false hopes. Kiyoura must have come along with Kikutani's brother to make sure that Kikutani didn't learn something from him. The postcard had tipped Kiyoura off, but Kikutani had the feeling that Kiyoura could see through him anyway. It was quite likely that his release depended on the impression he made on Kiyoura, and now he began to realize that sending the postcard to his brother had been a reckless act.

The next three months he spent in unbearable suspense, but when Kiyoura appeared at the end of that time, the expression on his face set Kikutani somewhat at ease. Kiyoura's eyes were as gentle as the first time they met, and he was almost friendly as he gestured for Kikutani to have a seat. Kikutani could find nothing in Kiyoura's tone that suggested the postcard had hurt his chances.

Kiyoura wanted to talk about Kikutani's brother's family. After Kikutani's trial, his brother had resigned his teaching job at the vocational high school and taken work in the accounting office of a friend's construction company. The work was steady, and, after disposing of their mother's house, he had been able to build a small place just outside town. In his free time he liked to fish.

"Your sister-in-law seems reliable," Kiyoura said with a slight frown. His brother's wife was the daughter of one of Kikutani's colleagues at the high school; Kikutani himself had been responsible for getting them together. She was a very methodical person; she began saving for a house, tiny though the deposits were, almost from the moment they were married. She was the image of "reliable," as Kiyoura put it, but Kikutani thought he could detect a hint of disapproval in the parole officer's tone. The fact was that not once had she come to visit Kikutani in prison or so much as sent him a letter. It was safe to say that she felt a deep loathing for him, in the wake of his horrible crime, and would have preferred to sever all ties with him. No doubt his brother, out of respect for her feelings, had made a secret of his visits and of the packages he sent. Powerful memories of what Kikutani had done would linger in the old castle town, and it must have been difficult for the family to live with such humiliation. Kikutani found nothing strange in her rejection of him.

As they spoke, Kikutani studied Kiyoura's expression and began to realize that his sister-in-law represented a significant obstacle to his parole. Even if his brother was willing to serve as guarantor for his release, his sister-in-law would never allow it.

"Do you like chickens?" Kiyoura asked suddenly, looking up at Kikutani. "I mean, I suppose I should really be asking if you hate them."

"I wouldn't say I hate them...," said Kikutani, not quite sure what the question meant. Kiyoura looked thoughtfully out the window and then changed the subject.

Kikutani spent much of his free time over the next few days wondering why Kiyoura had mentioned chickens. He recalled that his mother, about the time he entered elementary school, began keeping a few chickens in the backyard in order to have fresh eggs to feed to his ailing father. It was Kikutani's job to collect the eggs from the henhouse and bring them to his father. Taking a still-warm egg, his father would carefully make a hole in one end with a needle; then, putting his mouth to the hole, he would suck out the contents. But this lasted only a short time, because the neighbors soon began complaining about the noise from the henhouse at dawn. His parents were forced to give up the chickens, but Kikutani still felt something approaching affection for the birds. Perhaps his brother, sharing those memories, had begun raising chickens at his house on the edge of town, prompting Kiyoura's idle remark.

Six months later, in another interview with Kiyoura, Kikutani learned just how important chickens were to be to his parole.

"There's no telling when this might be," Kiyoura began, choosing his words carefully, "but if you were to be released, how would you feel about working on a poultry farm?" At the word "release," Kikutani fell into a kind of stupor and was unable to answer. "The president of the company where your brother works has a friend who runs a chicken farm; they've spoken about your situation, and it seems he's willing to take you on. I've met him myself, and he's a fine person." Kiyoura's tone was subdued. Kikutani could feel his heart pounding in his chest, and he grew weak. He knew he had to say something, so he began, haltingly, to talk about the chickens of his childhood.

"I like chickens. I like them a lot," he blurted, but he could hear the exaggeration in his voice and felt that he was simply trying to ingratiate himself with Kiyoura, and he blushed with embarrassment.

That night, back in his cell, he buried his face in his pillow and wept. It had been the first time Kiyoura gave any hint that Kikutani might be paroled, and it even seemed that this could happen soon. He knew there was almost no chance that his brother would serve as his guarantor, but perhaps they had arranged for this man who ran the poultry farm to sponsor him instead. Kiyoura had probably been to see his brother a number of times, and had probably also called on others who were involved. Kikutani felt deeply grateful to him for having spent so much time and effort on his behalf.

From that day on, Kikutani noticed a marked change in the way the guards looked at him. Their eyes were softer, and sometimes they even seemed to smile at him. He imagined that they knew that he was up for parole and were glad for him.

Five days earlier, as he was getting on line after breakfast to go to the workshop, a guard came by to tell him to step out of line. He was sure he had noticed a certain softness in the guard's eyes. Kikutani was led through the prison offices to the room where inmates were interviewed and parole cases reviewed. Against one wall was a large desk where a white-haired man, the section chief, was seated, his underlings standing around him. As Kikutani approached, they all turned to look at him.

"Congratulations," said the chief, taking a letter from his

desk and standing to meet Kikutani, "your certificate of parole has arrived from the prefectural board. You'll be released in five days, March 25. We've notified your brother, so all you need do is follow instructions and make the necessary preparations." A warmth spread in Kikutani's chest, and his knees wobbled, as if he might slump to the floor at any moment. He nodded silently and shuffled out of the room as best he could, tears streaming down his face. "Congratulations," he could hear the guard repeat behind him. "Thanks," he managed to mutter, waving feebly as he made his way down the corridor.

That day he was moved from his cell to a special holding room for prisoners who were about to be released. These new quarters were equipped with a TV, a teapot, and even a mirror on the wall. He turned on the TV, but his eyes stared uncomprehendingly at the screen, and his mind was a blank. His body felt light, featherlike, abstracted from the material realities of his existence; the physical functions of breathing, eating, digesting, excreting were somehow unrelated to him. He was relieved of his duties in the workshop and given permission to go wherever he wanted in the prison, but when he was alone in his room, he would weep for no reason, or else pace in great agitation.

Overcome by an urge to tell someone about his impending release, he scrawled tiny characters on postcards and addressed them to Kiyoura and to his brother, who he imagined had already been notified. He wrote essentially the same thing to both, about his gratitude to the guards and others at the prison who had been responsible for him, but on Kiyoura's postcard he added special thanks for the role

Kiyoura had played in securing his parole. When he finished, out of habit from his long years as a proofreader, he carefully inspected each character.

He was given two small cardboard boxes and told to pack his clothes and other personal belongings. From the thirty or so books he had accumulated, he chose the Japanese and English dictionaries, a guide to classical grammar, and a volume of history; the rest he gathered up and carried to the prison library, where he handed them over to the inmate in charge.

Late in the afternoon of the third day after he was moved to the temporary cell, his brother came to see him. "I'm happy for you," his brother said when they faced each other through the wire screen. Kikutani, his face covered with tears, could only nod. Before the interview, his brother had been to the prison office to make arrangements for what Kikutani would wear on the day he was released. The suit and shoes he wore when he arrived had been wrapped in heavy, oiled paper and held for him; but fifteen years and seven months had passed since then, and the material of the suit had deteriorated and the shoes had turned dry and hard. It was decided that his brother would buy a suit for him in town and have it sent to the prison, while someone else would make arrangements to buy a pair of shoes from the prison shoe shop. Kikutani was deeply grateful for his brother's kindness.

The following morning, a man from the prison office came to Kikutani's room with a pair of black shoes and a box wrapped in department-store paper. Kikutani carefully removed the paper and opened the box; inside he found a navy-blue suit, as well as two dress shirts, a dark-blue polka-dot tie, a belt, and socks. In the breast pocket of the suit coat, stuffed in a small plastic bag, was a square of matching material for mending holes. Kikutani made a line of his new possessions against the wall of his room, as if they were decorations, and gazed at them. The thought that he could dress himself in these clothes and walk about freely made him feel the reality of his release all the more powerfully. He picked up the shoes and tried them on. The measurements had been exact, so they fit perfectly, but he was surprised at their weight. They were made of leather, hand-sewn by the prisoners in the factory. Kikutani realized that what made them seem so heavy was the fact that he had worn nothing but canvas prison shoes for many years. He wondered whether he would really be able to get around in such heavy shoes, but when he tried imagining himself walking on paved streets or on the bare earth in them, he found the weight pleasant, and he strolled about the room gazing down at his feet with delight.

That afternoon, a man from the prison accounting office came to his room and handed him several sheets of paper that recorded his pay for the work he had done in the print shop.

"Quite a sum," the man said. "In fact, it's the most anyone has ever taken out of here." With a nod to the guard, the man left. Kikutani flipped through the pages, stopping at the column that gave the grand total: 1,027,525 yen. Before he went to jail, his take-home pay had been about 53,000 yen a month after taxes and his union dues were subtracted. Now he had saved more than twenty months' pay—a substantial sum, as the man from the accounting office said. From watching TV, however, Kikutani knew that wages and prices had gone up, and he doubted that it would seem like so much money once he was released. Still, it was a start, and he felt confident that it would be enough to tide him over until he readjusted to life on the outside. When he first started working in the prison shop, he was stunned by the low wages; but inmates aren't in a position to complain, so he resigned himself and worked as hard as he could. This, he thought, was the result.

In the first years, he earned less than 1000 yen a month; but as he rose through the system of privileges, his wages slowly increased. And after he reached the highest level, he was allowed to take work back to his cell, which meant that he could earn as much as ten times what the lowliest prisoners earned. There were, of course, opportunities to spend money on creature comforts, but Kikutani maintained a spartan life and parted with little of what he made. Nevertheless, he was surprised that his savings came to more than a million yen, and he stood checking the figures again and again.

That night, after lights-out, he lay awake in bed, exulting in the thought that he would be released the following day. He tried to smother alternating bursts of laughter and sobs by covering his head with his pillow. At last he turned to stare at the suit and shoes lined up against the wall.

Rising early the next morning, he washed his face, then cleaned his room until it was spotless. When he had finished breakfast, he sat down with his legs tucked under him properly and listened to the sound of the roll call in the distance. Soon afterward, he could hear footsteps as the inmates headed off to work. A profound silence fell over the prison. Kikutani sat motionless, his eyes half closed.

An hour later, he heard footsteps in the hall, and the head guard appeared in front of the cell with a man from the prison office. "Bring all your things," said the guard, opening the door. Kikutani stood and picked up a box and his shoes. The guard came in to help with the other box, and Kikutani walked out of the cell. He followed the two men down the corridor, staggering a bit as the feeling drained from his legs. They led him to a room in the prison office and told him to sit on a stool by the wall. Kikutani took his place and looked quietly down at his lap.

He looked up again as he heard the door open and saw a short man in his sixties, another prisoner he had seen many times, enter the room. The expression on the prisoner's face betrayed his anxiety. His hair was white and thinning, and his skin seemed almost transparent. Kikutani knew that the man had been in for fifteen years and that he had spent his time in the woodworking shop. It was said he won some citation for the tea cabinets he made. Kikutani noticed that the young guard who was following the old man carried a cardboard box under each arm; he must be getting out today as well. The prisoner bowed repeatedly to the officers sitting in the room and then lowered himself into a chair next to Kikutani's. The two of them sat in silence, eyes straight ahead.

Thirty minutes later, Kikutani and the other man left the room, surrounded by guards and a number of prison officials. They made their way through the office building and down a covered passage that led to the prison chapel. When the heavy door swung open, Kikutani could see a large group of men gathered near the rostrum, all of them looking their way. The warden, a tall man in a suit, was standing in front of the dais, and Kikutani quickly spotted Kiyoura among the men flanking the warden. Hovering behind Kiyoura was a plump woman in a kimono; she must have been the other prisoner's wife. The officials who brought the prisoners bowed toward the assembly at the front of the hall, and Kikutani and the old man followed suit. The guards took up their positions by the door, which had been shut after them. One of the officials turned to the two prisoners.

"You are here to receive your official parole papers," he said. "Advance toward the warden." Kikutani fell in step behind the other prisoner and walked slowly up the aisle between the rows of chairs. They stopped a few yards from the platform, straightening their backs and bowing their heads. The warden's eyes lowered slowly to the papers in his hand, and he read their names.

"You're the right ones?" The two men nodded that they were. The older prisoner's name was Igarashi. "You men have exemplary conduct records since coming to this institution, and you have applied yourselves to your work. Congratulations on your perseverance. At this time it is my pleasure to inform you that we have received your papers from the prefectural parole board, which has deemed you fit to return to society. You will leave this prison to take up your lives on the outside again. I am sure you must be pleased. You will undergo many hardships, but I am confident you will endure these and live the remainder of your lives as useful citizens." Kikutani could feel tears welling in his eyes.

"Now, I am sure that you are aware that your parole officer, Kiyoura, has been laboring long and hard on your behalf while you've been awaiting your parole, despite his numerous other duties. It's thanks to him that we've been able to secure guarantors and places to relocate you. I would just like to take this opportunity to express our gratitude to him for all his efforts." The warden bowed politely in Kiyoura's direction; Kiyoura bowed in turn. So Kiyoura had been working all the while on Igarashi's parole as well as on Kikutani's.

Now the chief of the records division approached the warden and called Igarashi's name, handing the warden a sheet of paper. The warden walked up to Igarashi and held the paper out to him. "I am pleased to present you with your official parole," he said. Like an elementary school student receiving a certificate of merit, Igarashi reached out to take the paper. "Your pleasure at this moment must be especially great, because your wife is here to be with you. I urge you to keep your debt to her in mind and do your best to live together in harmony. When difficulties arise, do not try to solve them on your own. Talk them over with your wife, and with your parole officer. Understood?"

"Yes," Igarashi managed.

Then the warden stood in front of Kikutani and handed him his paper. "You, sir, were a teacher, a discerning individual. I urge you never again to be moved by the passions of the moment, but to use reason, swearing never to act rashly. Is that understood?"

"I swear," Kikutani answered in a loud, clear voice. The warden returned to the dais.

"The presentation of the official parole papers is concluded," said the head of the records division. With another bow to Kiyoura, the warden walked toward the door, accompanied by some of the officials. Kikutani and Igarashi were led to a waiting room in the chapel by Kiyoura and the remaining prison officers. The boxes containing their belongings had been left there, and they were instructed to change into the suits that had been bought for them.

Kikutani took off his shoes and slipped out of the pale-blue jacket and pants of his prison uniform, folding them neatly and stacking them on the counter. Next to them he placed the prison shoes, soles up. He stepped into the trousers of the suit and put on the shirt. Then, searching his memory, he managed to tie the tie. Finally, he slipped on the jacket. The suit seemed to fit, but the shirt didn't. The sleeves came down to the middle of his palms and the collar choked him slightly.

Igarashi changed into navy-blue pants and a brown jacket of some thin material. When the two were done, they were told to stand before one of the older officials, who re-cited for them a list of warnings about life on the outside. During the time they had been in prison, social conditions had changed a great deal, and it was invariably the case that prisoners paroled after long sentences experienced a certain amount of disorientation. In order to make their transition as easy as possible, a system of reeducation had been developed: halfway houses and a rehabilitation agency established to administer them. Volunteers with experience in helping ex-convicts had donated real estate and other personal property to these facilities. Kiyoura was the director of one of them.

It was up to the parolee whether or not he chose to live in one of these facilities, the officer continued, but they all hoped that Kikutani and Igarashi would spend at least some time there, until they had familiarized themselves with society once again and were ready to return to their homes or be placed with their guarantors. For Kikutani, who had no place to go and no one to rely on except Kiyoura, the decision was simple. But Igarashi as well decided to go to the halfway house managed by Kiyoura, perhaps out of the anxiety he felt at the idea of returning immediately to a normal life.

"Well, then," said the man in his most official tone, turning to Kiyoura, "we are counting on you." Kikutani and Igarashi, boxes in hand, left the chapel. The shoes seemed even heavier to Kikutani than when he tried them out in the cell, and they made a loud noise with each step. His ankles began to hurt as he walked through the courtyard, and his thighs were stiff. The official told Kiyoura that he would contact them at the halfway house with further parole procedures. A small green van was parked under the enormous crown of a zelkova tree. Kiyoura told the parolees to put their boxes in the back. The guard who had responsibility for Kikutani's section approached Kikutani.

"Take care of yourself," he said. "Make the most of it."

Kikutani pulled himself up and bowed formally. "Thank you for everything. You take care, too," he said.

Kiyoura exchanged a few words with the prison staff and then climbed into the driver's seat. Kikutani, Igarashi, and Igarashi's wife took their seats, and the van pulled out, following a small lead car driven by a guard. When they reached the steel gates of the courtyard, the driver of the lead car stuck his head out the window. The young guard bowed, and the gate swung open. The van crept through the gate after the car and then slowly began to pick up speed. Passing the prison office, they turned right and out into the spacious prison grounds, dotted here and there with flower beds. There was a line of cherry trees in front of the martial arts hall on the left, but it would still be some time before they bloomed. The branches bore just the slightest trace of crimson.

The gate in the high metal fence came into view ahead, and the car slowed and stopped beside the guardhouse. Kikutani and Igarashi were told to leave the van and stand before the gate. The official entered the guardhouse, showed some papers, and had a few words with the guards. There were bows all around, and soon he was outside again. He told the two parolees to get back in, and when they were seated, the gate slid open and the van began to move. Kiyoura nodded to the guards as they passed through the gate, then made a left turn and accelerated. Kikutani remembered hearing the sound of patrol car tires on gravel while he was in the prison, but this road was wide and paved.

"Well, how does it feel to be out?" Kiyoura asked without turning around. Kikutani wasn't sure how to answer, and Igarashi, too, said nothing.

They drove past rows of closely built, identical houses, which gave way to the long concrete fence of a factory. An industrial park, Kikutani thought they called it now, with rows of buildings and warehouses and trucks going back and forth. Eventually a highway came into view ahead, and the van turned onto the entrance ramp. Kiyoura drove through the tollbooth and merged with the traffic. Kikutani had never been on a highway before. They were rare in Japan before he went to prison, and he saw them only on television. The real thing seemed much bigger, and the cars were moving much faster than he expected they would—and so close together. At this speed, he realized, the slightest contact with the car next to them would result in a terrible accident.

He reached for the hand strap above the window and sat rigid.

The highway passed over a wide river plain that seemed to have been made into a golf course. Men in white caps and women in red uniforms were strolling over lawns. Rowboats dotted the river itself. On the other side, the rows of houses on the streets below began to be punctuated by taller buildings; and soon, flanking them, there were large, coffee-brown apartment houses. As the van made its way deeper into the city, clusters of even taller buildings began to appear among the apartments. There were enormous towers hung with banners—probably department stores—and red-and-white advertisement balloons flying overhead. The balloons caught Kikutani's eye, still and peaceful against the blue sky.

The cars on either side began to converge on their lane, and the van slowed as it reached a place where two highways came together. Eventually, the cars were bumper-to-bumper, and the van crept along, stopping briefly and then moving again. The tension from the high speed melted away, and Kikutani's eyes began to cloud over. He yawned. Then, to his shame, he began to feel carsick. Tall buildings towered over them now, looming down on the road, which seemed to run through a narrow valley, but Kikutani hardly noticed because of the chills that had gripped him. He was covered with sweat, and waves of nausea came and went. He kept his eyes down and prayed that the van would get where it was going soon and he could get out.

A few moments later they pulled out of the line of cars and left the highway, driving through streets lined with government buildings that flanked the palace. Groups of men, and even some women, were running slowly along the paths by the moat. Kikutani had heard of the fad known as jogging, but he assumed that it was something done on weekends or in the evening; here were men with jobs running in the middle of the day. The van turned off the street that followed the moat, drove up a gently sloping lane, and passed through the gate of a white concrete building on the right. Kiyoura pulled into a parking space.

"Lunchtime," he said, checking his watch. He took a large bundle wrapped in paper on the seat next to him and stepped out of the van. The parolees and Igarashi's wife scrambled out and followed him through a Plexiglas door into the building and down a hall to a room marked WAITING AREA, where they found three desks surrounded by chairs, but no people. Kiyoura told them to sit. He unwrapped his package and handed box lunches to Kikutani and the Igarashis. Then he left the room briefly, returning with a tray filled with cups of tea. As Kiyoura sat down, Kikutani slid his chopsticks from their wrapper and split them. He lifted the lid of the lunch box and examined the contents: on one side was a mound of rice, so brilliantly white that it dazzled him for a moment. In the exact center of the white field was a single pickled plum, like a drop of crimson ink. On the other side of the box, in colorful array, were bits of omelet, earthtone beans, slices of salmon, simmered carrot with burdock root, pale-pink pickled daikon, and shreds of seaweed. He extended his chopsticks ever so slowly and brought a bite of rice to his mouth. As he chewed, he savored the slightly sweet flavor and the velvety texture, so different from the mixture of rice and rye that had been the staple for all his long years in prison; and each of the other foods, as he tasted them one by one, seemed to be of the best ingredients skill-fully seasoned. The thought occurred to him that he was now free to eat such colorful, delicious food and such snow-white rice every day, and his spirits soared. Igarashi sat next to him, silently working his chopsticks.

When Kikutani had eaten the last grain of rice, he re-placed the lid on the box, retied the string, and reached for his teacup. The tea, lukewarm by now, was much like what they'd had in prison, but the cup itself, made of china, felt much heavier than the plastic ones to which he was accus-tomed. Kiyoura had taken out a cigarette and was about to return the pack to his pocket, but then he offered one to Kikutani, to Igarashi. Kikutani shook his head, and Igarashi bowed slightly in refusal. Before the "incident," Kikutani had smoked two packs a day; and even after going to prison, he had often had dreams in which he was puffing on a ciga-rette. But now he felt as he had back in his student days, when he smoked for the first time, a bit afraid that the smoke would sicken him, make him dizzy. He had no desire to reach out to the extended pack.

Looking up at the clock on the wall, Kiyoura turned to Igarashi's wife. "We're here to meet with someone from the supervisory office, but they're all at lunch right now. I won-der if you wouldn't mind waiting here while I take these men out for a short walk? It's time they begin getting used to the way things are out here."

"Of course," she said, folding her hands in her lap and nodding.

"Fine," said Kiyoura, stubbing out his cigarette in an ash-tray. "Let's go have a look around." He rose, and the men followed him out of the room and through the entrance.

Kiyoura walked at a leisurely pace, hands in his pockets, taking the sloping path uphill; Kikutani and Igarashi, out of long habit, fell in behind him single file, swinging their hands in step. Eventually Kiyoura glanced back, and an amused look flitted across his face. "You can forget the military drill," he said, laughing. "You're out here now, and you can relax." After that, however, he did not pay further attention to them, knowing perhaps that it was useless at this point. He walked on up the hill, eyes straight ahead.

In prison they had been required to form lines and walk in step; if they forgot, it was recorded as an infraction of the rules. Kikutani, who was always thinking about his chances for parole, had carefully avoided breaking any rule; he marched in lockstep even when there were no other prisoners around. Now, he was out and no longer had to be so careful; but his body had become accustomed to walking with his arms waving at his side, his knees rising with each stride, as if that were the only way he could get himself to move forward. A man approached them coming down the hill, eyeing their strange gait suspiciously. After he passed, they could feel his gaze on their backs.

Reaching the top of the hill, they passed under a large torii gate. A path spread with white pebbles led to the main shrine; but Kiyoura, apparently worried about the time, headed toward a smaller pavilion. In the woods at the back of the tiny shrine, he stopped.

"You two need to try to look around a little while you walk," he said. "The plum trees are blooming. A little past their peak, I guess." At Kiyoura's urging, Kikutani shifted his gaze to the trees around them. There were more than twenty plum trees, white and red; some flowers had pale petals with broad smears of pink, while others had faintly golden centers. He remembered the small red plum tree he had bought at a flower market and planted in his garden. Kiyoura was right, these trees were beginning to fade; the ground beneath them was covered with petals, some of which had already begun to dissolve into the earth.

"I meant to tell you," said Kiyoura, as if suddenly remembering, "I'm holding the money you saved while you were inside. It's in the safe at the halfway house, so if you need it, just let me know. I've got to warn you, though: it may seem like a lot of money to you now, but prices have gone way up. I hate to be a killjoy, but you'd better keep that in mind."

"We know," said Kikutani, a gloomy feeling coming over him as he spoke. "Before I went away, postcard stamps were seven yen; now they're forty. That's nearly six times as much, so I figure everything else must have gone up, too." It worried him to think that his million yen in savings was worth less than 200,000.

"Seven yen, was it?" said Kiyoura, cocking his head. Then, glancing at his watch, he said they should get back. He started for the gate, with Kikutani and Igarashi in tow.

When they reached the waiting room, Kiyoura disappeared for a moment and then returned, asking the two men to follow him. They climbed a flight of stairs to a room marked REHABILITATION DIVISION and were shown into the office of a small man in a dark-blue suit. He seemed to be waiting for them, standing with his hands resting on his desk. Kikutani guessed the man was about forty-five years old, but his hair was still jet black and his skin was pale and lustrous like that of a much younger man. Kiyoura introduced his two charges.

"I see," the man said in a pleasant tone and turned toward them. "Congratulations on your parole. You've earned it." His voice was clear, his eyes sparkling. Still standing by his desk, he began to enumerate for them all the conditions of their release, pausing after each item for emphasis.

"Beginning today, you will undergo a course of study at the halfway house run by Mr. Kiyoura to reeducate you in the ways of society. This generally lasts three months. You will be granted an extension, if you wish, barring unforeseen circumstances. For the time being, your room and two meals a day at Kiyoura's facility will be paid for you, but you will be responsible for buying your own lunches. After twenty-five days have passed, you will pay for all of your meals.

"These halfway-house facilities are designed to help you become a normal, functioning member of society once again. We will create a schedule for this to be accomplished, and your training will begin. We will expect you to observe scrupulously all the rules laid out by the men and women who will be looking after you at the halfway house. But at the same time, we want you to move beyond your dependence on others and learn to stand on your own two legs. Be sure you take proper care of the bedding and other necessities that will be supplied by the house. Disturbing the staff or residents of the house with drinking or rowdy behavior is strictly prohibited. In time, you will find employment, and when your period of adjustment has ended, you will be able to leave the house and move to an apartment or other residence. You will be expected to devote yourselves to your jobs and to establish yourselves as useful members of society.

"During your readjustment period, and even after you have left the halfway house, you will be required to report twice a month to the officer in charge of your case. And you are required to obtain his permission before you travel or change your place of residence." The official then addressed Igarashi and explained that he had been released three years prior to the end of his sentence. If during the next three years he violated his parole, he would be returned to prison. But if there were no infractions during that time, he would be considered to have served his sentence and his parole would come to an end. Then, turning to Kikutani, the official continued.

"In your case, you have served more than fifteen years of an indefinite sentence, but technically you have not discharged your debt to society, and the rules require that you remain under the supervision of your parole officer for the rest of your life. However, in ten years' time, if your record remains absolutely clean, you will have served twenty-five years total. Since Japanese law doesn't provide for sentences in excess of twenty years, in such cases a careful review is performed by the parole board and a petition for a general pardon can be issued by the central examining body. If the case is viewed as having merit, then the Justice Minister may commute the sentence. Admittedly, the number of people who have managed this is relatively small; still, they are out there, and they should be your inspiration—apply yourself to becoming the next man to receive a pardon. We wish you every success in your efforts," he concluded smoothly.

"I'll do my best," said Kikutani, pulling himself up straight to answer. But in the official's words he could detect the enormous distance between his situation and Igarashi's, despite the fact that they were both on parole. A fifteen-year sentence suggested that Igarashi, too, had been convicted of murder, but it was clear there must have been a number of mitigating circumstances. If Igarashi could serve the rest of his time without a violation, he would be free of the parole board's supervision. For Kikutani, however, the official's words hung heavy: supervision of the board for life.

Kiyoura approached the desk and handed the official some papers he had pulled from an envelope. The official glanced at them briefly and then looked up again. The two exchanged a few friendly remarks, mentioning a number of names. The inspector asked about the various residents of Kiyoura's facility, and Kiyoura responded with a long litany: one man who managed to obey the rule against drinking in the house but who staggered home dead drunk virtually every night; another who had exceeded his allotted stay but refused to move out; a volatile man who got into an argument with another resident. As he went on with his list of problems, with only the occasional grunt from the official for encouragement, Kiyoura seemed to have forgotten the presence of Kikutani and Igarashi. Some of the infractions Kiyoura was inclined to overlook; others had already sorted themselves out. In a few cases, he told the official he would be writing up a report. The two concluded their business, and the official thanked Kiyoura.

"And you two," he said, turning toward them, "don't let us down." With a bow, Kikutani and Igarashi followed Kiyoura from the room. They stopped by the waiting room, where Mrs. Igarashi was sitting, hands folded in her lap, and the four of them returned to the van.

"That's it, then," Kiyoura murmured as he started the engine and pulled out into the street.

2

Shiro Kikutani opened his eyes and sat up in bed. For a moment he was disoriented and stared wildly around the room. The first thing that struck him was the tatami matting under his mattress; then he noticed that the door was made of wood and glass, not iron bars. His body felt as though it had just bobbed up on the surface of the day. His eyes sparkled. With a mixture of delight and relief, he realized that he was in his room at the halfway house instead of in his cell. But when he realized that the light coming through the door was daylight and not from the bulbs in the corridor, he began to feel anxious. He missed the chimes in the prison that would have had him out of bed by six and ready for his routine. Did they have chimes here? Among the house rules that Kiyoura had ticked off for them the day before, he had said that breakfast was from six until seven-thirty. The men who were headed to jobs ate early, and some of the day laborers skipped breakfast in order to get out to look for work as soon as they could. But Kikutani had been awake much of the night, too keyed up to sleep, and now he had probably overslept. It must be past seven-thirty.

He got to his feet and went out into the hall, still in his underwear. Creeping halfway down the stairs, he crouched over to catch a glimpse of the clock on the office wall. His body relaxed. Just past six. He sat on the stairs for a moment.

Back in his room, as he was carefully folding his futon, it occurred to him that after all those years of waking at the same hour, he would wake up now even without the chimes. He got the broom and dustpan he'd noticed in the hall and swept out his room. Then he dressed and went down to the washroom. There were three men there; Kikutani joined them to brush his teeth. They glanced his way briefly, then went back to what they were doing; no one spoke to him. A middle-aged man was drying his face with a towel. Kikutani noticed that the back of his arm was covered with a deep-blue tattoo.

He took his soap, towel, and toothbrush to his room, went back downstairs, and slid open the glass door of the dining hall. Two men were plying their chopsticks in front of steaming bowls of rice. As Kikutani sat down, one of them motioned toward a pot in the middle of the table.

"Miso soup," he said. Kikutani nodded, took the lid off the pot, and ladled some soup into a bowl. There were pickles and fermented beans to go with the rice; and the soup, with cubes of tofu, was delicious. In prison, they had brought the soup around to the cells on a pushcart in a big metal bowl, letting it get cold along the way. A steaming bowl of miso broth was no more than a distant memory to him at this point. As he stared down at the table, he was struck again by the admirable harmony between the white rice and the warm soup.

The two men stood to go as three more came in, Igarashi among them. He sat down next to Kikutani, who took the bowl in front of Igarashi and filled it with soup from the pot. In prison the men had been forbidden to talk among themselves, and now, out of habit, they sat eating in silence. When he finished, Kikutani took his dishes to the sink and washed them. Then he went back upstairs to sit quietly in the middle of his room, his legs folded neatly under him. About now, he thought, roll call would have ended at the prison; the doors of the cells would be opened, and the inmates would be lining up to go to the workshops.

Last night he had heard all kinds of noises, among them the siren of an ambulance or police car that passed several times. Now the room was quiet, with only the distant sound of the announcements from the train station. The clamor of the city, which had grown louder as the night deepened, subsided as morning approached. Kikutani had imagined that the halfway house would be somewhere in the outlying suburbs of Tokyo, so he was surprised when Kiyoura drove the van into the heart of Shinjuku, turned off a busy shopping thoroughfare into a narrow street, and stopped. The street was lined with neon signs identifying the cluster of hourly hotels, and sandwiched between them were crumbling, two-story stucco buildings. On one of these, above a sliding glass door, was a wooden sign that read INN OF THE SUMMER BREEZE. Kikutani guessed that the halfway house was here because Kiyoura happened to own the building, but he wondered whether this location might not be too provocative for a group of parolees. Unless the idea was to reintroduce them to the real world by putting them right in the middle of it rather than off in some pastoral setting on the edge of nowhere. In any case, the house looked completely out of place in its surroundings.

Kikutani sat in his room, legs folded, eyes half closed. He knew that no one would bother him now if he decided to walk around or simply roll over and go to sleep, but this was how he had always sat in his cell, and it was the only way he could relax and let time pass. Two hours later, he heard footsteps in the hall, and the glass door opened.

"Please get dressed and come to the reception room. The chief is waiting for you," said a man in his twenties wearing jeans. As soon as he had delivered this message, he turned and left. Kikutani stood up, put on his suit, tied his tie, and went out into the hall. The reception room was next to the office. When he opened the door, he found Igarashi seated on an old couch. Kikutani joined him, and the two sat quietly, facing forward. In a few minutes, the door to the office opened, and Kiyoura, also in a suit, came into the room.

"So, did you get any sleep?" he asked, lowering himself into an armchair on the other side of the table. The two men said that they had. "From the looks of you, I'd say you didn't get much. If you didn't sleep, don't be afraid to say so. You no longer have to go around answering 'Yes, yes' to everything." From the table he picked up a cigarette and a lighter.

Kikutani felt like laughing. Kiyoura had been around so many inmates that he knew exactly what they were thinking. It was easy talking to him, and Kikutani felt he could rely on him for anything.

"As I said yesterday, you'll start work in two weeks. But until then we want you to try to get used to things again.

Unfortunately, I'm pretty busy right now, so you'll have to do a lot of this on your own. Today, we'll take you to a department store, so you can see for yourself what's happened to prices. And if there's something you need, you can do some shopping while we're there. Give some thought to what you want to buy." The phone rang in the office, and a young man opened the door. Kiyoura left them for a moment.

An alarm clock, thought Kikutani. This morning I woke up right at six, but who's to say that will last? Before the incident, an alarm clock had been about 1500 yen. If a postcard stamp was six times as much, then a clock was probably ten times as much. A frightening amount of money; but getting up on time in the morning was fundamental, and he decided he had to have a clock.

The door opened, and Kiyoura came back with two envelopes. He sat down and placed one in front of Kikutani, one in front of Igarashi. "Your savings from the workshops are in here," he said. "You'd probably have trouble guessing how much you need for shopping, so why don't you each take 20,000 for now?"

"All right," said Kikutani, opening the envelope and removing the stack of bills. He remembered seeing reports on TV when the new currency was issued, but the 10,000 bill was smaller than he thought and a bit slippery. In prison, they never handled money of any kind; when they wanted to buy something, they simply gave the guard an order slip with the name of the item written on it, and the price was deducted from their savings. Kikutani slipped two bills from the stack and returned the rest to the envelope. He recorded the amount in the register that Kiyoura had passed across the table and stamped the receipt.

"I'll give you change for one of those," Kiyoura said, taking the envelopes and their bills to the office. He returned almost immediately and in front of each of them put a stack of 1000-yen bills and a pile of coins. "They don't make 500s anymore; it's just this now," he said, pointing to a large coin. Kikutani stuffed the bills in his coat pocket, shoved the coins in his pants, and rose from his chair. They waited outside until Kiyoura joined them.

"I don't want to see any more marching today," he said. "You're out in the real world now, and people will wonder about you if you walk like that. Why don't I walk in the middle, just in case." Stepping between them, he grabbed their wrists and set off. As they walked, their hands began to swing and their knees rose in step, but Kiyoura held firm. Kikutani could feel his muscles stiffen and his knees lock.

They turned a corner and entered a street lined with shops. Although the traffic here was barely inching along, none of the drivers seemed particularly upset; not a horn could be heard. Kikutani stared at the tranquil, creeping line of cars in wonder. A moment later, he was enveloped in thick, overpowering odors. Food, gasoline, chemicals, paint, perfume…his head was filled with a complex cocktail of smells. He grimaced, feeling suffocated.

The crush of people became overwhelming as well. Since the three were no longer able to walk abreast, Kiyoura let go of their wrists and went ahead. With his hands free, Kikutani could feel his arms falling into the swinging oscillation of the prison march, so he grabbed the sides of his pants to keep them still. He tried to avoid people as they came toward him, but his body was stiff and slow to respond. On more than one occasion he was bumped, and would stagger a few steps before regaining his balance. It was frightening to be surrounded by so many bodies, and he could not keep up; but he became suddenly terrified of losing Kiyoura and began charging ahead, colliding with anyone in his way.

They came to the elevated tracks of the National Railway. A train was just pulling out of the station, the cars gradually picking up speed. Kiyoura stopped and waited for Kikutani to catch up, then entered the station.

"When you went away to prison, they still had windows with live people selling tickets, didn't they?" he said, stopping and speaking quietly. "Except in the smallest stations out in the country, ticket windows are a thing of the past for commuter lines. It's all done with these vending machines now. Stand here a while and watch how they work." Kikutani had seen characters on TV shows use these machines to buy tickets, but he had no idea what was involved. A young man approached one of the vending machines, put some coins in the slot, and quickly punched one of the buttons that lit up. A ticket fell out of the slot at the bottom of the machine, and the man picked it up and moved on. From the almost unconscious way the young man went through this procedure, Kikutani could see how completely these machines had become a fact of daily life. A woman came and put her money in the machine, collecting coins that fell out with the ticket before she hurried away. So, thought Kikutani, they even make change.

"They don't take 500-yen coins. We're going to Shinjuku, so use the 100-yen coins I gave you. There are some machines that take 1000-yen bills." Kiyoura went up to the machine at the end of the line, put a 1000 in the slot, and retrieved the ticket and change. Kikutani fished the coins from his pocket, but then realized he didn't know the fare to Shinjuku and stood puzzled.

"Check the map up there," said Kiyoura. "The numbers written over Shinjuku are the fare from here." Kikutani studied the illuminated diagram above the vending machines, then selected two 100-yen coins and inserted them in the machine. He pushed the button and dutifully gathered up his ticket and change. Igarashi took longer looking at the map, but he finally found the right amount and went to buy his ticket. As they made their way through the gate and up the stairs to the platform, Kikutani realized with horror that they had paid 120 yen to go just one stop. The minimum fare when he had last been on a train was 20. Money, it seemed, had lost all its value.

The train was crowded. Kikutani stood near the door and looked out the window. Rows of astonishingly tall towers loomed up behind the small, aging buildings that lined the track. Some of them were squared off like normal buildings, but others traced improbable arcs in the air, and they were all sheathed in subtle, shifting colors. He thought of the armies of men who must have worked to build these massive structures while he was locked away in prison, and he began to realize just how far he had been left behind.

Kikutani felt a wave of panic as he stepped off the train and into the jostling crowd on the platform at Shinjuku Station. He huddled close to Kiyoura as they trotted through the gate and down into an underground pedestrian passage. As Kiyoura walked, he looked back from time to time to make sure the two men were still with him. Eventually, he turned and went up some stairs, coming out in the food section of a department store.

Now Kikutani was even more overwhelmed. He couldn't stop himself from grabbing Kiyoura's arm for reassurance. He felt himself drowning in a flood of intense odors from foods he couldn't even identify. The shoppers were packed closely together as they jostled their way through the aisles, assailed from all sides by the high-pitched chorus of calls from the salesgirls. The counters seethed with people and products. Kikutani was shoved and bumped as he staggered along, dazed and bleary-eyed. At last they managed to force their way through the crowd and into an elevator. The door closed, and the car started up. Kikutani felt queasy; his stomach dropped the way it had when he was a child. With each stop, the blood seemed to rush out of him, only to come rushing back when the elevator started again.

Finally the door opened, and they got out. Kikutani noticed that Igarashi was pale and had broken into a sweat, and he realized he must look the same. On this floor, at least, the crowd was thinner. Birdcages and potted plants were lined up for sale. Behind the noisy birds were cages full of puppies. The parolees were in a small space on the top floor that sold pets and garden supplies. Walking past the display shelves, they came out onto the spacious roof, dotted here and there with rows of red and blue chairs. Off in another corner was a pavilion that sold refreshments. The sky was overcast.

"So, what do you think of a department store?" asked Kiyoura as he continued to stroll along.

"I've never seen so many people," said Kikutani, wiping the sweat from his brow with the back of his hand. Igarashi said nothing. Kiyoura stopped and sat in one of the red chairs, signaling for them to join him. Looking a little tired, he crossed his legs and lit a cigarette. Kikutani sat stiffly in his chair, knees together. He watched a woman sitting nearby. Her eyes followed a small child in a white hood who was toddling around the roof. Kikutani realized that he must have seen lots of women yesterday and today, must even have brushed against some when they walked in the crowds, but as he stared at this young mother, he felt he was seeing a woman for the first time since he went to prison. His eyes moved naturally to her chest, but the folds of beige material in her blouse made it hard to tell whether or not her breasts were large. The back of her neck was white, and her lips glistened a brilliant crimson.

"So," said Kiyoura, leaning back in his chair, "what are you planning to buy?"

"An alarm clock," Kikutani stammered, sure that Kiyoura had caught him studying the woman. He wondered, too, whether the money he'd brought with him would be enough for the clock. Kiyoura nodded and looked at Igarashi.

"A parasol and galoshes," Igarashi said as if by reflex.

"Good idea to be prepared for rain," Kiyoura agreed. "But almost everybody carries umbrellas now. And galoshes? They may have them here; I know they have them for kids. We'll see....Okay, then, let's get at it. You're not here just to buy; you should study the prices of things as you're shopping." He crushed his cigarette into an ashtray and stood up. They went down two flights of stairs to a corner of the store where clocks were sold.

In contrast to the food section in the basement, this area was almost empty, with neatly dressed clerks standing at attention. The wares on the shelves were so elegant, the atmosphere so refined and formal, that Kikutani felt himself shrink. Kiyoura, however, wandered through the aisles and stopped in front of a display cabinet. The two men followed a step behind him. In the case were clocks of a sort that Kikutani had never seen before. One was a glass dome in which four gold spheres revolved. After a half turn, they would swing back the other way. There was an emerald-green wall clock with hands in the shape of airplanes. Kikutani stared in total fascination. Finally he remembered that he was shopping and took hold of the price tag hanging from a fancy little clock framed in wood. He was sure that this was the sort of clock that only rich people bought, something rare and expensive, so he was surprised that the price was only 6800 yen; he checked the tag several times to be sure he hadn't misread it. Puzzled, he studied the prices of the other clocks hanging nearby; most were more than 10,000, but there were several that cost less. He walked off to look at other clocks, conscious that his expression had relaxed. There's nothing to worry about, he told himself.

Kiyoura was waiting for him by a counter lined with alarm clocks. "You probably remember the old wind-up kind. Most now have something called a quartz movement; there's a little battery inside that keeps them running for a long time. There are elaborate ones with bells or chimes, but I imagine you want something simple. The cheap ones work just as well; these are only 2800." Kiyoura reached out and picked up a small, square, red clock and handed it to Kikutani. It was light, and Kikutani liked the design.

"I'll buy this one," he said.

"There are lots to choose from," Kiyoura said. "You've

got to make your own decisions." Kikutani nodded and studied the other clocks for a moment, but none of them seemed better than the one he held, and the price was right.

"This one's fine," he said.

"Okay, then, buy it and let's go," said Kiyoura, glancing up at the woman who was standing behind the counter. Kikutani slipped three bills from his jacket pocket and walked over to the clerk.

"I'd like this one," he said. Taking the clock and the money, the woman went off to the cash register, returning a moment later with his receipt and change on a little dish and the clock in a neatly wrapped package. Kikutani took the clock and his change and bowed to the woman.

"Was it more than you expected?" asked Kiyoura as they continued their tour of the store.

"Not really," said Kikutani.

"Is that so?" said Kiyoura. "All the better, then."

As they approached the escalator, Kiyoura stopped. "You two go first," he said. Kikutani hesitated at the top. He wasn't frightened, exactly, but it had been a long time since he'd ridden an escalator and it looked strange to him. The little steps with their sharp teeth came sliding out at the level of the floor and then gradually formed themselves into stairs on the way down. If he lost his footing getting on, would he fall between the teeth and be torn to bits?

"What's the matter?" Kiyoura asked. "Hop on." His eyes were laughing. Kikutani was sure that Kiyoura had waited for them to get on first because he knew that men just out on parole were likely to be frightened of escalators. Kikutani screwed up his courage and set his foot firmly on the escalator. As his body lurched forward and started down, he bent his knees and gripped the handrails. He could feel the blood rushing to his face, and he wondered if he was about to collapse. At last the floor rose up to meet him, and he thrust out his leg to step off. Turning around, he saw Igarashi, eyes fixed and glassy, following close behind, but with Kiyoura holding his arm.

They set off again through the store, the parolees sticking as close as they could to Kiyoura. They wandered through department after department: men's clothing, accessories, pajamas, stationery, electrical appliances. In each, Kiyoura told them to check prices. Almost everything was astonishingly expensive, with the sole exception of televisions, which were cheap, only a fraction of what the parolees imagined they would cost. As they moved from floor to floor, shopping and studying, Kiyoura led them each time to the escalator, even when the stairs were closer. As Kikutani practiced getting on and off, he could feel his confidence growing.

When they reached the ground floor, Kiyoura made his way to the department that sold umbrellas. Most of them had colorful designs, but Kiyoura found a dark-blue one that seemed right for Igarashi. It was about four times the price that Kikutani remembered. The woman behind the counter pushed a button on the handle, and the umbrella unfolded in front of them. Igarashi's eyes danced, and he laughed out loud like a small child. It occurred to Kikutani that he'd need something, too, when it rained, so he bought an umbrella just like Igarashi's. As they were finishing the transaction, Kiyoura said something to the clerk. Listening to her answer, he turned and set off down the stairs to the men's shoe department. In one corner was a line of rain boots.

After having his feet measured, Igarashi chose a pair of shiny black boots, and Kikutani again followed suit. This time the price was almost the same as when he went away to prison. It was quite strange: while public services, like stamps and train fares, were several times more expensive, some commodities hadn't gone up at all.

3

Kiyoura served as a priest at the Buddhist temple where he had been born and raised. But his father, who was the chief priest, seemed to understand the importance of his son's work and, despite his own failing health, took care of the temple with only the help of some younger monks. This allowed Kiyoura to devote himself completely to the halfway house, a job that kept him extremely busy. He seemed to be constantly in motion, going off in the van, showing up with yet another group of newly released prisoners, or talking with visitors in the reception room. Among these visitors was a man who was clearly an ex-convict. He would come with a woman who seemed to be his wife, and the residents would catch sight of them through the glass door deep in conversation with Kiyoura.

As busy as Kiyoura was, he still found time to work out a schedule for Kikutani and Igarashi's readjustment to society. He took them to a nearby restaurant, where the men from the house could go without feeling self-conscious, and he showed them around Shinjuku Imperial Gardens. In the afternoon, on the fourth day after their release, he took them to the office of a tour-bus company at the station, so they could see for themselves how much the city had changed.

"What will you tell the tour guide if she asks where you come from?" Kiyoura asked, his eyes smiling. Such a question was natural, since most of the customers were sightseers from the countryside. When the bus was empty, like today, such a question was almost unavoidable. Neither Kikutani nor Igarashi had an answer. "If you tell them you're from a halfway house, they'll want to know halfway from where. I don't think you want to go into that, so just smile and say you're from Ibaraki or Fukushima." Kikutani nodded.

As soon as Kikutani found a seat by the window, the bus started to move. The columns of tall buildings slid past beyond the broad expanse of glass. He listened attentively to the guide's patter, looking back and forth as she pointed out the various sights. Every street in the city seemed to be jammed with traffic, and among the long lines of cars, Kikutani noticed some with odd shapes he had never seen, not even on the TV in prison. They stopped at the parade grounds in front of the palace, and the passengers filed off for the customary group picture in front of Niju Bridge. As they were trudging through the gravel back to the bus, the guide slowed down to walk beside them and ask her question, just as Kiyoura had predicted. "Ibaraki," Kikutani mumbled. Igarashi just nodded.

The trip lasted only three hours, but the relentless stream of new sights and sounds left Kikutani exhausted and barely able to stumble off the bus. Apparently, the sightseeing trip marked the end of their initial reorientation, and Kiyoura seemed to pay them less attention. Kikutani responded by spending almost the whole day shut up in his room, venturing out with Igarashi only at lunch for a bowl of ramen or a plate of curry at the place Kiyoura had shown them. In prison, the food was invariably cold by the time they got it, so they found the hot ramen especially delicious, drinking the broth right to the bottom of the bowl.

After a week, Kiyoura gave Igarashi permission to spend a night at home with his wife. Igarashi's wife had moved to a different part of the city following his conviction, so Igarashi did not need to worry now about curious neighbors. When he came back, his eyes were shining, and he looked like a different person. Kikutani felt a pang of envy that Igarashi had a home to go to. Igarashi returned on bath day, which was every other day for the house residents. In prison, they bathed only twice a week, so this arrangement seemed a great luxury. Still, out of prison habit, they soaped up quickly and barely dunked themselves in the hot tub. When Kikutani got back to his room, he sat down in his usual position, legs tucked under his hips. He could hear feet padding down the hall and stopping in front of his room, then the door slid open a crack. Igarashi peered in and held out an oblong package wrapped in paper, signaling for him to take it. Then he backed out and disappeared down the hall. Kikutani unwrapped the package to find a block of sweet bean jelly, no doubt something Igarashi had received from his wife. As he let a small piece of the candy dissolve on his tongue, he stared at the lustrous mass, lost in the sweet flavor he had all but forgotten. Igarashi's wordless pantomime, Kikutani knew, was from long years of being under threat of punishment should the guards catch you talking between cells.

When Kiyoura realized that Kikutani and Igarashi were going out for their lunch and shopping only in each other's company, he told them in no uncertain terms that they must learn to make their way around the city alone. Kikutani's heart sank when he heard this new requirement, but he resolved to go for lunch by himself. He boarded the train to Shinjuku and retraced his steps to the department store where Kiyoura had taken them. He found an empty bench in the roof garden and watched the people coming and going and the clouds floating above. Later, as he was leaving the train on his way home, it started to rain. He felt a thrill, because in prison they were not allowed to get wet, and as he walked along under the shop awnings, savoring the drops that made their way through to his skin, he had an overwhelming sense of freedom. He turned off the busy street into the alley and stopped to look up at the sky. The shower had almost passed, and a pale light spread across the space between the buildings. It was pleasant to let the last drops splash on his face. His head still tilted back, he opened his mouth and began walking again toward the house.

He got to the point where he would spend an hour or two a day outdoors, but he was still anxious whenever he was away from the halfway house, and as often as he could, he shut himself up in his room. He noticed how different he was from men who came to the house after a shorter stay in prison. They would wander out the very day they arrived, and soon they would go off drinking in the evening, stumbling back late. Some of them smoked, and some ate their dinner elsewhere, heading off for the public bath with a towel and a bar of soap. They didn't seem to need the moral support of the other men in the house; after a few days, they would find work, and then they would disappear altogether.

On the twelfth day after their release, Igarashi was allowed to go home with his wife. Kikutani joined Kiyoura in seeing them off at the door. Smiling faintly to Kikutani and bowing to Kiyoura, Igarashi turned and followed his wife down the alley. The thought that he would probably never see Igarashi again made Kikutani sad. They had met only when they were paroled, and they had spoken little on their outings from the house, but Kikutani felt they had understood each other. He watched quietly until Igarashi turned the corner and disappeared from view.

That evening, Kiyoura mentioned that the manager of the chicken farm that had agreed to hire Kikutani wanted to interview him the next day. "I know you feel like you're not really used to things out here yet, but the first step in getting back to normal is settling into a job. Most of the men who get out after a long sentence like yours start work after two weeks. If they can manage it, so can you." Kiyoura's words were meant to encourage Kikutani.

"I understand," he muttered. He knew he would have to go out and work eventually, but didn't feel up to it just yet. It wasn't the work itself he minded, it was having to be around people. The idea of having to make small talk or kill time with his future coworkers filled him with anxiety.

"You're to go there tomorrow morning," repeated Kiyoura, as if not noticing Kikutani's worried look, and went back into the office.

That night, Kikutani lay in bed tossing and turning. He

knew that Kiyoura had helped a great many parolees, and found work for them as well. Kikutani told himself to stop fretting and trust this man who had so much experience and was willing to help him.

The next morning, he rose earlier than usual, shaved, put on his suit, and sat waiting in his room. A little after eight, one of the young men who worked at the house came to call him. Kikutani went downstairs and stood in front of the office until Kiyoura emerged carrying a paper bag. Together they set off for the station. The platform was crowded with commuters, but the commuters were all pushing onto the inbound trains, leaving almost empty the outbound one that Kiyoura and Kikutani boarded. After a few stops, they transferred to an express. Kikutani watched as the tall buildings thinned out and patches of green became more common. The farther they went, the more people left the train, and eventually Kiyoura and Kikutani found seats together. A purple outline of mountains became visible in the distance against the blue of the sky, and lower hills began to push up against the tracks from either side. They had been riding for about fifty minutes when Kiyoura signaled to Kikutani that it was time to get off.

A small supermarket and some shops fronted the open area outside the station, where a line of buses stood waiting. They boarded one and were soon riding through quiet streets past rows of houses. Eventually, the bus turned onto a road that ran through open fields, with hills pressing in from the right. Crossing a bridge over a clear flowing stream, they headed up a slope. There were very few houses here; at last, next to some woods, Kiyoura stood to get off.

"Middle of nowhere," he muttered as he fished a scrap of

paper out of his pocket. After a quick look at the map, he set off down a road that skirted the trees. As they rounded a gentle curve, a cluster of buildings came into view. The largest one was the stucco shed nearest them. As they approached, the unmistakable odor of a henhouse filled the air, and they knew this was the right place. A sign reading AKIYAMA POULTRY hung over the gate, and two white container trucks were parked just inside the compound. Kiyoura passed through the gate and pushed open the glass door of a small prefabricated office building that stood on the right. He said a few words to a middle-aged woman who had come out from behind her desk to meet him, and then he beckoned to Kikutani. They were shown into a meeting room adjoining the office, which was decorated with a calendar featuring large photographs of chickens. In one corner was a bookshelf filled with magazines and books about the poultry business: *Poultry Managers' Companion, Diagnosis and Treatment of Disease in Chickens, Complete Poultry*. Five minutes later, a tall man in his forties came into the room.

"I'm Akiyama," he said, exchanging business cards with Kiyoura. Following Kiyoura's lead, Kikutani sat down on the edge of the couch. "Did you have any trouble finding us?" Akiyama continued. When Kiyoura assured him that the map had been perfect, Akiyama launched into an explanation of why it was necessary to build the chicken farm in such a remote spot. Until five years ago, he said, they had been located much closer to town, but the stench of the chickens and the swarms of flies from the dung brought complaints from the neighbors, so they finally decided to move. "When we got here, there were almost no houses in the area, but a couple of years ago they started building. Still, they're far enough away that we don't hear too much about the smell. When the flies swarm, though, we get an angry phone call or two." Behind his glasses, Akiyama's eyes seemed sparkling and clear.

Kiyoura asked about the size of the farm. Akiyama replied that they had some 160,000 chickens laying approximately 130,000 eggs per day, which they trucked off to supermarkets and coops all over the country. Kiyoura looked surprised by these figures; Kikutani, too, was amazed that there was so much demand for eggs.

"This is Shiro Kikutani," Kiyoura began, as if remembering why they'd come. "As you know from the records we sent you, he's just been paroled. We'd like you to take him on for a trial period, and if things work out, hire him as a regular employee."

Kikutani stood. "At your service," he said, bowing.

Akiyama looked him over for a moment and then turned back to Kiyoura. "That's what we agreed," he said. "In this line of work, we hire a lot of people who quit right away. From my point of view, the man who can stick it out is the one I want helping me." The hours, he explained, were from eight to five, with no overtime. The farm employed twenty-five women and ten men; the men were responsible for shipping the eggs, mixing the feed, and taking care of the henhouse. Since Kikutani had no driver's license, he would not be able to work on the shipping; and all the feed was mixed by an employee with more experience. That left the henhouse, Akiyama concluded. Kikutani had been listening, nodding as the poultry farmer spoke, but he realized that Akiyama didn't look in his direction. "Shall we have a look around?" Akiyama said, getting up.

Kikutani followed Kiyoura from the office and out into the compound. They entered a large steel-frame building, where they found stacks of cardboard boxes against the walls. Beyond these, they came to a conveyor belt carrying a steady stream of eggs. Akiyama stopped in front of a metal box and explained that it was an egg cleaner. The damp eggs coming out the other side went straight into the dryer, and from there to a woman who sat by a lamp and examined the insides of the eggs as the eggs passed. Every so often, when she found a cracked shell or a spot of blood in the yolk, her hand would reach out to remove an egg from the line. The eggs went on to a scale, where they were automatically sorted into small, medium, and large sizes. Finally, they arrived at the end of the line, where three women nimbly fit them into egg cartons. All along the line, no one spoke.

Falling in step with the conveyor belt, Akiyama led his visitors out of the building. Before them was another large raised structure from which the belt, loaded with eggs, was emerging. Here they discovered the source of the overpowering stench: the mound of chicken excrement spreading out beneath the floor of this building. As they followed Akiyama up the stairs, they could hear the cackling and clucking of the chickens. Entering the henhouse, Kikutani was enveloped by the odd noise: more like the restless clacking of countless tiny machines than the voices of birds.

Several rows of metal cages, stacked double, stretched off toward the far end of the long building. In each cage were two leghorn chickens, and at the moment they all seemed to be craning their necks out of the cages, pecking at their feed. Thousands of heads bobbed up and down, shaking countless tufts of feathers in a hypnotic dance. Akiyama was explaining that there were sixteen hundred birds in each row of cages, but the noise made it almost impossible to hear him. The henhouse was staffed by a single man who worked at one end; the rest of the operation was automated. The feeding equipment was mounted on rails and moved slowly along the row of cages, dispensing grain into long conduits; and the eggs that came rolling out of the bottom of the cages landed on the conveyor belt that took them to the packing room. The temperature in the building was kept quite warm.

They followed Akiyama out the door and down the stairs.

"Very impressive," said Kiyoura when they were seated once more in the meeting room. "It's really an egg factory, isn't it?" Akiyama explained that egg prices had been unstable in the past few years, and that two years ago a nationwide surplus had caused a crisis, driving even some large producers, those with a million birds or more, out of business. But after that, production controls were put in place and a balance struck between supply and demand. Also working in their favor was the fact that most of the feed was imported, since the strong yen had brought costs down and made business profitable.

The talk moved to Kikutani's commute. It would take him something over an hour from the station near the halfway house—a long way but not impossible. Akiyama said that the other employees all lived nearby, and they might be able to find Kikutani a room in the company dormitory.

"What do you think?" Kiyoura said.

"I'd prefer to commute from the house," Kikutani answered emphatically. Since leaving prison, he had come to think of the halfway house as his one refuge. The thought of moving out and living near the farm had no appeal at all. With that settled, Akiyama moved on to the matter of reimbursement for Kikutani's commute. There were, he said, employees who used the bus, but Kikutani's fare was bound to be much higher, and it would be unfair for the employer to fund the whole thing. Akiyama said he was willing to pay for half. Kikutani agreed, and they decided he would start work the day after next. Akiyama left the room for a moment and returned with two red net bags of the sort used for carrying fruit.

"These are double-yolk eggs, and these are regular ones," he said. "They're about as fresh as you can get. Please, take them as a souvenir of your visit." Kiyoura thanked him, and then he and Kikutani took their leave. As they walked back to the bus stop, Kikutani realized that he had been worried about his new job, but now that he'd seen the place, he thought he would be able to handle it. His greatest worry had been his coworkers, and he found it particularly reassuring that the henhouse was completely automated. What a relief to think that he'd be surrounded by chickens instead of people. He was happy, too, to be working far from the city, near the woods and fields, sights he hadn't seen in many years.

What's more, he'd come away with a good impression of Akiyama. That the man was willing to hire someone with a background like Kikutani's was proof of a broad-minded and generous spirit. There was no trace of the hard-nosed, miserly attitude usual with managers; rather, he seemed relaxed and friendly. The only thing that troubled Kikutani was that Akiyama had kept his eyes fixed on Kiyoura almost the entire time, hardly even glancing in Kikutani's direction.

No doubt he avoided looking at him because he was acutely conscious of his past.

"Sensei," he began, to get Kiyoura's attention.

"I've told you that you should stop calling me sensei," Kiyoura interrupted, chuckling. "Kiyoura is enough. It sounds funny to be called sensei by an older man."

"I just wanted to ask you before I start there: does the boss know that I killed someone?" The sound of birds chirping in the woods rose to a crescendo.

"Of course he knows. I didn't go into details, and he didn't ask, but I did tell him that there were extenuating circumstances." Kiyoura glanced at Kikutani and then back at the road.

"Do you think he'll tell the other people who work there about me?" Kikutani continued.

"I've asked him not to, and he seems to understand. He said that only he and his wife will know." As they came out onto the gravel road, Kiyoura turned to look at him. Kikutani could see the concern in his eyes about the long and difficult path that lay ahead of Kikutani.

They reached the bus stop. Kiyoura contemplated the fields.

"The air out here is wonderful, isn't it?" he said, shading his eyes and looking up at the sky. At last the bus came into view along the winding road, threading its way among the widely scattered houses, a few of which still had ancient thatched roofs.

The next day, Kiyoura gave Kikutani directions to a store that sold work clothes. The racks were filled with bluish outfits, but these reminded Kikutani of the prison uniforms, so he ended up with a light-brown shirt and pants. His next stop was a sporting goods store, where he bought a pair of white canvas shoes. He finished his shopping trip at a men's shop, where he found three pairs of socks for 1000 yen.

He returned to the house, but felt tense and restless. It wasn't that he wasn't used to work; he'd worked hard at the prison. But there everything had been laid out for him: his work clothes, choice of jobs, everything. He had simply done as he was told. Now things were different. It was all very well to say that he should simply relax and let things happen as they would, but he knew he had to take care of himself, had to buy his own clothes and do all the other things necessary to hold down a job. He began to worry that he had forgotten something, that he had overlooked some important point.

He ran through his schedule for the following day. In order to reach the farm by 8:00, when work started, he would have to leave the house around 6:15. Breakfast would have to be at 6:00. Since he was going to work at a chicken farm, it made sense for him to wear his work clothes on the train, yet he wanted to do things the way he'd done them when he was a teacher: he wanted to wear his suit for the commute. He could tie his work clothes and shoes in a bundle and carry them on the train. He reviewed the transfer to the bus in his mind, imagined himself arriving at the farm and entering the henhouse. Then it struck him: he hadn't given any thought to what he would do for lunch. Since the house didn't provide lunches, it wasn't likely they would pack anything for him. And he couldn't remember seeing anything resembling a restaurant anywhere near the farm. He would make do with some bread and milk. But the stores were not likely to be open that early in the morning. He would have to buy something tonight.

After dinner, he went out to the shops to get some pastries and milk. He was surprised to learn that milk was now sold in containers made of heavy paper rather than glass. He would have liked to keep looking for a bottle, but it didn't seem worth the effort, so he bought a carton and went back to his room. Finally able to relax, he took a pen and paper from one of his cardboard boxes and wrote a letter to his brother. He quoted Kiyoura: finding a job was the first step in reentering society. But it also meant that he was taking his first steps out into an unknown world after fifteen years of prison life. There would be no walls, no guards to watch his every move—something he'd dreamed about for a long time, but now that it was about to come true, he was oddly nervous. He wanted to tell his brother about his fear of the life that awaited him, but he found himself writing the standard sort of letter he had written from prison: he was happy to have found work, and he would try to apply himself to the job. As he folded the letter and slid it into the envelope, he felt a wave of sadness that he had no one to write to but his brother.

He wrapped his work clothes and boots in a neat bundle and placed it next to his futon before going to sleep, which he did earlier than usual. The next morning, he woke to the alarm he had bought. He shaved, then raced through breakfast in the dining hall. He put on his suit and, taking his package, went downstairs. Kiyoura, looking sleepy, poked his head out of the office.

"Good luck," he said. Kikutani realized that he had risen early just to see him off on his first day of work.

"Thanks," he said. "I'll be back this evening." Outside in the street, the shutters on the shops were still closed tight, but the sidewalk was already crowded with commuters hurrying to the station. His pace quickened to match theirs, and he was soon pushing his way through the turnstile and up to the platform.

As on the previous day, the trains heading downtown were packed with people, but his outbound car was relatively empty. He stood near the door and looked out the window. Sunlight flooded the streets along the track; they were lined with tall white buildings. Here and there he could make out a school, a hospital, an apartment tower. As they left the city, trees and houses began to appear among the buildings. Eventually, the train arrived at the station near his job, and he got off and made his way down to the bus depot. He boarded the bus, which was full of high school students, and it set off almost immediately. The bus made one pass through the town and then headed out into more rural streets. A school, built up against the hills on the right, came into view, and the students got off, leaving behind the faint odor of young bodies.

The bus reached the stop at the edge of the woods, and Kikutani got off. He hurried along the road, glancing at the men and women working in the fields and at their trucks and plows parked along the paths. He passed through the gate to the chicken farm and peeked into the office. The clock on the wall said he was fifteen minutes early. Relieved, he opened the office door a few inches.

"Good morning," he called to the woman at the desk, then closed the door and stood waiting outside. A few minutes later, a line of men and women streamed in through the gate, passing the office and heading for the processing center and the buildings beyond. A few of the women turned to eye Kikutani doubtfully. Looking back into the office, he caught sight of Akiyama entering from the rear. Akiyama seemed to see him at the same moment, and after saying a few words to the woman at the desk, he came out to join Kikutani.

"Good morning," Kikutani said, his voice eager.

Akiyama looked down at his suit. "You can't work in that," he muttered.

"I brought work clothes with me," Kikutani said.

"Fine. Come with me," said Akiyama, leading him to a door at the end of one of the buildings. They entered a large room that appeared to be the employee dining hall: rows of wooden tables and benches on a concrete floor, and one wall lined with wooden lockers. Akiyama opened one of the lockers. "Get changed, please," he said. "You can leave your clothes in here."

Kikutani got out of his suit and folded it carefully with his dress shirt. He laid his good clothes in the locker on top of the cloth in which his work clothes had been wrapped, arranged his shoes and lunch on the shelf below, and closed the door. He hurried to put on his work clothes and canvas shoes. When he was finished, Akiyama, who had been waiting on one of the benches, rose and led the way outside. In front of the processing center, a young man in a white uniform and cap was loading a truck with cartons printed with the words FRESH EGGS: AKIYAMA FARMS. They stopped at the bottom of the stairs that led to the henhouse, where a short, stout man in his fifties was smoking a cigarette. Tufts of white hair protruded from under his work cap. Pausing between puffs, he nodded slightly and wished Akiyama good morning in a voice that was as thin and high-pitched as a child's.

"This is Koinuma," said Akiyama. "And this is Kikutani, the man I told you about yesterday. I want you to show him around and teach him the ropes." The introductions made, Akiyama spoke with Koinuma briefly about the day's work and then went back to the office. Kikutani bowed again, wondering what Akiyama had told Koinuma about him. But there was no hint of distrust in the eyes that returned his look, and he felt he could believe Kiyoura's reassurances that Akiyama would not discuss his past.

Koinuma tossed his cigarette aside and began climbing the stairs. "Just stick close and watch everything I do," he said over his shoulder. "In a month you'll know everything you need to, more or less. Usually there are two of us, but we take a day off on alternate weeks, and when you're alone here, it can get a little busy. The other guy's off today, but when he comes back, the three of us will have it easy." His tone was cheerful and encouraging, but as he opened the door to the henhouse, the squawking seemed to rush out and envelop Kikutani. "Almost everything's done by machine," Koinuma continued. "A timer turns things on in the morning. All we have to do is make sure the system's working and take care of a few things the machines don't cover." The conveyor belt dappled with eggs was already moving through the building. Koinuma checked the feeding and watering systems and then strolled slowly down the aisle between the cages, turning left and right to look in each as he passed. When the men approached, the birds started and cackled; heads bobbed and wings flapped.

The cages were raised to allow the droppings to fall onto

a shelf that ran below; from there, they fell again to a hold-ing area under the floor. The purpose of the shelf was to al-low some of the moisture from the droppings to evaporate right there in the henhouse. Under the floor, big fans spun continually to further dry them. Wet droppings gave off a tremendous stench, which, when the wind was in a certain direction, brought complaints from the nearby houses. Thus, all the fuss and precautions. From time to time Koinuma would stop and use a pole he carried with him to dislodge piles of droppings and send them tumbling to the lower level. This, he told Kikutani, was a big part of the job.

At one point Koinuma stopped and peered into a cage. Kikutani came up beside him. "This one's been eating poorly for a couple of days. Doesn't look like she's had much today either," he said. Unlike the other hens, whose necks seemed to be continually shooting out toward the feed trough, this bird sat quite still, her head almost motionless. "Until about ten years ago, it used to be that some disease would get into a henhouse, and you'd have tens of thousands of chickens die overnight. Nowadays we vaccinate them, and it's pretty rare we lose any. Still, sometimes you have one like this that gets sick. You watch it for a couple of days, and if it still looks bad, you get it out of there." He looked up from the cage and started down the row.

They continued this stop-and-start pace for a long while, and Kikutani could feel his legs growing heavy. And the incessant, restless motion of bird's heads tired his eyes. At some point, however, without his noticing it, the smell of the droppings and the deafening clucking began to bother him less.

At noon, they left the henhouse and went to the dining hall. At the long tables, lines of men and women sat with their lunch boxes in front of them. "This is Kikutani," Koinuma called out to the room as he fished in his locker for his lunch. "He just started today, and he'll be working with me." Kikutani straightened himself, bowed in the direction of the tables, and gave the required greeting. He could feel eyes on him, and he was beginning to have difficulty breathing, but there were several friendly replies to his words, and then people went back to their chatter and their lunches. He sat at the corner of one table and began to chew on his bread, washing it down with the milk. Before long Koinuma came with a teakettle and cups and, sitting next to him, poured him some tea.

"Mind if I ask how old you are?" he said, peering around to look Kikutani in the eye.

"Fifty," Kikutani replied, reaching for the teacup.

"Two years older than I am. You look younger—forty-five at most, I'd have guessed." He glanced at Kikutani again as he lit a cigarette. "Where were you born?"

"Chiba prefecture," Kikutani said.

"Chiba, huh? When I was young, I worked for a whole-sale fish place in Choshi. Whereabouts in Chiba?"

"Sakura," Kikutani muttered, stammering a bit. As soon as he opened his mouth, he regretted not having picked some other place for his home. What if someone working at this chicken farm was from Sakura, or had relatives there, or friends? Even if it was seventeen years ago now, they'd probably still remember the incident that had been the talk of the town for months. Because it involved a teacher, the newspapers were full of it, and it was been written up in the weekly magazines. Lots of people must still remember his name. He looked away from Koinuma.

"Sakura? Isn't that near Narita? I've been through there in the truck lots of times on my way to Tokyo or Chiba. Quiet spot, isn't it?" Koinuma propped his elbow on the table and puffed on his cigarette. Kikutani relaxed a little, feeling fairly sure that Koinuma didn't know any more about his hometown. Nestling his teacup in both hands, he sipped in silence. His heart sank at the thought that from now on he would have to live with the fear that his past might become known.

"The boss said that the print shop where you were working went belly-up. So things are even worse in the print business, huh?" Kikutani could feel himself begin to sweat. Kiyoura must have told Akiyama that he'd worked as a proofreader for the prison printing house, and Akiyama had told Koinuma that it was for a regular printer.

"The printing business has changed a lot, and companies that don't keep up don't make it," Kikutani answered haltingly, mouthing something he'd heard in the prison shop.

"Makes sense," said Koinuma. "That's the way it works when everything's riding on machines. You take this business—ten years ago we used buckets to fill the feed boxes. It took a lot of men and a lot of hard work to keep those chickens fed. But the boss was smart: he tore down the old henhouse and built this new, American-style mechanized operation. First time I saw it in action, you could have knocked me over with a feather." Koinuma laughed, and Kikutani smiled back at him.

In the afternoon, Koinuma took a chicken from its cage.

Its eyes fluttered open and closed sluggishly, and its wings seemed almost limp. They took it out to one corner of the grounds, where Koinuma deftly wrung its neck. It hadn't been eating for four days, Koinuma explained, instructing Kikutani to dig a hole. The tiny tongue jutted out from the beak as Kikutani tossed the dirt on the body.

The automatic feeder was set up to operate at specified hours, moving feed from the hopper into the troughs and finally to the individual cages. The cycle repeated four times a day. At closing time, Koinuma locked the henhouse, and they walked down the stairs. Kikutani changed into his suit in the dining hall while the other workers filed out in their work clothes.

It was past six-thirty when he arrived back at the house. Exhausted, he barely managed to strip off his suit jacket before flopping on the tatami. A half hour later, he made his way down to the dining room. While he was eating dinner, Kiyoura came in to say that he wanted to talk to him, so when Kikutani finished, he went to the office. Kiyoura told him to wait in the meeting room. A moment later he came in himself and nodded to Kikutani to have a seat on the couch. He questioned him about his first day at work. Kikutani was able to answer honestly that he was completely satisfied and didn't see any reason why he couldn't go on there indefinitely.

"That's wonderful," said Kiyoura, nodding. "You know," he continued, "I had a call from Akiyama a little while ago." Kikutani looked up. Akiyama had seemed friendly enough, but he must have had second thoughts about hiring Kikutani. Perhaps he phoned to say Kikutani didn't need to come tomorrow. Akiyami had been willing to try to conceal

Kikutani's past from the other employees, but it proved too difficult and now he was losing his nerve. If it became known in the neighborhood that he had a man working for him who had received an indefinite prison sentence, the little farming village would begin to gossip and the other employees would be up in arms. Some of them would probably demand that Kikutani be fired. It was undoubtedly something like this that led Akiyama to phone Kiyoura after Kikutani left the farm.

"It's about your head," Kiyoura said, studying him. Kikutani looked puzzled. "You either need to cut your hair shorter or grow it out. The way it is now, Akiyama is worried the people at the farm will suspect something." There was a hint of laughter in his eyes. "Now that he mentions it, you do look a little odd with your hair like that." Once parole was granted, a prisoner was allowed to begin growing his hair back so that it wouldn't attract attention outside. But Kikutani's last prison haircut had been just two weeks before he was notified of his release, and now his hair was at a particularly awkward length. "You can shave it back to the way it was if you want," Kiyoura continued, "but it looks a little strange this way. It probably makes sense to grow it out. Why don't you go to a barber and get it trimmed for the time being." As Kiyoura spoke, the purpose of Akiyama's phone call became clear, and Kikutani could feel the tension draining from his body.

"At most barbers," Kiyoura said, taking out a scrap of paper and beginning to draw a map, "they'll want to make small talk with a new customer, ask him where he lives, that kind of thing. That's a little awkward for our residents, so I usually suggest they go to a place near the station. It's half the price of other shops, and that means they really have to move the customers through. A haircut there takes about a third the usual time, so the barber can't chitchat." He finished the map and held it out to Kikutani. Running his hand over his head and smiling sheepishly, Kikutani took the paper and left the room.

He went upstairs, put on his suit, and set out in the direction of the station. As he walked, he thought about the care that Akiyama had shown in worrying about such a minor detail, and a feeling of deep gratitude welled up in him. Also, if Akiyama was willing to go to the trouble to phone Kiyoura about Kikutani's hair, then he must be planning to keep him on at the farm. Kikutani was already keenly aware how lucky he was having someone like Kiyoura to take such good care of him; it seemed almost more than he could hope for to have yet another person he could trust and depend on.

The barbershop turned out to be a big place with a long row of chairs. All the barbers were young men. The waiting area was full, but the customers were called one after another, and within ten minutes Kikutani was being led to a chair in front of the long mirror.

"I'd like to let my hair grow out…," he managed, looking up at the barber, a man in his early twenties with long sideburns.

"Very well," the barber replied, and without another word he began to move his hands nimbly around Kikutani's head. He trimmed around the edges with scissors, did a quick shave along the neck, and then shampooed his hair. When Kikutani looked up and saw himself in the mirror, he thought he looked younger, thanks to the haircut. The barber removed the white towel that had been wrapped around his neck, and Kikutani stood and walked over to the cash register. The bill came to 1200 yen. Kikutani reached into his jacket pocket for the money, waited for his change, then made his way out to the street. He had thought he was becoming used to the way prices had gone up, but the haircut shocked him. His old barbershop, before the trial, had charged 450, a third of what he had just paid—and this was an exceptionally cheap place, as Kiyoura had said. How much would it have cost at a normal barber? He looked around at the men passing on the sidewalk and marveled that their hair looked neatly tended and freshly cut; no doubt they were all paying these prices for haircuts and still managing to make ends meet. The next morning, he looked in at the office on the way to the henhouse. Akiyama, sitting at his desk, glanced up as the door opened, and a smile spread across his face. Kikutani bowed deeply without saying a word.

Koinuma's partner in the henhouse, a man in his mid-twenties named Shirakawa, was back from his day off. As Kikutani had done the day before, he followed Koinuma through the rows of cages. Then Shirakawa asked him to load boxes of eggs in the container truck and clean the floor of the henhouse. It was decided that Kikutani's day off would be Wednesday.

After he began working at the farm, Kikutani rarely left the halfway house except for his commute. When he arrived back at his room after a long day at work, he would feel the familiar relief that had always come over him when he returned to his cell. Taking up his position on the tatami, he would sit quietly until bedtime, never even going down to watch the television in the dining hall. On his day off, things were much the same: he stayed in his room as much as he could. At one point, Akiyama said that Kikutani needed a resident's card in order to sign up for insurance, so Kiyoura took him to the Ward Office to fill out the necessary papers. As agreed, Akiyama deducted half the cost of Kikutani's commute from his salary and bought the train and bus passes for him. Before Kikutani knew it, the cherry trees along the tracks had shed their blossoms, and a deep green was saturating the landscape.

The month during which he was allowed to eat a free breakfast and dinner in the dining hall expired, and he began to stop at a cheap restaurant near the station on his way to work. He discovered a chain store that sold boxed meals, and he took these for lunches at the farm. The menu changed from day to day, and Shirakawa noticed how good they looked, even asking Kikutani to buy one for him from time to time.

As the days got warmer, swarms of flies appeared beneath the floors of the henhouse. It seemed that the mounds of chicken excrement made an ideal place for them to lay their eggs. As the droppings accumulated, they were scooped up by a small backhoe, loaded into a truck, and shipped about a mile away to a second factory, near the hills, that the farm owned. Here they had a new, windowless brooder house, but also a machine that automatically dried and pulverized the endless stream of excrement. When it had been reduced to a fine powder, it was packed in bags and sold to nurseries and landscapers. At times, Kikutani was sent over to help pack the powdered droppings.

He had grown used to making small talk with the other employees, but one day early in May, Koinuma came up with an unexpected question. "You're single, aren't you?" he asked. "I hear that your wife got sick and died." Kikutani looked up from his lunch and met his gaze. He knew that Koinuma had been around the farm longer than anyone else and that he and Akiyama were friendly. He had probably asked about Kikutani's background, and Akiyama had come up with this story. Soon after starting the job, Kikutani realized that there was a good chance that at some point someone would ask him about his family; he had even given some thought to how he should answer. But Koinuma's question came out of the blue, and he was flustered.

"Uhh," he stammered, nodding vaguely and looking down at his lunch. He knew that he should answer the question evenly and calmly, with no hint of agitation, but he could feel himself losing control of his emotions as his face contracted into a grimace. The endless months and years in prison had been one long battle with those horrible memories, one long reflection on the awful inevitability of his actions. No doubt the court that handed down his sentence hoped that he would use his time in prison to repent his crime and rehabilitate himself, but he had remained unable to find any remorse in his heart. Yet time had eventually turned his memories into pale, still shadows that were no longer able to stir him. He had, in the end, found a kind of peace, and he was reluctant now to let anyone disturb it.

"Must be hard living by yourself," said Koinuma, puffing on a cigarette. "And it can't be much fun coming all the way out here from Shinjuku. There are plenty of houses around here that would rent you a room. You should think about moving. I can think of a couple of places that might suit you. Want me to ask around?"

"It's really nice of you to think of it, but I've lived in town where there are lots of people, ever since I left home, and I'm used to it...." He began to work his chopsticks again.

"I get it. But going to Tokyo makes me feel dizzy, like I can't even breathe." After that, Koinuma fell silent.

Kikutani had known that these questions were coming. His story had some holes in it, holes that he must try to fill. If the print shop where he had worked went out of business, there must have been other places in the city where he could have found work. Why would he come all the way out here for a job at a chicken farm? Also, there was his suit—not exactly the normal commuting attire for someone who tended hens, who spent a good bit of his time shoveling chicken shit.

Koinuma sat quietly smoking his cigarette. Kikutani knew he must be wondering what he had said to hurt his feelings, and Kikutani was overcome with a sense of hopelessness. His past was still coiled tightly about his heart, despite all the blank days in prison cut off from the world, and that past was waiting to be stirred up by any trivial question, was waiting to destroy him.

4

The rainy season had begun, and the fly population was exploding. Anyone approaching the henhouse was greeted by an enormous swarm, and even in the dining hall the workers constantly had to brush them away just to be able to eat. The flies also seemed to be riding the wind into the nearby residential areas, which brought irate calls to the office. Koinuma had Kikutani spray pesticide on the droppings piled under the building and treat them with a powder meant to kill the maggots, but nothing helped. The air was filled with buzzing.

One evening, when Kikutani returned to the halfway house, he was called into the reception room. "I mentioned when you moved in that in principle you're allowed to stay here three months," said Kiyoura, reaching for a cup of instant coffee. "Part of the process of readjusting to life outside is getting your own place away from the house and learning to live by yourself. In a couple of weeks, you'll have reached the three-month limit, so I thought we should talk this over. We understand that there's a big difference between living here for free and renting, and that you've got to have enough money. That's why we let some residents stay for up to six months; we don't want you to feel rushed. So, what do you have in mind? Do you think you'll be going, or sticking around for a while?" Kikutani sat, silently absorbing this generous offer. He would have liked to stay where he was, but he knew he had to stop depending on Kiyoura's kindness and move out according to the rules. But what sort of place could he find? And how much would it cost? "What do you think?" Kiyoura prompted, lighting a cigarette.

Kikutani looked down at his lap. "I'll find a place somewhere...."

"I would like to tell you that you don't have to go if you're not ready, but to be honest I think the best thing for you would be to get out of here. You have a job, and as far as I can see, you've made a good start at readjusting. You can't lose your nerve now. Who knows, living alone may give you a real sense of freedom, open you up to new things. I think you should find a room and move out." From the look on his face, Kiyoura had got the answer he wanted.

"Do I need to talk to a realtor to find a room?" Kikutani asked. He remembered seeing slips of paper taped in the windows of the offices near the station; they described apartments of various sizes, but he knew he wouldn't have the courage to go in alone.

"I can help with that," said Kiyoura, watching Kikutani's reaction. "Now, you'll probably want a place somewhere nearer your job...."

Kikutani panicked. It was hard enough having to move

out, but he couldn't imagine living in a strange place far from the house, even if it meant shortening his commute. He didn't think he could live someplace where he couldn't stop by the house whenever he wanted, where he couldn't see Kiyoura every day.

"Actually, I think I'd like to be as close to here as possible," he said, determined to have his way on this one point.

A faint smile appeared on Kiyoura's face. "I see," he said. "So you're not so different from the others. Everyone who gets out after a long sentence wants a place near the house. I understand how you feel. But you need to think it over carefully. We're right next to Shinjuku, and all the people who work at the bars and clubs live around here, which means rents are high. You should get as far away from here as possible. It would make things simpler for you." Kiyoura's words piled up like a heavy weight on Kikutani's back.

"When you say rents are high, about what do they cost?" He stared up at Kiyoura.

"Well, a four-and-a-half tatami-mat room with a kitchen runs from 35,000 to 40,000 yen a month. Plus, when you move in, you need to pay the deposit and the equivalent of a month's rent for the realtor and the landlord."

The sum dismayed Kikutani. The rent would cost a third of his salary, and there would be bills for gas, electricity, water. He would be inviting disaster if took on such a rent. Even so, he couldn't think of moving far away from the house. If he cut his expenses to the bone, he could probably manage the rent, and the money he had saved in prison would cover the deposit and fees.

"It's too expensive, I know," said Kiyoura, pressing his point. "You really should look somewhere else, someplace close to work. It'd be much cheaper. You have your savings, but if you dip into them every month to make up what your salary can't cover, they'll be gone in no time. It would be a shame to see the money it took you all those years to earn get eaten up for no good reason. What do you say?"

Kikutani looked down again. He wanted to listen to Kiyoura, to obey him without question, but he wanted to live close to the halfway house even more. "I'm sorry, but I would still like to stay near here," he muttered.

"I see. Well, in that case we'll look in the neighborhood. Perhaps you'll change your mind in a few months and want to get rid of that long commute." Kiyoura seemed to have regained his good spirits.

Kikutani stood, bowed, and left without a word. Back in his room, he began to feel depressed that he had gone against Kiyoura's wishes. He had known that the time was coming when he would have to move out of the house, and he had tried to prepare himself, but he hadn't foreseen that Kiyoura would want him to move far away. Kiyoura was only thinking in practical, financial terms, but for Kikutani the house and Kiyoura were a lifeline to which he was desperately clinging. He knew that if they pushed him away, he would drift off into oblivion. A strange thought occurred to him, and he smiled bitterly to himself: if they forced him to move to the distant suburbs, he would be better off simply going back to his cell. How ironic this was; he thought of the great joy he felt when they gave him the release he had dreamed of for so long.

What was it that made him so uneasy at the prospect of separation from the house? In prison the high walls and steel bars had given him a sense of security. After long years of that environment, he experienced panic when he was left out in empty space with no restrictions or boundaries, like the fear of a mole suddenly forced out into the sunlight. The halfway house, a place where he could burrow in and escape that emptiness, was almost an extension of the prison. And Kiyoura was there too, Kiyoura who knew everything about his past and was always ready to offer the right advice or word of encouragement. To leave him, Kikutani felt, would be to lose himself. The best plan was to settle someplace near the house for as long as possible while he gradually grew accustomed to this vast, borderless expanse known as society; then, eventually, he might reach the point where he could live somewhere farther away.

The next evening, when Kikutani returned from work, Kiyoura called to him from the office as Kikutani was about to go upstairs.

"You're not going to believe this," he said, coming out of the office, "but you turn around these days, and things go up. It seems that a four-and-a-half mat room with a kitchen is 45,000 yen, plus one month's rent for fees and two months' rent for deposit. And that's on the cheap side, they tell me!" His scowl was almost comical.

"Is it near here?" asked Kikutani, studying his face.

"Do you know the noodle shop on the other side of the main street? You turn at that corner and then right again at the second cross street; there's an apartment building there. I went to have a look. The room's not too bad, but the rent's just too high." Kiyoura seemed irritated.

"But it's quite nearby," Kikutani stammered. "It sounds fine."

"Are you sure? Even at that rent? Think it over. I don't

know how you'll manage month after month." His eyes bore into Kikutani's.

"I'll manage, somehow," Kikutani mumbled. He knew that Kiyoura was against his living close to the house, and his intensity was distressing.

"Well, you're the one signing the lease, and if you don't care about the rent, then go look at the place. You'll decide whether it's what you want or whether you should look for somewhere else. When you finish dinner, let me know, and we can go together. I'll be in the office."

Kikutani hurried through his meal and then cracked open the office door. Kiyoura appeared a moment later, and they walked through the shopping district in silence. They passed under the train tracks and stopped at a realtor's office. Sliding open the door, they were greeted by a middle-aged man in a loud checkered suit. Kiyoura told him their business, and the realtor picked up the phone and dialed a number. Telling the man on the other end of the line, presumably the manager of the apartments, that they were on their way, he hung up and escorted them from the office. He walked ahead with Kiyoura, explaining in a tone that sounded defensive that the recent rise in land prices had encouraged all the landlords to raise rents.

The streets through which he led them were lined with stucco apartment buildings and small condominiums. He turned into the entrance of one of them and knocked on the manager's door. A man in a polo shirt appeared and gave them the key. Back out in the street, the realtor told them that the woman who owned this building, as well as two others nearby, had the manager living on the premises to keep an eye on things. The room Kikutani was to rent was off a small alley next to the building. The realtor led them up a metal staircase that clung to the building, and fit the key into the lock of the apartment on the end. He groped around in the dark and at last found the light switch. As Kikutani followed the two men into the narrow entrance and removed his shoes, he found himself in a small, Japanese-style room with a kitchen and bath to his left. The walls were dingy, but the tatami mats and the sliding doors on the closet were new. He stood, silently looking around the room.

"Well?" asked Kiyoura, trying the faucets in the kitchen.

"It's fine," said Kikutani, almost without thinking. Unlike the larger room at the halfway house, this one was almost exactly the dimensions of his cell; the walls pressing in on him made him feel at home. The stark facade of the condominium just outside the window was also to his liking.

"You shouldn't make up your mind so fast," Kiyoura cautioned. "At any rate, the rent's too high." He seemed angry. Kikutani looked around the room again; he opened the door to the bathroom and peered up at the ceiling. "Well?" repeated Kiyoura.

"I like it," Kikutani replied almost inaudibly.

"If that's the case...," Kiyoura murmured.

The realtor was studying them closely. "You'll take it, then?" he asked. At Kiyoura's nod, he slipped on his gold-buckle shoes and led the way out of the room, waiting to lock the door behind them. They followed him down the stairs, and after returning the key to the manager, he led them back to his office. He pulled a standard contract from his files and spread it out on the desk for them to look at, and then Kikutani signed and marked the signature with his seal, followed by Kiyoura, who served as his guarantor. The day after tomorrow was Kikutani's day off, and they decided he would move in then, paying the deposit and fees when he actually took possession.

"Did he know that I just got out of prison?" asked Kikutani when they were in the street again. He had noticed that the man avoided looking him in the eye.

"Probably," said Kiyoura. "Almost certainly. I'm sure he knows what sort of place I run. But if there's one thing you can say for this realtor, he's tight-lipped. He won't say a word to the landlord or the manager; otherwise, I wouldn't use him." Kikutani followed Kiyoura back to the house in silence.

Two days later, it was moving day, and Kikutani was busy from early morning. The envelope containing his savings was removed from the safe in the office. He checked the account book, verifying the balance, and then went with Kiyoura to a bank near the station. He deposited all but 300,000 yen, receiving a bank book and the promise of a cash card in the mail. Then they met the manager of the apartment building at the realtor's and, having paid the advance rent, deposit, and fees, received the key. They paid the realtor his fee as well. They went to the shopping district to buy some of the items Kikutani would need to set up house. Kiyoura took him first to a bedding store. After a friendly conversation with the owner, he picked out a futon, sheets, and a pillow, and asked to have them delivered in the evening. Next was a hardware store for cooking equipment. Kikutani would have to begin cooking for himself in order to economize,

Kiyoura explained. They bought a rice cooker, a kettle, a saucepan, a frying pan, and a kitchen knife, as well as teacups, plates, chopsticks, and even a small low table. As he walked along with Kiyoura, both carrying the purchases, Kikutani felt his spirits sinking at the thought that he had just spent more than 230,000 yen. An amount it had taken him two and a half years to earn in prison was gone in less than three hours.

Kiyoura pointed out the public bath and a laundromat. They went back to the house. Kiyoura made him some instant coffee in the reception room, which Kikutani sat and drank, recovering from the morning's ordeal. Kiyoura took out a cigarette, and then he said something unexpected. While Kikutani had been living in the house, Kiyoura served as his parole officer, managing his readjustment, but once Kikutani moved out, his case would be taken over by the parole officer for the district where he would be living. As Kiyoura said this, Kikutani's face went pale, and he sat, cup in hand, staring at Kiyoura.

"I'll work with you until the end of the month, but then you'll be switched to a man named Takebayashi. I'll send the forms for the transfer off to the parole board. In the meantime, I don't want you to worry; Takebayashi is a wonderful man." His tone was light, almost careless. But Kikutani felt he was being abandoned: not only did he have to leave the house but his ties with Kiyoura were to be cut as well.

Some of the young staff members helped Kikutani carry his boxes of clothes and cooking utensils down to the car. "I'll come visit," said Kiyoura, smiling at Kikutani as Kikutani crawled into the passenger seat. At the apartment building, they helped him move the boxes to the bottom of the stairs, after which Kikutani carried things up and arranged them in his room. When he was done, he locked the door and sat in the middle of the small area of tatami mats, crossing his legs more comfortably than he had before. He had left the house and found his own place. From now on, he told himself, he was free to do as he liked—and the first thing he would change was the stiff, uncomfortably formal, bent-leg way of sitting to which he had become accustomed in prison. But he found that it had been so long since he'd sat any other way, this more relaxed position actually made his thighs and calves ache. He stretched his legs out across the tatami. It was a devastating discovery, that the habits of prison life were still deeply rooted in his body. Perhaps it was too soon for him to be out on his own. But it was Kiyoura himself, with his long experience with parolees, who had decided it was time for Kikutani to go, and Kikutani would have to do his best to prove him right.

The room had grown dark. He stood and turned on the lights. The outlines of furniture from previous residents appeared as white shadows on the walls. A knock at the door startled him from his inspection of the walls. "Futon delivery," said a voice. Kikutani opened the door to find a young man with a large bundle on his shoulders. "I've brought your bed," the man said, setting his load down in the entrance. He began unwrapping the bedding and laying it out. When he finished, he had Kikutani sign a receipt and left. Kikutani put the futon away in the closet. Through the wall he could hear the sound of an old romantic ballad playing on and on; it stopped at last. Then someone left the apartment, locking the door and charging down the stairs. Suddenly Kikutani realized he was hungry, so he went out to buy some bread. The alley in front of the apartment building was deserted, but as soon as he turned the corner, he could see the lights and the crowds of the shopping district. Clutching the key in his pocket, he set off down the street.

5

On his first day off in July, Kikutani went to see Kiyoura in order to be introduced to the man who would be taking over as his parole officer. When they were settled in the reception room, Kiyoura launched into a description: Kyutaro Takebayashi was seventy-five and the owner of a rice shop and a market attached to it, though he had turned the management of these over to his eldest son and his son's wife. Kikutani noticed that Kiyoura's face was sterner than usual.

Parole officers, Kiyoura explained, were appointed by the Ministry of Justice and were invariably people of impeccable character who had earned the trust of society. They were given the title of part-time civil servants, but they received no compensation whatsoever; their work was really a form of charity. Dealing with the difficulties encountered during the rehabilitation of men on parole required extraordinary amounts of time and energy. With that in mind, Kikutani should make sure that he didn't create any additional burden for Takebayashi and should follow all the rules set up under the code governing parolees. Twice a month he was to call on his parole officer and sit for an interview in which he would give a detailed and accurate report on every aspect of his activities. If he wanted to move, or take a trip lasting more than seven days, he was to submit a request to the board through his parole officer and obtain prior permission. In the case of trips lasting less than seven days, he was to explain the reason for the trip and obtain verbal permission from the officer.

When Kiyoura finished his instructions, his expression softened. "'Parole officer' sounds serious and impressive, but you can think of him as a wise old man in the neighborhood who is there to offer advice about anything at all—work, your health, problems you can't handle yourself. Your parole officer is well connected and knows about life; he'll find a way to help you. Understand?"

"Yes," said Kikutani.

"Good. Then let's go," said Kiyoura, rising from the couch. A car was waiting for them in front of the house. The day was hot, the streets pale and shimmering. Posters announcing a big summer sale hung in front of a dress shop. Takebayashi's house was close by; Kiyoura pulled into the garage of a large, venerable-looking rice store. A supermarket was attached to the right side. Standing in the spacious entrance of the shop, Kiyoura called out a greeting, and almost immediately a woman appeared and then retreated back down the hall. A white-haired old man emerged from the garden in back and urged them to come in. When they removed their shoes, they were shown into a large living room with one side open to a veranda looking out on a garden. Delicate bamboo blinds had been hung in the room and veranda, and through these they could see the mottled orange, gold, and white of carp in a pond. After being introduced by Kiyoura, Kikutani bowed very deeply.

"I'm Takebayashi," the old man began. "It's a pleasure to meet you. As I see it, this is really pretty simple: you stop by here a couple of times a month for a chat, and that's about it. If something's bothering you, you should feel free to tell me. If it's something I can help with, I'll do what I can...," he said, breaking into a smile. His wife brought chilled wheat tea and some old-fashioned sweets. She sat down next to her husband. Kikutani was tense in the unfamiliar surroundings, but as he listened to the quiet conversation between Kiyoura and the elderly couple, he gradually began to feel more at ease.

"Do you drink?" Takebayashi asked. Kikutani replied that he did not. "Most men don't right after they get out," Takebayashi continued. "But a little drink now and then could do you good. Helps you unwind. Me, I couldn't do without it. In my younger days, I used to spend a lot of time at the geisha houses, but I'm getting a bit old for that now. Still, the old woman here keeps me company, and we have a glass or two." His wife laughed as he finished speaking.

"It must be lonely, living by yourself," she said. "You should come have dinner with us from time to time." Takebayashi seconded this invitation and then asked about Kikutani's job, his apartment, and the other details of his life. Kikutani went through each point, expressing his satisfaction

with the way things had been arranged, as Takebayashi nodded in approval. A half hour later, they left Takebayashi's
shop.

"He's a fine man," said Kiyoura as he climbed in the car
and headed back to the halfway house. "He understands the
job. He should, I suppose; he's been at it almost twenty
years."

A wave of relief and gratitude washed over Kikutani
with the realization that there was another person he could
rely on besides Kiyoura. Yet at the same time it seemed
strange that there were people like these two who were willing to extend a helping hand to men just out of prison, who
exhausted themselves making sure the parolees found their
footing and didn't return to dissolution or crime. Why were
they willing to take on this kind of work, even when it
meant giving up any semblance of a normal existence? And
they didn't take credit publicly for it, keeping secret the fact
that they were parole officers. Clearly, they were in it not
for the glory but because they believed in the possibility of
rehabilitation and in the value of social service. Kikutani
knew he would not have to be convinced to pay his regular
visits to Takebayashi.

The flies in the henhouse multiplied prodigiously, and
the workers spent a good portion of their time spraying pes-
ticides. Also the droppings where the flies bred had to be removed more frequently. Kikutani spent several days at the
farm annex stuffing bags with dried excrement to be sold as
fertilizer.

Since moving into the apartment, Kikutani had started
making a simple breakfast for himself and then a lunch to

take to work. He gave up eating out. It seemed that most of the other people in his building worked at night; there was hardly any sound to be heard before he left for work early in the morning or after he got back in the evening. If he woke in the middle of the night, however, he would hear the faint sounds of people talking or a radio playing, then someone humming to himself as he came up the stairs, then a door opening, a door slamming. Once, on his day off, he ran into the man who lived next door, and they exchanged nods. The man was young and wore his hair in a permanent wave. Kikutani guessed he must work in a bar. But the man vanished into his room without a word before Kikutani could say anything.

Toward the end of the month, he went to visit Takebayashi. He found him standing at the edge of the pond in his garden. "Oh, good to see you. You're looking well," Takebayashi said, glancing up when Kikutani appeared. Then his attention returned to the pond. Kikutani stood beside him, gazing into the murky yellow water. The shadows of large carp were dimly visible beneath the surface. "They're infested with fish lice," Takebayashi said. "I was just about to treat the pond. Used to be when this happened, most of the fish would die. But this new stuff pretty much takes care of the problem." He studied the water. Kikutani remembered the brightly colored carp swimming in the moat of the castle near the high school where he taught. Originally released as tiny things, they had grown year by year despite the fact that no one fed them, until they were a swarming mass of color, gracefully weaving their way amid the duckweed. It was said that there were nearly two hundred of them; but one year in midsummer, some started floating belly-up on the surface of the moat, and in ten days more than half were dead. He had heard that a pest had infected the fish—perhaps this fish lice that Takebayashi had mentioned.

Takebayashi sat down on the edge of the veranda, and Kikutani sat beside him. As they sipped tea that had been brought by his son's wife, Takebayashi listened intently to Kikutani's report on his daily activities. He asked whether Kikutani was in touch with his brother. Kikutani said that his brother had sent him rice, coffee, and other supplies. "Fine," said Takebayashi in his usual calm voice. At last Kikutani rose to go, promising that he would come again the next month.

When August arrived, they were suddenly quite busy at the farm. Thirty thousand adult chickens in the henhouse had to be replaced with younger birds. The process began with rearing thirty thousand chicks at the annex. On the grounds of the annex were four windowless concrete buildings: a brooder and three houses for raising the young chicks. They would buy hatchlings from a dealer and transfer them to cages in the brooder, twenty-six chicks to a cage. Sixty days later, the chicks would be moved to the other houses, where they would spend sixty more days until they reached the size where they were ready to lay. Then they would be used to replace chickens in the henhouse whose egg production had fallen off.

Before the young birds could be moved to the house, preparations had to be made. A number of men, recruited from the nearby farms, set to work in the rearing houses under Koinuma's supervision. These buildings were equipped with the latest technology from America, which kept the internal temperature constant and ensured proper ventilation.

The feeding and watering, too, were done automatically, and the droppings were removed on a conveyor belt, so that a whole building could be managed by just two men. During the night, the houses were unmanned, but if the temperature or ventilation showed an abnormal reading, a signal to Akiyama's house was triggered. If he was out, the call transferred automatically to the homes of several relatives in succession, and a recorded message reported the malfunction.

Before the young birds could be moved into the main henhouse, they had to be vaccinated against infectious diseases and treated with eyedrops. The men worked in groups of three: one to take the bird from the cage, one to administer the vaccine and the eyedrops, and one to return the bird to the cage. Kikutani joined one of these groups scattered throughout the henhouse, and in five days they had finished treating all thirty thousand birds. Next, they had to clip the beaks. If the chickens' beaks were left sharp, there was the danger they would peck one another to death in the cages. Also, sharp beaks were less efficient for pecking, and the hens tended to get less nourishment. To prevent both these problems, the men cut off the ends of the beaks. Again they worked in groups of three, using a red-hot pair of shears to cauterize the tip.

At the end of eight days, all the preparations were completed, and it was up to the specialists to select the birds that were to be replaced and dispose of them. One morning a dozen men showed up in a truck piled high with baskets. Entering the henhouse, they made their selections with startling speed and pulled the doomed birds from the cages, hauling them off stuffed ten to a basket. The baskets were piled back in the truck, and by the end of the first day, ten thousand chickens had vanished. These birds were destined to be plucked by means of a giant centrifuge, after which they would be cut up and processed for use as canned meat or in sausage.

When all thirty thousand had been carted off, Kikutani and the other men brought the young chickens from the annex in the container truck and transferred them to cages in the henhouse. This was heavy work, and Kikutani was so exhausted at the end of the day that he would find himself dozing off on the train home and missing his stop. When he finally reached his room, he had no energy left to make dinner and would simply lie on his back on the tatami mats.

Toward the end of August, the flies let up a bit, and by the beginning of September they were noticeably fewer in number. It grew cooler, and there were signs of autumn. The din in the henhouse was higher in pitch after the arrival of the young birds. The days passed peacefully. As Kiyoura had feared, Kikutani's rent proved to be a burden, but Akiyama called Kikutani in one day and told him he was raising his wages now that Kikutani was used to the job. So in the end Kikutani was able to manage without touching his savings, and he began to feel that he was achieving a degree of stability.

On payday, he stopped at a liquor store and bought some cans of beer before returning to his apartment. Prior to the incident, he was not in the habit of drinking at home in the evening, but there were times when he would go out with some of the other teachers and discuss work over a few drinks. He had never been able to drink much, but he found that he enjoyed feeling a little tipsy. Now, pouring the beer in a glass and taking a sip, he was reminded of the first time he had a drink, soon after starting at the university. Just as it had then, the beer tasted bitter, and he grimaced. He was amazed that anyone would think this was a treat; but before he even finished the glass, his belly began to feel warm, then his chest, and the feeling went to his head. In an instant he was reeling; the walls began to sway, and the tatami seemed to roll under him. It was difficult to sit up, but he planted his hands in front of him and looked around the room. Laughter came welling up in his throat: he had supposedly made some progress getting used to life again, but it amazed him to discover that it took only a sip of beer to make him drunk. The sixteen-year void in his life seemed huge to him now, and he realized how hard he would still have to work to bury those years, to make his life indistinguishable from other people's. If he drank a lot, eventually he'd get used to it again! A kind of euphoria enveloped him, and he sat in the middle of his room, laughing and laughing.

The leaves in the woods along the road from the bus stop to the chicken farm turned to their fall colors, then to brown, and soon they were dropping. When the wind blew through the branches, the withered leaves would whirl up like a flock of starlings and come fluttering down on the road and in the fields beyond. The days grew cooler, and gradually some of the commuters on the train appeared in coats. Fine autumn days followed one after another. The air outside the train window was crisp and clear, and the outline of mountains in the distance appeared sharp and vivid. The flies disappeared altogether. The heat in the henhouse was turned on, and when Kikutani opened the door, warm air enveloped him. It poured from thick conduits and was circulated through the building by the slowly revolving ventilation fans.

One day, when the temperature had fallen even more, Kikutani returned to his apartment to find a note from the building superintendent in his mailbox. It was a reminder that his contract stipulated that he could not have gas or oil heaters due to the fire hazard; he could use only an electric heater.

"Heat...," he muttered as he stared at the paper. He recalled the beginning of his first winter in prison, when he realized there would be no heat. After work, they returned to their cells for dinner and inspection. Then they had five minutes of "meditation," when they sat quietly on the floor. He could still remember how he shivered and his teeth chattered during those five minutes. When that was over, it was only a little after six o'clock, but they laid out their futons and climbed in, because that was the only way to endure the cold. He had heard from a man who worked with him in the print shop that prisons in colder places like Hokkaido had kerosene stoves that were brought out in September or October and set along the corridors that ran between the cells. Inmates in the north, it seemed, actually kept warmer. Here, the prisoners dreaded winter, but Kikutani found that as the years passed, he gradually became used to the cold, and even after the meditation time, he would continue his proofreading, rubbing his hands together or blowing on them to keep them warm.

Having put up with those hardships, Kikutani was sure that his apartment would be much warmer than his concrete cell. He didn't need to waste his money on a heater; if he was cold, he would simply go to bed early. But then he thought that prison life was meant to be different, that it had nothing to do with his life now. Since the dawn of time, when people felt cold, they lit fires to warm themselves. The technologies had changed, but even today this was a basic human instinct: to have heat in winter. He may have learned to stand the cold in prison, or to go to bed to keep warm, but that was not normal. Now that he was a free man, he should buy a heater like everyone else.

On his day off, he left his apartment, wearing his suit. His plan was to go to the street lined with shops and buy a heater at the appliance store, but when he remembered the day he spent with Kiyoura shopping to furnish his apartment, he hesitated. Kiyoura had been so at ease when the shopkeepers approached him, answering casually while he made his selections. Kikutani doubted he could manage such composure. But at the department store, almost no one had come up to them; he could shop there in peace.

So he boarded the train for Shinjuku, then took the underground passage to the basement of the department store. As before, the high-pitched voices of the clerks in the food section washed over him while he wove his way through the shoppers and got on the escalator. The electrical appliances were on the sixth floor. A few shoppers poked around among the rows of flickering televisions stacked against the walls. He spotted a sign for heaters, and there, next to the kerosene models, was a row of electric space heaters. Unlike the old wire-coil models he remembered, most of these were long and thin, with what appeared to be fluorescent lightbulbs in them. Most were nearly 20,000 yen. Among them, however, was a small model that was just under 6000; on it was a tag that read WITH FAN. He remembered the enormous fans that circulated the warm air in the henhouse; it must be something like that.

He stood for a long while in front of the small heaters, until at last he pointed to a white one and said to a nearby clerk, "This one, please...." The clerk went to get the heater from the stockroom, wrapped it, and handed it to Kikutani. As he rode down the escalator, package in hand, Kikutani felt a sense of satisfaction that he had been able to do his shopping without Kiyoura. Nothing to be afraid of, he told himself; you simply hand over the money, and they give you the goods.

As he walked through the crowded food section in the basement, he realized that he was no longer startled by the voices of the clerks hawking their products. He dodged through the mass of shoppers toward the exit that led to the underground passage and back to the station, but then it occurred to him that he was just one stop away from home. He could just as easily walk. Going back up the stairs and cutting through the first floor of the store, he went out into the street. Shinjuku was full of young men and women strolling the sidewalks. Kikutani found a crosswalk and made his way to the other side of the wide avenue, setting off in the general direction of his neighborhood. He left the main street and turned into a narrow alley next to a liquor store. The alley was lined with bars and small restaurants, none of which seemed open. Only a few of the cheapest eateries and cafes were doing business, and an odd quiet pervaded the area. Kikutani walked along quickly, eyeing the black plastic bags bulging with garbage that were set out in front of most of the shops. A man moved steadily down the alley, gathering the bags and tossing them in the back of the blue cart he pushed.

Kikutani emerged from the alley, crossed the street ahead, ducked into yet another small passageway next to a cafe. This new district, he discovered, was given over to seedy hourly hotels. There was no one in sight except for a woman who was scrubbing down the entrance to one of the hotels with a brush. As he walked along, studying the buildings on either side of the alley, he noticed a couple who rushed out from behind the stone wall of a hotel just ahead. They stood a moment and then came walking in his direction. Kikutani started to look away, but he stopped and stared at the woman as she passed, her eyes downcast. She walked a few steps behind the man as they hurried toward the corner and disappeared to the right. Kikutani stood gazing at the spot where the woman had disappeared; he could feel his heart pounding in his chest, and he sensed that his face had gone pale. For a moment he had been convinced it was his wife, so closely did the woman resemble her. From behind, too, she was almost identical. The man, in his forties, had walked by quite nonchalantly, but in the woman's face Kikutani could see the heat and excitement of their encounter in the hotel.

Behind him, suddenly, a horn sounded, and he turned to see a taxi coming down the alley. He pressed against the wall to avoid being hit. When the taxi passed, he walked to the corner where the couple had turned and looked to the right, but they were gone. He smiled bitterly to himself, realizing how ludicrous his hallucination had been. His wife? If she were alive, she'd be forty-six; her hair would be turning gray. He saw the humor in confusing this thirty-year-old woman with his wife as she had been sixteen years ago. But though it was only a hallucination, his agitation didn't go away. This woman must be married too. If she was spending time with a man at a hotel during the day, it was because she didn't want her husband to find out. Kikutani's wife must have followed Mochizuki from some hotel with that same expression on her face, with those same hurried steps. He remembered that she had almost always been home when he got back from the school, and so, he realized later, her affair with Mochizuki had been confined to the daytime. It was this association, the row of illicit hotels, that had brought on the momentary confusion.

He walked on, his face blank. Crossing a broad avenue, he entered a street that led through a residential district. There were small hotels here and there, but when he passed them, he found himself in the shopping street in front of his station. He made his way to his building and climbed the stairs. Once inside, he sat on the tatami and hung his head. He had seen something he should not have seen, and now a terrible memory had come back to haunt him. He should have known better than to walk about the city; he should have simply taken the train. The nightmares began while he was on trial and continued when he was in prison; but even during the day these thoughts often came to plague him. He never once regretted killing his wife, not for a moment. For her and for Mochizuki, he had nothing but rage and resentment. Yet, as the years went by, the intensity of these feelings lessened, and the nightmares stopped. That had been his one comfort. So now it was unbearable that all this had been stirred up again at the sight of the woman leaving the hotel.

Kikutani got up and paced the room, rubbing his head vigorously. Mochizuki's face came back to him, and with it an overwhelming desire to rip that face to shreds with his bare hands. A groan escaped his throat. He wished he could drive every swirling thought out of his head.

The remaining leaves had fallen from the trees on the road to the farm, and he saw frost on the fields. As winter approached, the hens were somewhat less productive, but the trucks still left the farm loaded with eggs to deliver. The young man named Shirakawa quit, and in his place a couple was hired to live on the farm. The man worked in the henhouse, and the woman was placed in the packing building. They lasted less than a week. They had said they were married, but the consensus around the farm was that they had run away together; after all, he was at least ten years younger than she.

Kikutani and Koinuma were left to manage in the henhouse by themselves. Mondays, when Koinuma was off, were especially hectic, and though Kikutani was used to the work now, he was still exhausted at the end of the day. On the train, the face of the woman at the hotel drifted into his thoughts, and he would return to his room oppressed with memories of his wife. All that had happened long ago, he told himself, and he'd had more than fifteen years to forget. Still, the moment of mistaking the woman for his wife had left him shaken. He took to drinking in the evenings. The alcohol no longer affected him as quickly as it had that first evening, so instead of beer he began to warm single-serving cups of sake in a pan of hot water on the stove. Though drinking helped him sleep, his wife began appearing in his dreams, always in the same scene: she sat quietly in front of him while he screamed at her, accusing her of adultery. She never moved or answered, staring into space as if she didn't hear him. A hard light shone in her eyes, and her mouth was twisted into a pout. Finally, his anger would grow to a fever pitch, and he would reach for a knife to plunge into her face—at which point he always woke up. His heart would be racing; sweat would be pouring from his body. It usually took a long time to get back to sleep, so he was tired the next day. He often dozed off on the train.

On the scheduled day, he went to Takebayashi's house for their meeting. The old man studied Kikutani as he sat down across from him.

"Something the matter?" he said almost immediately. His tone was calm, but his eyes were inquisitive. Kikutani had the distinct impression that Takebayashi had guessed his problem, that he somehow knew Kikutani had seen a woman resembling his wife and it had upset him.

"Nothing in particular," he said.

"Really?" said Takebayashi. Kikutani told him that he and Koinuma were managing the henhouse by themselves and that he had begun drinking. Takebayashi nodded at everything Kikutani told him, but right to the end he seemed to be trying to peer into Kikutani's soul.

One day, Kikutani woke to the first snowfall of the winter. It melted almost immediately in the city, but in the fields and woods around the farm it stayed on the ground for some time. The end of the year came, and on December 30 in the afternoon, they stopped work early and drank beer and sake with Akiyama in the cafeteria. All the employees were given a holiday until January 3, while Akiyama and his family looked after the henhouse and the brooder. A bit unsteady on his feet, Kikutani walked slowly in the direction of the bus stop.

On New Year's morning, he made soup from some rice cakes he had bought at a nearby store, and the next day he went to the halfway house. Kiyoura urged him to come in, but Kikutani paid his respects standing in the entrance and then set off for Takebayashi's house. There, too, he wished his benefactor a Happy New Year without so much as removing his shoes. He had made up his mind that he would not intrude on their celebrations.

The shopping district was deserted, and there wasn't a car to be seen on the streets. It was as if the city had died. Tokyo, he realized, had become a place inhabited by recent transplants from the outlying prefectures. These newcomers had all taken their cars and gone home for the holidays. The apartment building, too, was empty and deathly still. Kikutani, with nothing to do, waited for nightfall and his sake.

He thought about New Years long ago. The people in his town would visit the Makata Shrine near the walls of the old castle, dedicated to the former lord of the region. Offertory dances were performed in front of the main hall of the shrine, and stalls selling all sorts of food and souvenirs lined the approach. The celebration attracted visitors from the whole area, and the great shrine bell rang continuously. Once they had finished at the shrine, the revelers would call on family and friends, exchanging cups of sake late into the night. The lights of the town burned until dawn, and the doors of the houses were adorned with pine branches and bamboo. Kites danced overhead. The warmth in the celebration came from the gathering of people, the crush of bodies; but in Tokyo he could see nothing but empty concrete buildings and deserted asphalt streets. He found himself longing for the lively festivities of his little town, but he knew that he would never set foot in that place again.

His brother had assumed the job of looking after the ancestral graves at the family temple. Kikutani had forfeited the right to be buried there when he died. Someday, he imagined, he would be killed in an accident or die of a sudden illness. His parole officer would contact his brother, who would come to collect the body without even letting the relatives know what had happened. There would be no wake, no funeral, just a quick trip to the crematorium and a plain urn. Kikutani couldn't imagine where his brother would put the urn when it was all over. Families almost never came to collect the bodies of prisoners who were executed. The prisoners who thought about this in advance usually put into their wills that they wanted their bodies donated to science. Then, when the sentence was carried out, the prison would hand over the cadaver to a medical school, where organs would be harvested for transplants and other uses. The body would end up on the dissecting tables of medical students, and a year or so later, whatever was left would be cremated and placed in some anonymous mausoleum. Kikutani pictured his brother wondering what to do with his ashes. The parole officer would probably suggest some potter's field where no one kept records, no families tended graves.

He felt uneasy about how much the mere sight of the hotel woman had affected him. He had no idea how many more years he might live, but he felt sure now that there would constantly be these small disturbances that would cause him sleepless nights. He had done everything he could to forget the past, but the thing for which he had received an indefinite sentence continued to exist and could never be erased. If he were to spend the time that was left to him averting his eyes from his past, until at last his body was worn out and death came, he would probably still not find peace. Instead, he needed to face squarely what he had done, what his crime meant; and to do that, he would have to go back to that town. There, he would find the man he was eighteen years ago; there, he would find his wife.

Work began again on the fourth, and Kikutani immersed himself in the cackling of the henhouse. A fine rain was falling as the truck, flying a festive flag, left to make its first delivery of the year. On his day off, he went to visit Takebayashi. As he was shown into the sitting room, he turned to Takebayashi. "I'd like to go home to my town," he said. Kikutani's birthplace was a two-hour train ride away, so he could make the trip in a day; still, it was clearly a trip, and according to the rules he needed Takebayashi's permission.

"You came from Sakura, didn't you? Why do you want to go?" asked Takebayashi, fingering his teacup.

Kikutani was quiet for a moment. "I'd like to say a prayer at the grave of the mother of the man my wife was seeing," he said, his voice faltering. The fact that Mochizuki's mother had died in the fire right after the incident had initially seemed to him inevitable, a natural retribution for Mochizuki's betrayal. He'd even taken pleasure in the symmetry. But during the prosecutor's interrogation, he realized the horror of what he'd done and broke into tears. The old woman had been crippled and lived on the second floor of the house with only a small bird for company. When they found her body after the fire, lying next to it was a charred and twisted birdcage.

Mochizuki's family grave was in the same cemetery as Kikutani's, and he assumed that the old woman must be buried there as well. During the trial, the prosecutor had admitted that there were mitigating circumstances in the murder of Kikutani's wife and in the assault on Mochizuki, but Kikutani's unforgivable crime had been to cause the death of Mochizuki's mother, who had nothing to do with the matter. It was that aspect of the case that had resulted in the indefinite sentence. Feeling the justice of this decision, Kikutani refused to appeal and went straight to prison.

"To her grave?" said Takebayashi, nodding as he looked up at Kikutani. "I understand how you feel, but I wonder," he said, cocking his head. Assuming that Takebayashi would give his permission, Kikutani was caught off guard. In prison they were encouraged to feel remorse for their crimes and reform themselves so they wouldn't repeat their mistakes; then they were sent back out into society. It was the duty of the parole officer to make doubly sure that a man had reformed, so Kikutani thought that Takebayashi would approve of his wish to visit the old woman's grave. He wondered why Takebayashi was reluctant.

"I think it would be best to wait a bit," Takebayashi said, glancing at Kikutani. "I can't tell you exactly why I feel that way, but I do. It's fine to want to visit her grave, but it's less than a year since you've been out of prison, and that worries me. But perhaps it's just me. I think you should go talk to Kiyoura about this. He's known lots of men in your situation, and he'll know what's best. If he says it's all right to go, then you can," he concluded in his habitually calm tone of voice. Kikutani murmured his compliance as he rose to leave.

Making his way down the narrow alley in Shinjuku, he

pushed open the door to the halfway house. Through the receptionist's window, he could see Kiyoura sitting at his desk. He was shown to the conference room, and Kiyoura joined him almost immediately. Kikutani bowed and sat down on the couch. Kiyoura, who had caught a cold, was a little pale. Kikutani told him a few things about his recent activities and then made his request, just as he had made it to Takebayashi, adding that Takebayashi had told him to seek Kiyoura's opinion.

"I can understand why you want to do this," said Kiyoura almost casually, "but I think you should wait. Give yourself some time to think it over." Dumbfounded, Kikutani sat staring across the table. He had thought that a man as generous as Kiyoura would not only permit him to go but would actively encourage him. "For one thing, I'm not sure it would be as simple as just visiting the grave. There would be no way to avoid being seen in the town, and I wonder if you're ready for that. I don't know if the family or relatives of the victims are still there, but you have to consider that you might run into one of them. What would you do in that case? I don't mean to be cruel, but no matter how sincerely you apologized, you'd be forcing them to remember something they might just as soon forget, and I doubt they'd appreciate it. It's a difficult problem, and that's why I think you should give yourself time to think it through." Kiyoura had not skipped a beat in making this argument, and Kikutani found he had nothing to say in response. He looked down; he himself could see the sense in Kiyoura's reasoning—no doubt the same problem had occurred to Takebayashi. Kikutani realized that despite his parole, his crime was still with him like an enormous weight on his back.

"While I was in prison, I thought that the one thing I'd do if I ever got out would be to visit that grave," he said, trying one last time to explain.

"That's precisely the attitude that we all want you to have. That's what they mean by 'repenting your misdeeds.' But in this case you have to think about how the other people involved might feel. This isn't something you can do without thinking about it; give yourself some time. The right moment will come." Kiyoura's eyes shone as he finished. The conviction in his voice, Kikutani knew, was based on long years of experience; it had its own power and left no room for argument. Kikutani rose to leave, saying that he understood. Bowing, he pushed open the door to the reception room and found his way out into the narrow street, and from there into the busy shopping quarter. He headed automatically in the direction of the station and he passed under the elevated tracks.

He had been under the impression that he lived in the midst of a society that stretched without limits around him, but the reality now seemed quite different. Of the people he came in contact with on a regular basis, the only ones who knew about his past were Kiyoura, Takebayashi, and the Akiyamas; as for the others, he did his best to keep them in the dark. Therefore he was constantly watching what he did and said, straining every nerve to detect how people reacted to him. Also, his time was not completely his own: twice a month on the appointed day, he had to go to Takebayashi and deliver a detailed report of his activities. Perhaps to avoid making him nervous, Takebayashi never took notes during their meetings, but he knew that Takebayashi wrote a complete summary afterward and forwarded it to the parole board. At the moment Kikutani left the prison, he wanted to shout with joy at the feeling of liberation; but now he saw his liberation was an illusion. It seemed to him that he was surrounded by thick walls barring his way, limiting his movements. He felt as though he were bound hand and foot, and it struck him that he had perhaps been freer in prison. He wandered on through the unfamiliar streets with an empty look in his eyes.

That evening, as he sipped his sake, he muttered to himself, "I'm not a child. I don't have to do everything that Kiyoura and Takebayashi tell me to." It was just a quick day trip, not long enough to fall under the parole board's travel restriction. If he went without telling them, he probably wouldn't be breaking any rules; and if they did object to a little thing like this, then what was the point of letting him out of prison in the first place? His mood grew blacker as he continued to drink. As long as he didn't leave the prescribed area, he told himself, he could go where he wanted. He no longer received a thing from the government; he had become completely self-supporting. So there was no reason for them to interfere in the details of his life. "I'm going," he murmured. If he was ever to gain some measure of independence, he couldn't continue living in fear of the past. And if he was going, the sooner the better—his next day off, if he could manage it.

As he refilled his cup, he began to plan the best way to get in and out of the town unnoticed. In a small community like his, the position of high school teacher had been an important one. Nearly everyone knew him by sight, so he could never walk around town during the day. And even at night, when he got off the train at the station, he was bound to be seen by someone. So, to avoid that danger, he would get off one stop early and walk the rest of the way into town at night. On his way to work the next day, he checked the schedule for the Sobu Line, writing down the departure times. He decided to leave the night before his day off.

Clear winter days followed one after another, and from the train window he could see mountains clad in glittering snow off in the distance. Flocks of chickadees fluttered among the bare branches of the forest near the farm, while the buds on the plum trees were beginning to swell.

6

Arriving home from work just before seven o'clock, Kikutani left his lunch box in his room, gathered up the sticks of incense he had bought the day before, and headed back to the station. As he was boarding the train, he realized that he had forgotten matches to light the incense, so when the train reached Tokyo Station, where he had to transfer, he went to a newsstand. He asked the woman for matches, but as he was waiting, he noticed Koinuma's brand of cigarettes in the display case and decided to buy a pack of those as well. He was drinking again, so why not smoke, too?

He had some difficulty finding the Sobu Line, since it was located deep under the station, but at last he descended a long escalator to the platform. Most of the men and women waiting for the train seemed to be commuters, and the thought occurred to him that some of them might be from his town. Once on the train, he positioned himself by the door across the way and stared out the window. A bell sounded, the doors closed, and the train pulled out of the station. As it emerged aboveground, it began to pick up speed, crossing the Arakawa River. Kikutani could see car lights streaming back and forth on a parallel bridge. He was shocked by the march of tall concrete buildings on either side of the tracks. Around the stations in particular were thick clusters of high-rise apartments, department stores, hotels, and banks, all lit up in neon lights. He could barely make out the names of the stations as his express flew by, but he was amazed to see how many sleepy little whistle-stops had become bustling forests of big buildings. The transformation was so complete that he worried that he had somehow got on the wrong line.

The rows of concrete structures continued as the train moved away from the center of the city, and his astonishment grew that all sign of fields and trees had vanished in less than twenty years. There weren't even many normal houses; almost every inch was covered with tall buildings. He wondered whether he would even know Sakura when he got there, whether it too hadn't altered beyond recognition.

At Chiba Station he transferred to a local train and once again took up his position staring out the window by the door. As the train approached his home, he could feel his heart beating harder. While he had been in prison, he had dreamed of the river that flowed through town, of the earthworks surrounding the old castle and the stone stairs leading up to the shrine; but eventually these images had faded. Now, though, he was sure that even if the rest had changed, those old landmarks would remain. He peered into the darkness. Against the starry sky he could make out the black forms of hills, and he could tell that the train was now passing through woodlands. It seemed that out here, at least, things had not changed completely from the way he remembered them, and this thought calmed him. Still, apartments had been built near the stations where they were stopping, and there was a good bit of traffic on the wide streets. Between stations, however, it was dark along the tracks, except for the lights of houses in the distance. There were fewer passengers on the train now, and a number of seats were empty, but Kikutani remained standing by the door out of fear of being recognized.

When the train stopped at the station before Sakura, he got out. The other passengers hurried along the platform toward the exit. Kikutani followed more slowly, turning up the collar of his coat as he passed through the ticket gate. The station clock said just after nine-thirty. Once outside, he turned down an unpaved road that followed the tracks. This was the way to Sakura. He became acutely conscious of the feel of the earth beneath his feet. The lights of the train receded to the north.

The anxiety that his town would be unrecognizable began to fade as he saw the fields on either side of the road and the rolling hills beyond. Here and there were faint glimmers of light from what must have been farmhouses. The look of this place in the dark was familiar and reassuring, and the night air smelled of home. He quickened his pace. The road followed the tracks through the fields, and for a while he saw no one, until the headlights of a car appeared and rushed past, followed by a motorcycle. The road eventually turned next to a small stream, leading to a larger, paved avenue, which crossed a short bridge. Soon Kikutani found himself climbing gently through a dark wood that loomed over him from both sides. Among the high branches were glints of starlight, but the ground beneath his feet was pitch black. The smell of damp bark came to him from the darkness. The road twisted and turned as it climbed through the woods; at the top he paused before a small roadside shrine to Jizo, then descended toward the town.

As the trees thinned and then disappeared altogether, he stopped, the lights of the town spread out in front of him. Ahead to the right was a handsome white building that must have replaced the old wooden station. It faced a broad square flooded with light. As the view came into focus, he was overcome with emotion and stood quite still for some time before slowly continuing.

The road ended at the river: the Takasaki, where he had often fished for bitterling with a small pole. Just as he had then, he walked along the bank, watching the surface of the water. Reaching the bridge, he crossed over and came out into the main street, which had been covered with gravel when he left but had since been widened and paved. He looked up and down the street but saw no sign of either headlights or people, so he crossed and started along another road that led up the hill. The row of old samurai mansions was exactly as it had been. As he was passing them, he noticed two figures coming toward him, apparently a mother and daughter, though only dimly visible in the starlight. He moved to the side of the road, looking away as they passed. Narrow beams of light escaped from cracks in the walls of houses on either side, but there was not a sound to be heard.

The road he was following came to an end. To the left was the police station. The memory of the time he'd spent detained there made him reluctant to turn that way. Retracing his steps, he entered an alley that ran between the walls of the mansions. The way was narrow and quickly left the houses and descended along stone steps through a bamboo grove. Ahead he could see a bent old man leaning on a stick as he climbed toward him. Kikutani tried to avoid his eyes, but as they passed, the old man looked up and gasped out a friendly "Good evening." Kikutani's reply was barely audible as he hurried on down the steps, a cold sweat spreading over his skin.

His detour rejoined the main road, which had changed little from what he remembered. Old plum trees were visible here and there. He hurried along among the familiar houses, coming out suddenly into a deserted street of tightly shuttered shops. A short way farther, he turned into another alley, which climbed the hill and branched to the right. He stopped when the temple gate came into view ahead, and after checking to be sure no one was about, he crept quietly through it. The great, leafless limbs of the ancient ginkgo trees spread over the temple grounds, casting deep shadows, and there was a familiar stand of bamboo. It seemed they were restoring the main hall just ahead of him; it was covered with scaffolding and surrounded by piles of pale lumber. A faint light burned in the priests' quarters off to the right. The old man who had been chief priest would almost surely be dead, having been succeeded by his son.

Passing quietly under the ginkgo trees, Kikutani made his way along the stepping-stones that led around the main hall to the cemetery at the back. As his eyes adjusted to the darkness, he could see the weathered pagoda beyond the rows of gravestones. His family's grave was to the left amid some trees, while the Mochizukis' was somewhere at the back of the cemetery. He threaded his way among the graves, stopping when he came to a stone enclosure. A dark mass of trees stretched off into the distance beyond a simple grave that bore the inscription TOMB OF THE MOCHIZUKIS FROM GENERATION TO GENERATION.

When he saw the characters for *Mochizuki*, the brilliant colors of the fire eighteen years ago flared again before him in the night sky. He had brought a can of lamp oil from the trunk of his car and splashed the oil on cardboard boxes stacked against the wooden walls of Mochizuki's house, drizzling what was left inside an attached shed. It was dark in the house, but he was sure that the wounded Mochizuki had taken refuge there and was holding his breath, hoping Kikutani would go away. Noticing a plastic container of gasoline in the shed, Kikutani took it and circled the house, dousing the walls. Finally, he used his lighter to ignite one of the boxes, tossing it into the shed as he retreated. The flames sprang up almost immediately, turning the shed into an inferno and illuminating the whole area, and soon they spread to the walls of the house. Kikutani, his eyes ablaze, stood watching the fire scatter clouds of sparks and listening to the explosive sound of timbers shattering. Then, suddenly, from inside the house there was a hysterical wailing, and Mochizuki's wife burst through the flames clutching a child. Amid shrill shouts and the vague realization that many people were running around him, he stood frozen and watched the collapsing house and the countless embers it sent screaming gaudily into the night sky. At some point, he was grabbed roughly by several men. They pinned his arms and dragged him from the scene, shouting curses at him, but his memory after that was dim.

But now Kikutani was confused. Other than these memories, no real emotion came to him as he stood before this grave. Mochizuki's elderly mother had burned to death in that fire, and her bones were buried beneath this marker, but the only thing that struck him now was the beauty of the flames: he felt no remorse. Rather, a sense of satisfaction crept over him at having destroyed Mochizuki's house. Was it merely an act when he wept before the prosecutor, a ploy to lighten his sentence? And coming here with this incense…was it to atone for his sin or merely a pretext for visiting his hometown? He stood before the grave, searching his heart for the answers to these questions.

A faint sound roused him from his thoughts. A few yards off, a white dog crouched, staring at him. He wondered whether it was a stray or a dog kept by the temple. At any rate, it was not growling, just watching him closely from a safe distance. It was the first dog he'd faced since getting out of prison, and though he wasn't really frightened, he did feel uncomfortable and found himself backing away from the grave. Following the stepping-stones around to the front of the main hall, he glanced toward the priests' quarters and then passed under the ginkgos and out the gate.

He knew that the trains had stopped running for the night, so he decided to pass the time on the grounds of a nearby shrine. He walked quickly up a narrow path and through an old torii gate. There was a small caretaker's house to the right, but the shrine was communally kept and no one lived there. In front of him stood a stone lantern, and beyond that the tiny main building of the shrine, no larger than a roadside memorial. He sat down on the short flight of steps leading up to the shrine.

The night air—a mixture of earth, bark, grasses, and river water—reminded him that he was home. The smell was familiar, but bound up with it were memories that choked him. He sat utterly still and looked out at the gate, faintly visible in the darkness.

You could say that it all started with a letter. He returned to the teachers' room after his last class one day to find an envelope on his desk. On the back it said simply "From a friend." The fact that it was anonymous meant it was probably a complaint about his teaching or one student slandering another. Feeling depressed, he sat down and slit open the envelope. The handwriting was obviously a woman's, and the letter began: "I am herewith relating to you some important facts." The pretension of this greeting depressed him still more, but as he read on, he found that it had nothing to do with school but concerned him personally. The writer claimed to have witnessed a number of occasions when Kikutani's wife made daytime visits to a motel on the outskirts of Chiba City in the company of Sadao Mochizuki, and the letter gave a list of the dates and times. Furthermore, it said, when Kikutani made overnight fishing trips on his days off, Mochizuki parked his car in the woods near Kikutani's house and stayed until close to dawn.

"You are a teacher worthy of respect not only from your students but from their families, and thus we cannot sanction this sort of lewdness that comes as an affront to your position as a husband. Since you seem unaware of these facts, we take the liberty of informing you of them here," it concluded. Kikutani sat frozen in his chair, the letter dangling in his hand.

His first reaction was that this had been written by the mother of a student who bore him a grudge, looking to cause problems for him at home. If she had said that she happened to witness something on one occasion, it might have been more believable, but to record their every movement, every date and time, like some professional private detective, and then to follow Mochizuki to his house at night and wait until he left at dawn...that strained credulity. The whole thing was clearly a hoax. Some of his students' mothers were, in fact, a bit peculiar, and he'd had trouble with them before, a number of times. The letter was just the sort of thing one of them might send, he thought, as he tried to picture these women in his mind.

Returning the letter to the envelope and shoving it into his coat pocket, he thought about his wife, Emiko. They had met while he was still at the university, one summer when he worked at a big discount clothing store. His job was in the stockroom: he would unpack incoming shipments, check them for style and quantity, attach price tags, and get them out to the various departments in the store before it opened in the morning. Emiko had come to Tokyo from a city in Fukushima prefecture to study home economics at a junior college. She went to school at night, and during the day she worked in the lingerie department of the same store. Slender and slightly pale, she gave the impression of being naive and inexperienced, but she was good with the customers and well liked at the store. He noticed her almost immediately.

The store was open year-round, seven days a week, so

the employees took one day off a week, staggering the schedule. On his day off, Kikutani would go to the pool at a nearby amusement park, and it was there that he met Emiko and a group of her friends who apparently had the same day off. Emiko in a bathing suit was completely different from the young woman in her uniform at work; she was cheerful, more relaxed, sipping iced coffee with the other girls at the edge of the pool. After that, Kikutani and Emiko began to go out together every week. They were both living independently, away from their families, working while they went to school, and their similar circumstances made them comfortable with each other. Her dream, she told him, was to go back to Fukushima after she graduated and become a kindergarten teacher.

He finished at the university a year early and found a job teaching Japanese at a high school for girls back in his hometown of Sakura; but every Sunday he would come into the city to meet Emiko after work, catching the last train home that night. They would sit on a bench in the park, hugging and kissing, but he never tried to push things further. Shortly before she was due to graduate, he went to the uncle who had been looking after Emiko and asked for permission to marry her. The uncle, who liked Kikutani, made the trip back to Fukushima to relay Kikutani's request, but Emiko's parents, who had been hoping that she would come home to marry, objected at first. But when they learned that Kikutani was a teacher and that, while not rich, his family did own some land, they decided to make the best of things and give their blessing. The wedding was held in the fall of that year, and the couple moved into a new house that Kikutani had built on the outskirts of Sakura.

He was satisfied with his new life. Things with Emiko were going well, and he loved his work. The days seemed rich and full. There was just one thing that spoiled their happiness: as the months passed, Emiko showed no signs of getting pregnant. She consulted an obstetrician in Chiba City, and was finally told that she would not be able to bear children. For Emiko, this was heartbreaking news. Her desire to become a kindergarten teacher was really just an expression of her love of children, and to find out that she would never have her own devastated her. Kikutani, too, was disappointed, but knowing how she felt, he tried to make light of it, telling her that they would be happy, just the two of them. He was careful never to mention children in her presence.

Emiko planted flowers around the house and made a little vegetable garden, and it seemed to Kikutani that she was getting over her grief. Before long, a friend from the neighborhood invited her to an exhibition of traditional dyeing techniques in Chiba, and a new interest developed. Emiko joined the club that sponsored the exhibit and began taking lessons three times a month. At home, she would busy herself cutting out stencils and dyeing bits of cloth. At first she made only small objects, wall hangings and table runners; but after a few years she progressed to the point where she was dyeing material for kimonos and sashes. She seemed to have a gift for the work, and the pieces she sent off to the annual exhibition invariably sold immediately. This success gave her self-confidence and sent her back to her dyeing with an even greater passion. When she began receiving requests from people in Sakura to dye cloth for kimonos to be worn on festival days, it was clear that her work had moved beyond a mere hobby to become a paying job. Kikutani was delighted at his wife's occupation, and he would often help her stretch cloth, whole rooms full, in preparation for dyeing. Their home life was stable, and their sex life was satisfying. He found it hard to believe that his wife, busy as she was with her work, would be having an affair with one of his fishing companions.

When he finished writing his class reports, he left the teachers' room and went out to watch the softball team scrimmage. They would be going to the prefectural tournament, and two of his students were on the team. The game had just started, and he joined some other teachers who were clapping and yelling, but the letter kept returning to his mind and he couldn't relax. Halfway through the game, he got up and went back to his desk. A short time later, he left the school and was walking along the main street of Sakura.

The cherry trees along the avenue had finished blooming. From time to time one of the students would fly by on a bicycle, calling out a greeting. The street came to a fork. Kikutani usually took the left turn, which led past the castle ruins and toward home, but today he hesitated and went to the right. Descending a gentle, wooded slope, he came to the shores of Crone's Pond and sat down on the grass. Legend had it that a castle wet nurse once came to the pond carrying the lord's infant daughter and dropped her in the water while trying to pick some flowers. The baby drowned, and as her punishment, the nurse was drowned as well.

Kikutani pulled the envelope from his pocket and unfolded it. He studied the dates for the two-month period during which Emiko had supposedly been meeting Mochizuki at the motel in Chiba: they corresponded exactly to the days Emiko had gone to her club meetings, and the times were just after the meetings ended. If the whole thing was a fabrication, someone had gone to a lot of trouble to make it convincing. The author of the letter knew that Emiko was going to the meetings, and she also knew that Mochizuki made a believable partner.

Mochizuki was about five years older than Kikutani and managed a construction company in Sakura. They became friends when they joined the same fishing club. The Kashima River, which ran north of town, was good for roach, and a tributary upstream, the Takasaki, was known for bitterling. Fishermen came from all over the eastern suburbs of Tokyo when the club held its fishing derbies to celebrate the roach and bitterling seasons, and at certain times of year, the members would go deep-sea fishing, often staying overnight near the docks. Mochizuki, who was particularly fond of deep-sea fishing and owned elaborate equipment, always went on these trips; but in the summer of the previous year he began skipping the overnight outings. He explained that his company was busy and that it would set a bad example for his employees if he missed two days of work. But this also meant that Mochizuki knew when Kikutani would be out of town on a fishing trip. He gazed at the leaves of a water lily floating on the surface of the pond.

On days when his wife went to her meetings, she was always home making dinner when he got back from school; and as far as he could remember, when he returned from his fishing trips, everything seemed normal, her manner unchanged. She would watch as he brought out the fish he had caught, and then help him take some around to share with the neighbors. When he held her at night, she felt the same.... Impossible! he told himself, but he was as agitated as before. The words of the letter filled his head, and he wondered what sort of woman would write such a thing.

Emiko had been the first woman he slept with, and that first night he was a little unsure of himself. After they were married, he was completely faithful, unable even to imagine sex with anyone else. When other teachers at school talked about the women they knew in the world of bars and brothels, he wasn't interested. And he had always believed that Emiko was satisfied as well. But if the letter was true, then another man had been making love to her, and perhaps doing it better than he did. Maybe she'd found a kind of pleasure with Mochizuki that she'd never known before and went on with the relationship despite her fear.

Kikutani had heard stories about Mochizuki's way with women. Mochizuki was sensitive about gossip close to home, so he tended to look farther afield for his fun. He was not inclined to keep a mistress or get entangled with children, preferring to pay for a woman once and be rid of her afterward. He was the type who liked to keep things neat and uncomplicated, and not just with women. He was good at avoiding anything that might involve responsibilities, and to that end he liked to keep a low profile. When they needed approval from the city for their fishing derbies, the members of the club went as a group to see the mayor, but Mochizuki made some excuse to avoid joining them. He probably didn't want to be mixed up in anything that could damage his chances for the city construction contracts he depended on. But after a number of similar incidents, he gained a reputation among the club members for selfishness. It was also said that he was extremely rigid when it came to collecting bills for his company, and there were quite a few people in town who refused to do business with him because of it. You could almost see this attitude in his face, in the cold gleam of his eyes.

The sunlight playing on the surface of the pond faded, and the air grew cool. Kikutani rose and walked slowly back up the hill. That evening he spread out his fishing gear in the living room. He checked the lines, hooks, floats, and sinkers, then arranged them neatly with his poles and fishing clothes. The next day after his last class, he was going to Iioka, near Inubozaki, to fish for sillocks on the beach. Then the club members would sleep in an inn near the docks and leave early the next morning for some deep-water flounder fishing. The trip had been scheduled for the previous weekend, but the weather had been doubtful and they'd put it off.

He felt stiffness in his face, but tried to go about his preparations as naturally as possible, sneaking an occasional glance at Emiko. She had finished cleaning up after dinner and was watching a drama on TV; everything seemed to be completely normal. When she went to have a bath, he took the letter from his suit and put it in the pocket of his fishing jacket. He had a drink and crawled into his futon, but he couldn't fall asleep. Instead, he lay listening to the sound of Emiko's breathing. Toward dawn, just after he had dozed off, Emiko woke him. He had a quick breakfast and left the house in his fishing clothes, hat, and boots, carrying his gear. He left his equipment at the home of one of the club members, where they would be gathering that evening, and went to school.

He taught his classes with a blank face, staring out the window much of the time. The sky was blue and cloudless, the sunlight blinding. From time to time a student would say something to call him back to reality. Between classes he went to the teachers' room, where he ran into a woman who had been at the school for many years and was approaching retirement. She was something of an old maid, and at faculty meetings she tended to come out with ludicrous proposals, but she understood the students and they liked her.

"Is something wrong?" she asked. "You look blue."

"I think I'm coming down with a cold," Kikutani mumbled.

"Well, you should take it easy. Try some sake with an egg stirred in and get to bed early." His thanks were barely audible. When classes were over, he left the school grounds and followed the road that led to the ruins of the main keep of the castle. Skirting the dry moat, he came out onto a gravel path and went to the electrician's shop where the fishing club was to meet. Several cars were already parked in front, and around them a group of men in fishing clothes and wide-brimmed hats stood smoking and chatting. Kikutani circled to the back of the house and changed into his clothes and boots on the veranda. He went to put his pole and tackle in the trunk of one of the cars, then waited with the others until it was time to leave.

When the members had all arrived, they split up among the cars. There were two women in the group, but no sign of Mochizuki. The line of cars left Sakura and headed east. Kikutani closed his eyes. Would Mochizuki be sneaking to his house tonight? He had built the place in a lonely spot at the edge of the woods; the nearest house was almost a hundred yards away. He had always had the impression that Emiko was not interested in other men, both before they were married and after. It seemed impossible that she could be sleeping with Mochizuki. And yet...now that he thought of it, about a year ago she had started to go on overnight trips, saying they were with friends from school or for club exhibitions in other parts of the country. He had always seen her off quite cheerfully, but now he wasn't sure who she had actually gone with, nor could he remember ever having seen pictures of the places she went to.

They followed good roads past Sanri Hill and through Yokaichiba. The other men talked fishing while Kikutani sat with his eyes shut. At last the line of cars reached the coastal road and stopped at an inn that they had used many times before. Just as the weather forecast predicted, the sea was calm. As the sun sank toward the horizon, setting the sea on fire, they began getting their gear ready for beach fishing. Kikutani, however, stayed behind at the inn, saying that he was feeling feverish and wanted to rest up for the next day's fishing. After they left, he sat for a few minutes on the tatami mats before going downstairs to borrow a thermometer from the innkeeper. When he pulled it from under his arm, it told him what he already knew; he did not have a temperature. But he shook down the mercury and muttered audibly, before returning to the room, that he did.

The sun set, and the fishermen came back to the inn. Most of them had caught two or three sillocks, and there was even a turbot on one man's stringer. After they'd had their baths, they sat down to a lively dinner. Kikutani refused the sake and barely touched his food, making a show of putting his hand to his forehead from time to time. Finally, the middle-aged city official sitting next to him grew concerned and asked what was wrong; Kikutani said he had a fever. He got up and went to explain to the club president that he had a high fever and chills and wouldn't be able to join them on the boat the next day. He would go home instead. There were worried looks all around and even a suggestion that he go to a nearby clinic, but he assured them that it was only a cold and he would be better off at home.

He planned to take the bus to Asahi City, where he could catch a train for Sakura, but the innkeeper offered to take him in his car, so Kikutani said goodbye to everyone and climbed into the passenger's seat with his fishing gear. It was late, and they made good time through the empty streets, arriving at the station just as the train for Sakura was announced. Kikutani hurried to get his ticket and ran out to the platform. Headlights approached along the tracks from the east, and the train pulled into the station. Only a few people got on, and Kikutani lowered himself into a window seat as the train started to move. The lights of the town thinned out, and the train rolled through the darkness, with only an occasional glimmer from a house in the distance. He stared out at these glimmers until suddenly a scarlet blur spread before his eyes. Blood rushed to his head, and his muscles tightened into hard knots. A sob escaped his throat as the image of his wife appeared before him, leaning back, breasts exposed....He was struck by the thought that he had never known another woman's body, but now his wife might be wrapped in Mochizuki's arms.

The train made its way in the direction of Sakura, stopping methodically at every station. He grew irritated by its slow progress. After about an hour, they finally pulled into Sakura, and a few people got off. Kikutani hurried from the station. The inn across the way had lights in the windows, but the noodle shop and the cigarette stand were closed. He crossed a small bridge and set off at a jog along the road that followed the stream. Half doubting and half believing, he hurried along, fighting for air. He passed the old moat, came out onto the banks of the Kashima River, and crossed another bridge. At last he turned into an alley and stopped for a moment. Ahead of him were the woods, black against the starry sky. In the shadows where the trees came to an end, there was a house.

Suddenly he could see how ridiculous he looked, creeping through the woods, having pretended to be sick in order to come home early from his trip. His wife was probably hard at work making stencils for one of her projects, or maybe she was just watching TV. Or maybe she had already gone to bed. She would think it strange that he cut his trip short, but he could say that he'd thought he was coming down with a cold. Better that she never knew how stupid he had been, believing in some anonymous letter and planning to sneak up on his own house. But as he stood staring through the trees, his eyes narrowed again to a sneer. There had been an undeniable plausibility to the letter, and he knew he had to see for himself whether it was true or not. He started walking. A slender moon like the blade of a sickle hung above the treetops in the cool night air. He passed a small house built right near the road. It belonged to a young man who worked for the farming cooperative, and Kikutani could hear a baby crying inside.

As he came to the edge of the wood, he slowed down and began to move more cautiously. The smell of wet wood was in the air, and from time to time he heard the piercing call of a bird and the flutter of wings. Long branches hung over him, leaving him deep in shadow as he made his way along the gently curving road. He stopped again. Ahead he could see his house, surrounded by its bamboo fence. A dim light was shining through the curtains. The road came to a fork at this point. He took the right branch, which ran into the woods. He stopped again, his mouth open. A few yards ahead was a small car parked on the side of the road. From the color and make, he knew that it was Mochizuki's—exactly as the letter had said, he thought, his body going rigid. The scarlet blur took shape and grew brighter, staining the car and the road and the shadows under the trees. He began walking toward the house, conscious only of the earth under his feet. A storm raged in his body, and his head was filled with a hissing sound, like foam dissolving into the air.

He crept through the gate in the bamboo fence. Peeking in at the gap between the curtains, he could see the table in the living room, and the room beyond, which was in half-light. The corner of the futon was visible behind the sliding door, and on it something white was moving. It was a leg, bent at the knee, writhing back and forth rhythmically, extending and then contracting. And pressing into the leg from above was a hip, bobbing up and down with the same motion. The scarlet mass grew brighter. The hissing sound stopped, and his body grew cold, as a profound calm came over him. He crept around to the back of the house and stood at the kitchen door. He quietly dropped his tackle box and slid his pole case from his shoulder. Finding the door latched, he fumbled for a hook and line and threaded them through the tiny crack between the door and the frame. By pulling on the line a little at a time, he was able to catch the hook on the latch; when he pulled, the latch lifted and the door opened. At that moment, he could hear Emiko's voice gasping and crying, shriller than when he was with her, and building to even more intensity. There was a man's voice as well, moaning softly.

Kikutani stepped up to the wooden floor of the kitchen and bent over the cabinet under the sink. Straining his eyes in the dark, he grabbed the handle of a kitchen knife that he used for scaling fish. Then, holding it, he stood by the glass door that separated the kitchen from the living room. His wife's voice reached a ragged squeal, and he realized there was no need to be cautious any longer. Throwing open the door, he dashed across the living room and was confronted by a man with wildly flashing eyes. Without a word, Kikutani, planted the knife in the man's shoulder. The man screamed and rolled out of the way into a corner of the room, pressing his back against the wall. The red blur ignited, and as it enveloped Kikutani he pinned his wife's body under his knees and raised the knife over his head. Emiko stretched her arms toward him, fending off the blade, but her face was cold and expressionless as he plunged it into her chest.

The man in the corner scrambled to his feet, back still pressed to the wall, and stumbled toward the kitchen. Kikutani knew that he was getting away, but he continued to stab his wife's body over and over. At last he stood and dropped the knife to the tatami. He felt inexplicably at peace, even satisfied, and he began to think what he should do next. It struck him as absurd that Mochizuki should escape with only a wound; he decided to burn down the house where he must be hiding. He went to the kitchen and switched on the light. The pump outside by the well groaned to life as he turned the faucet and water gushed from the tap. He rinsed the blood from his hands, then lathered his face with soap. As he was drying himself, he realized that his fishing jacket was stained with blood, so he took it off and dropped it on the floor before leaving the house. The slender crescent moon had risen higher above the woods, throwing a silvery light on the road and the fields beyond.

Kikutani took two cans of oil from the shed and tied them to the luggage rack of his car. He noticed that the scarlet haze that had filled his vision had faded, replaced by the pale moonlight. He got into the car and started it. As he drove away, he saw that the steering wheel was rocking back and forth and realized that he was trembling.

Kikutani shook himself and pulled the pack of cigarettes from his coat pocket. As he struck a match, he recalled that people who were off tobacco for a long time usually got dizzy when they started again. That didn't seem to be the case with him. True, it tasted bitter, his tongue got a bit numb, and his throat hurt, but he took another puff. He felt a sudden resolve, a determination to stop hesitating and do things.

After his arrest, he was taken to the prosecutor's office and formally charged. In the process, he learned a good deal. The author of the mysterious letter was Mochizuki's sister-in-law, who had been a member of Emiko's dyeing club. After a meeting, she happened to spot Emiko getting into Mochizuki's car near Chiba Station. Her suspicions aroused, she followed them in a taxi until they pulled into a motel. In the weeks that followed, she began pursuing them with unusual tenacity, and was able to confirm that Emiko and Mochizuki spent time at the motel after almost every meeting. She also learned that when Kikutani was away on school business or fishing, Mochizuki would stay at his house almost without bothering to make a secret of it. She agonized over what to do with this information, worried that her sister, who was in frail health, would be unable to stand the shock. Finally she decided to send the anonymous letter to Kikutani, in the hope of forcing Emiko to break things off.

He also learned that Emiko had died quickly, from eight stab wounds, and while Mochizuki's injury had healed, there was nerve damage that paralyzed his right hand. The incident received heavy media coverage, and Mochizuki was forced to quit his job. Shortly after the trial, he left town with his wife and children. Why had a cautious man like Mochizuki carried on his affair with Emiko under Kikutani's own roof? During the trial, he testified that he believed Kikutani, a fishing fanatic, would never cut short one of his beloved deep-sea excursions. He said that Emiko assured him of this, adding that she seemed to be stimulated by having sex with him in her own house, that the whole thing had been mostly her idea. Eventually they got so used to it that the sense of danger disappeared.

Mochizuki's description of having sex with his wife devastated Kikutani. Eyes closed tight, he was unable to hold his head up. The person he had thought was a chaste woman was really the opposite. As he listened to the detailed testimony about how much she had loved fornicating with Mochizuki, he became convinced that he'd been right to kill her. His only regret was that he had merely wounded Mochizuki. Still, he wondered, why should his wife, who seemed so satisfied with her life, have taken up with Mochizuki? Kikutani had never chased after other women, never gambled away his salary; she'd always been able to count on his coming straight home to her. But something had been lacking. And when Mochizuki came along, with more than a few faults, she'd been unable to resist him. Kikutani imagined her succumbing to Mochizuki's superior sexual technique, experiencing heights of pleasure she'd never known before. "And you had no idea that your wife was having an affair with Mochizuki?" the prosecutor asked. In the faintest of voices, Kikutani said he hadn't.

After going to prison, he thought through every detail hundreds of times but found no clue. Emiko had shown no sign of anything out of the ordinary on the days she went to her meetings, and when Kikutani came home from his fishing trips, the house was exactly as he left it, down to the ashtrays on the coffee table and the cushions on the tatami mats. "Still, you must have noticed that something was going on?" the prosecutor pressed, the hint of a smile playing around his mouth. He was clearly amused that anyone could have been so oblivious. But Kikutani merely cocked his head to one side and looked him in the eye, fighting his embarrassment. Why hadn't he been suspicious? Emiko's acting had been too good. He had not known his wife.

During the first years he spent in prison, he often dreamed that the scarlet blur returned, and he woke up groaning. The crimson dye flooded his vision, and from that moment he moved inexorably to the murder. He could feel the motion as the knife plunged into Emiko's body, the jarring in his arm as the blade hit bone. Her arms stretched out in front of her to ward off the blows seemed pitiful, but her eyes were weirdly devoid of remorse. Obviously she no longer felt any love for him; she had discovered real pleasure with Mochizuki and even in those last seconds felt no regret. That utterly expressionless face was her final challenge to him.

The tiny light of a bicycle bounced along the road at the bottom of the hill below the shrine. But most of the lights in the town had gone dark, and a deep silence descended. Why had he come here? Perhaps because here, in his hometown, the past could come back to him in all its lurid detail, as if the intervening months and years meant nothing. He rose from the steps and went to the stone basin where visitors to the shrine washed their hands. He turned on the faucet and brought his mouth to the end of the hose. The taste was clean, free of the chlorine they used in the city: the taste of home.

He decided to go back to the next town and wait there until the first train left for Tokyo. Taking the sticks of incense from his pocket, he hurled them into the darkness and walked toward the gate.

7

The season for plum blossoms had passed, and the cherry trees had faded. He now had a secret to keep from Takebayashi. He went to Takebayashi's house on the appointed day but said nothing about his visit home, reporting only that he had started to smoke. At any rate, the trip had been within the boundaries they set for him and he had wanted to exercise his free will.

At work, whenever they had a moment, the employees took to discussing the egg market in worried tones. Until the end of the preceding year, prices had been relatively stable; but when the market reopened after the New Year, they fell almost forty percent in one session and showed no sign of recovering. The problem was overproduction: the majority of the chicken feed was imported, and the strong yen had raised profit margins, causing producers to increase the number of chickens laying. To make matters worse, egg production usually went down during the cold months, but it was a particularly mild winter and there had been no dip. All this added up to a price collapse.

Akiyama, the area representative for the egg producers' cooperative, was out frequently for meetings or had the other managers to his office. According to Koinuma, the government advisory office was recommending that the number of hens be brought back to normal levels by taking the older birds out of the houses early, after a shorter laying life. Akiyama and the other co-op officials argued that this was a good plan and tried to get the producers to comply, but few were doing so. In fact, this kind of thing had happened a number of times in the past, and there was really nothing to do but wait until a natural shakeout occurred and the weaker farms either closed up shop or went bankrupt. The key to survival was to stay afloat until things improved.

The workers at the farm were uneasy about what all this would mean to them, but Akiyama seemed unruffled. Meanwhile, Koinuma went around talking to the men and trying to calm their fears. "The boss runs this place with what they call 'modern management techniques.' He knows what he's doing. He's seen these slumps before, and according to him eggs are just like other farm products: prices go up, and they come down. If you take the ups and downs too seriously, you don't last in this business. That's what he says. During other bad years he's always managed to turn a profit, and even though this is a rough patch we're heading into, I'm sure he can get through it. We won't be taking on any extra help for a while, that's for sure, and there won't be much in the way of bonuses, but that's life. We'll have good years again."

If the farm closed, Kikutani would have to ask for Take-bayashi's help in finding a new job. But could he expect another employer as understanding as Akiyama? And, too, Kikutani had come to feel that there was little chance that anyone at the farm would find out about his past. Koinuma, whom he saw the most, had been curious about Kikutani's background for a while, but seemed to have given up on that. Kikutani wanted to continue spending his days with the chickens, if that was possible, and he was reassured by Koinuma's assessment of the farm's business practices.

Around the middle of July, they received their bonuses. The bonuses were about half what they'd been the year before, but for Kikutani it was a first. He bought a small color television with his windfall. He would turn the set on as soon as he got home in the evening and sit drinking sake and smoking as he stared at the screen. His day off, too, he spent in front of the TV.

He went to Takebayashi's for his regular interviews. Occasionally Takebayashi's wife would bring out jars of instant coffee or canned goods from their son's supermarket and pass them unceremoniously to Kikutani. Once she gave him a large bag of rice.

"Kiyoura wanted me to tell you to stop by for a visit sometime," Takebayashi said as he was seeing him off at the entrance to the rice shop.

"But I'm sure he must be busy," said Kikutani. "I don't want to bother him."

"He knew that's what you'd be thinking; that's why he told me to invite you. Of course he's busy, but he said you should come."

Kikutani nodded. As he walked home, it made him happy to know that Kiyoura was still thinking about him de-

spite the fact that they had no more direct contact and Kikutani had been entrusted to Takebayashi. He came to a corner
and without hesitating turned down the street that led to the
halfway house. He had not felt like visiting the house since
the last time he saw Kiyoura, before his trip to Sakura. It was
partly that he had no particular need to go there, but the real
reason was that he was afraid Kiyoura, with his special intu-
ition, would see immediately what he had done. Now, however, he was worried that his absence might arouse suspicion.
It would be better to put in an appearance. Also, he sincerely
wanted to see Kiyoura.

He pushed open the door and looked in at the small receptionist's window. Kiyoura, who was seated at this desk,
caught sight of him and rose with a pleased expression. As
Kikutani entered the meeting room, Kiyoura came in from
the office. "You look well," he said cheerfully, dropping into
a chair. It was true that Kikutani had filled out; according to
the scale at the public bath, he'd gained five pounds or so. "I
hear you're drinking a little and you've started to smoke. I
think that's great." Kikutani smiled faintly and looked down
at his lap. Apparently, Takebayashi had been reporting every
detail of his activities, and it made him nervous to have Kiyoura watching him. To a question about conditions at work,
he related the news about the collapse of the egg market, but
said that the farm management was holding firm. He also
told about receiving his first bonus. Kiyoura listened quietly,
nodding occasionally as he puffed on his cigarette. A young
man brought in cups of instant coffee and went back to the
office. Kiyoura spooned some powdered creamer into his coffee and looked up.

"And have you seen your brother?" he asked. Kikutani said he hadn't, shaking his head slightly for emphasis. Since last fall, he hadn't had a letter either. His brother sent a New Year's card, but Kikutani didn't send one back. When he was in Sakura, in fact, he had not even wanted to walk by his brother's house at the edge of town, much less actually see him. He was grateful that his brother wrote to him while he was in prison and even sent an occasional package, but now that Kikutani was out, he was acutely conscious of the disapproval of his sister-in-law and his brother's reluctance to ruffle her. It seemed to Kikutani there was no reason not to cut all ties with them. Why was Kiyoura bringing this up all of a sudden? Since his brother was Kikutani's only blood relative, perhaps it was only natural to ask how they were getting along, but he had the feeling that the question was really Kiyoura's way of prying into whether or not Kikutani had been home. He decided to change the subject.

"How is Igarashi doing?" he asked. The truth was, he felt closer to Igarashi, whom he'd known just a few days, than to a brother who was so solicitous of his wife.

"He was sick for a while after he left the house, but he's better now and working in a furniture factory. He has his wife to keep him in line, and quite a talent for woodworking, so he should get along fine," said Kiyoura, staring absently into space. Kikutani remembered how Igarashi looked, a small figure trailing his wife down the alley, bundle in hand, and he felt sad that that period had passed so soon. Kiyoura was silent for a moment. "Actually, I've had news from your brother. He wrote a couple of weeks ago to say that his eldest daughter was killed in a traffic accident in the town where she was working." Kikutani looked up. "He said he wondered whether he should let you know, but before he could decide, they had the wake and the funeral. He knew he had to tell you sometime, though, and he asked me to do it without making a big deal of it." Kiyoura heaved a sigh, but Kikutani said nothing. "In fact, I think it was better that you didn't go to the funeral," Kiyoura added. "It may sound harsh, but I worry that someone might recognize you and cause trouble for your brother. I would guess that's why he didn't contact you in the first place. I think you should respect his feelings and just write them to say you're sorry. At this point, I think you should leave it at that and not worry about going to pay your respects. I know we talked about this before, but I still think you aren't ready to go back there." His expression was troubled.

Pay my respects? Kikutani wondered. As if he would. His brother's daughter had been a round-faced, happy child. When she was little, he took her to the festival at Makata Shrine or bounced her on his knee while they sat drinking. It was hard for him to imagine that this little girl had become a grown woman with a job. He could only suppose that his sister-in-law's dislike for him had been passed along to her daughters. He had no wish to see his brother's family or any of his other relatives. He appreciated the fact that his brother had looked after him despite his wife's feelings, but now he wondered whether he would rush off to a funeral, even if it was his brother's. Kiyoura suggested he write a letter of condolence, but if he did, he was sure his brother would read it once and burn it or tear it up for fear his wife would find it.

"By the way," said Kiyoura, leaning back in his chair and lighting another cigarette, "how are you getting along living so far from work? What would you say to moving someplace closer? I could find you a parole officer out there."

"I'd prefer to stay where I am," Kikutani answered immediately. "I enjoy the visits I have now with Mr. Takebayashi." He was comfortable with Takebayashi's quiet way of listening to his report while staring out into his garden, and he couldn't imagine being supervised by anyone else. It calmed him somehow just to be near Takebayashi, and the kindness his wife showed him had deeply touched him.

"I can understand that," said Kiyoura, nodding and looking at the ceiling. "He's a lot like a Buddha." Kikutani at last rose to leave. "Don't be a stranger around here," Kiyoura added.

Kikutani paused outside the halfway house and turned down a street that led away from his apartment. He was worn out from meeting with Takebayashi and then with Kiyoura, and he wanted to relax on the roof of the department store in Shinjuku. He passed through the empty streets of the neighborhood of sleazy hotels. Turning a corner, he saw a narrow three-story building on his left with a soiled sign hanging over the street. Next to the entrance was a placard listing the prices for the various sorts of "baths" offered inside. He glanced in the empty doorway as he hurried past.

Koinuma had been taking an interest in Kikutani's private life, knowing he was single. A few weeks earlier, as they were talking during a break, he asked with a slight leer if Kikutani had a girlfriend. Kikutani simply laughed and said he didn't.

"Well, then, how do you take care of...you know? Oh, I

get it. Where you live, you're surrounded by those bath-houses, and from what I hear a man gets a lot more than a bath at those places. What exactly do they do, anyway?" Koinuma's eyes flashed with interest.

"To tell the truth, I've never been to one," said Kikutani, "though I'm sure they're around."

"Come on. You live alone; there's nothing to be ashamed of. Most natural thing in the world, if you ask me."

"But it's the truth. I've never been, and I never intend to go." The smile faded from Kikutani's face.

"But why not? Why wouldn't you want to?" Koinuma persisted.

"Because they're dirty," Kikutani answered impatiently.

"Dirty?" Koinuma howled. "Ever heard of little thing called a rubber? You're not going to catch anything. Sounds like paradise to me, having a pretty girl take care of you. I'd love to go myself sometime, but I'm the farmer type and wouldn't know where to find these places or what they charge. But you live right in the middle of them—and you've never been?!" He looked skeptically at Kikutani.

Now, as Kikutani walked past the bathhouses, he thought over this exchange with Koinuma. When he'd said the places were dirty, it wasn't so much that he was afraid of disease as that he couldn't imagine having sex with a woman who had been with other men that day. In an article from a sports newspaper that he read on the train, he had learned what bathhouse girls do. That kind of thing might interest some men, but he had only skimmed through the beginning of the article and skipped most of the rest. As he walked, he found himself thinking about another prisoner, named Suzuki, who had worked in the print shop with him. Suzuki graduated from the law department of a good school and worked for a company for nearly twenty years before being convicted of embezzlement and sent to prison. In his line of work, Suzuki had been accustomed to high living, and he would casually refer to the women from the bars and clubs he'd been involved with. It was the kind of talk that didn't go down well with the other prisoners, but they tolerated it because it had nothing to do with prison life. Suzuki, who was nearly the same age as Kikutani, was one of the few prisoners who knew about his crime, and when they were alone, they would rattle on like two old men chewing the fat.

"You really are a prude, you know that?" This was Suzuki's label for Kikutani, and it stuck with him. If everyone who caught his wife cheating killed her, Suzuki said, the courts would be clogged with murderers and the prisons would explode. True, when a man was married a few years and arrived at a certain station in life, he might secretly wish that his wife would kick off from some convenient disease so he could find a younger, more desirable woman. But as time went by and a man got used to his wife's ways, he stopped wishing for her death. And if a woman was unfaithful, Suzuki said, then you just got rid of her, found someone who would take her off your hands. "If it were me, I'd be glad to see her go and have the chance to look for something better. A wife's not the only woman around. But you…you lose your head and kill her like a prude, like somebody who doesn't know anything; and on top of that you get yourself thrown in prison. What could be more stupid?"

Suzuki seemed to know just how Kikutani felt, and it made Kikutani squirm, but somehow he didn't resent the criticism. It struck him as reasonable coming from a man who had lived a very different life, and he accepted it in silence. According to Suzuki, it was precisely because Kikutani had never fooled around with women that he went berserk over his wife's infidelity and killed her. This was probably only a justification for Suzuki's own wild life and not a universal truth. Still, there was no denying the link between Kikutani's fastidious attitude about sex and the murder. Several times since getting out of prison, he'd been overcome with the desire for a woman, but it had never occurred to him to go to a bathhouse, despite Koinuma's insinuations. He knew what would happen if he did: he'd hate the woman who gave her body to men for money, and whatever desire he felt would die.

He wandered on through the city, leaving behind the residential neighborhoods and coming into streets lined with bars and small restaurants. Finally, he crossed a broad avenue and entered the department store. Taking the elevator to the roof garden, he sank into one of the plastic chairs. Thick ropes were tied to one corner of the roof, and above them floated red and white advertisement balloons, motionless against the white clouds beyond. Since his trip back to Sakura, the whiteness of his wife's legs glimpsed through the curtains had come to haunt him. He felt the core of her lust in the way those white legs spread themselves, in the way the toes pointed and strained. He also relived his cold-blooded feeling as he crept in through the kitchen door and grabbed the knife. Suzuki said Kikutani had gone berserk, but the truth was that except for the crimson blur that engulfed him, Kikutani had felt strangely calm. He took out a cigarette and lit it with a disposable lighter.

Why had he been so cool? His body had proceeded with

utter confidence, without the slightest hesitation, as if he had practiced this precise set of movements many times. Mochizuki looked up at him just as he had imagined he would, and Kikutani planted the knife in his shoulder as if the whole thing had been carefully choreographed. And when he turned on his wife, he stabbed her with such a clear sense of purpose, like a carpenter driving nails in just the right places. His face must have been as expressionless as hers at the time.

When he was very young, his mother worried that his nerves were fragile. He could still remember how upset she'd been with his reaction when their dog got distemper. The dog was coughing violently and spitting up blood, and he had begged his mother frantically to do something. They rushed to the vet, but it was hopeless, and the next morning the dog died with blood pouring from its mouth. Kikutani stopped eating after that and cried incessantly, unable to calm down even when his mother slapped his face. Things were much the same after he started school; a high-strung boy, he was the object of endless taunts and torments. The other children would think up games like forcing blades of grass into the tails of dragonflies and setting them loose, or sticking a straw up the rear of a frog and blowing into it to inflate its abdomen, but Kikutani would go pale and shrink from these amusements. Seeing this, the children chased him and, pinning his arms, pressed the bug or frog against his face. On those nights, Kikutani invariably had nightmares and cried out in his sleep.

After he was grown, the old fears persisted. Once, when he happened on a traffic accident with serious injuries, he fled across the street in horror. Even when a bloody scene came on the TV, he would look away. When one of his students got hurt, he became so completely flustered that they laughed at him when it was all over. But if he hated blood and suffering so much, why had he been so calm and collected as he stabbed his wife to death? With each stroke, the blood gushed from her body; but when he recalled the sight even now, he felt nothing. He looked up at the balloons. An unknown element seemed to lurk inside him, the thing that had manifested itself in the red haze. Whatever it was that spurred him to murder, it could be described only in terms of this brilliant mass of color that was impossible to explain rationally, that he himself didn't understand. The murder had been vague and hazy; the only thing that was clear was that he felt no regret for it. Rather, it seemed to him that he had been right to kill his wife.

Perhaps I should travel, he told himself. His trip to Sakura had been a bitter journey through his past, but now he wanted to go somewhere and relax. He'd been out of prison a year, and he was getting settled in his ways. He'd even developed a taste for cigarettes and sake. He was relatively healthy, and with any luck he'd live another ten years or so. Still, he felt ill at ease, as if something was out of balance. A change might be good, a chance to get things back on the right footing. There were, of course, lots of ways to do this, but he thought the best might be to visit a place that held pleasant memories from the past.

The coastline at Urayasu, a town in the south of Chiba prefecture, came to mind. He had been there during his second year in the university, at the invitation of a friend whose grandfather ran a light-metals manufacturing company and was building a net-fishing boat at the Urayasu harbor.

Kikutani and his friend took the Sobu Line to Motoyawata Station and went by bus to Urayasu. They waited by the channel until the grandfather and his whole family came in their car. A line of small fishing boats was moored in the channel, and they boarded one of them and headed toward the mouth of the Edo River.

As the boat chugged along, the grandfather reminisced about the end of the war, when he was a student in a commercial high school. As part of the general mobilization, the students were sent to a factory on the left bank of the river that made wooden transport ships. They had been called in specifically to help with the launching of the ships, and it was their job to cross the river in small boats and pull on heavy ropes attached to the new ship until it slid into the water. That night, the students slept in the factory dormitory and were treated to a feast that was unimaginable in those days: mounds of crab and white rice on boiled nori. It had been an unforgettable meal, and it was because of those memories that the grandfather sometimes went out in his boat even today, he told them.

A hundred yards downriver, he pointed out the factory on the bank, but it was nothing more than a decaying wooden structure half-covered with weeds. They went a little farther, and the pilot cut the engine and sculled for a few yards until they came to a complete stop. A middle-aged fisherman stood and leaned far out over the bow to cast the net. When they pulled it up on the boat again, it was full of sea bass, mullet, and perch. The boat was tied to a pole that had been fixed in the river, and they continued casting the net. A shallow sandbar dotted with reeds stretched away from them downstream; shore birds passed by overhead. The pilot and the fisherman brought out a brazier, pots, and other utensils and made miso soup, cutting up the fish for sashimi or to fry as tempura. And from this they made their meal, washed down with beer and sake. As the sun at last began to set, the engine was started again and they headed back, the evening air cooling their flushed cheeks.

Urayasu, at the mouth of the Edo River, was a traditional fishing village that seemed unchanged despite its proximity to Tokyo. The whole town smelled of fish, and men with towels wrapped around their heads stood talking loudly by the docks. Women, the image of fishermen's wives, made their way through the streets, babies strapped tight to their backs. The day on the boat had been an extraordinary treat for the young Kikutani and made a big impression on him. Even years later, in prison, he occasionally recalled the flavors of the dishes the fishermen made them and the shimmering scene with the sound of the reeds rustling in the wind. I might just go have a look around Urayasu, he thought. He would take a walk out by the estuary and sit on the riverbank; he wanted to see the sandbar with its bed of river grass, even from a distance. Lighting another cigarette, he gazed up at the balloons.

The next week on his day off, Kikutani finished breakfast and made some rice balls and three boiled eggs. They probably had restaurants in the town, but he wanted to unpack his own lunch sitting out in the breeze by the river. He left his apartment and headed for the station, feeling like an excited schoolboy leaving on a field trip. Clutching the strap on the train, he stared out at the puffy white clouds left by the night's storm. He changed for the Sobu Line at

Ochanomizu Station and immediately found a seat in the empty car. Perching on his knees the bundle containing his lunch, he looked out the window. He remembered how surprised he'd been at the changes in the scenery on this line the night he went to Sakura; but now, in the sunlight, the shining concrete buildings were even more astounding, hanging over the tracks and impressing on him the extraordinary degree of transformation. He could also see the endless ribbon of an expressway following the broad river. Finally, after they passed Ichikawa Station, there began to be signs of green among the buildings. He rose to get off at Motoyawata.

He found a seat on the bus to Urayasu and waited for it to leave. Motoyawata seemed to be a quiet residential district, but there was a long line of taxicabs in front of the station and an endless stream of people going in and out of the shops. Here, too, nothing was as he remembered it, but he was confident that he would find Urayasu unchanged. It could be reached only by bus, and though it was close to Tokyo, separated from it only by the Edo River, it seemed almost like a solitary island. The wave of steel and concrete that swept out from the city had not reached all the way to Sakura. The area around the station in Sakura had changed, but the rest of the town was just as it was when he lived there. So Urayasu, which wasn't even on a train line, should be even freer of urban sprawl.

The bus began to move. It followed a broad, straight street through a bustling shopping district. As Kikutani remembered it, they should have come almost immediately to open fields, but now there were unbroken rows of houses as far as the eye could see. The sunlight had dried the road, leaving it almost white. The bus went up a ramp that led to a long bridge across the Edo River. Kikutani could distinctly recall the old route: a narrow, winding path through dark, ancient houses, some of which still had thatched roofs—the very picture of a fishing village. But the new road they were turning onto now was broad, with stoplights and wide sidewalks.

After a time, a recorded voice announced that the next stop would be Urayasu Station. Wondering if he had heard wrong, Kikutani strained forward to look out the front window, and there he could see an elevated train line and the roof of a platform above it. Apparently, the fishing village that could be reached only by bus now had a train line. As they passed under the tracks and came to a halt, Kikutani lined up behind the other passengers to get off. With a look of astonishment on his face, he stood staring at the station until he finally collected himself enough to walk inside. From the map above the ticket machines he discovered that his lonely village was now connected by subway with downtown Tokyo.

Outside the station, he stood for a while and looked about. Surrounding him was a solid phalanx of condominiums, supermarkets, banks, and other large buildings, and through them ran a wide, smoothly paved boulevard. The fishing village at the end of the dead-end road had vanished, and a city of concrete had risen in its place. He felt utterly ridiculous to have gone out of his way for a bumpy bus ride to a place that existed only in his memory. But, he thought, even if the town has grown beyond recognition, the estuary might still be the same; the river, at least, must be flowing as it always did. He had come to see the sandbar covered with reeds, to sit for a while and smell the brine. Stopping a woman who was pushing a baby carriage, he asked her how to find the river and set off in the direction she pointed.

The people he passed were dressed just like people in the city, and there was no sign anywhere of a fisherman. As Kikutani walked along between the shops, he had the unsettling feeling that he had come to some foreign territory. Then he stopped by a small shrine at a fork in the road, suddenly recalling that to the right there was a channel that ran through the town and was lined on both sides by narrow alleys. This little waterway was one of his fondest memories of Urayasu. Feeling his spirits lift, he took the right-hand fork, and as he walked, he became convinced that this was the same street he'd known from his university days. Small boats were moored in the channel, and among the houses along the banks were some older wooden boats that had silvered in the river breeze. And the women who stood talking in the doorways were different from those he had seen near the station; these were more like the fishermen's wives of his youth. Ahead he spotted a sign hanging amid the eaves of the houses, and he knew his memory hadn't deceived him: this was the same marina where he and his friend boarded the grandfather's boat all those years ago. It was as if the old village existed unchanged here on the banks of the channel.

Kikutani stopped and peered into the marina office. There was not a soul to be seen in the entranceway or in the sitting room beyond. He followed the channel, crossing a small bridge to the opposite bank. He remembered that these alleys had been paved with bleached shells that made the most wonderful crunching sound as you walked; now they were asphalt. He came to a floodgate, which had been reinforced on both sides with concrete dikes. The road turned here, with the dike, to the left, and Kikutani saw that he had reached the river at last. He walked until he came to a staircase carved into the dike and, hesitating for just a moment, began to climb. When he got to the top, he found himself looking out on the expanse of the Edo River. As he turned downstream, however, a groan of dismay filled his throat: on both sides of the estuary where the vast sandbar had been, a broad strip of reclaimed land stretched far out into the river, and on it was a line of high-rise buildings receding into the distance. An elevated freeway snaked through them, dotted with the glittering reflections of speeding cars. He stood, paralyzed by this surreal vision, then flinched and turned to look behind him. A wail rose in his throat as he was confronted by a forest of towering buildings unlike anything he had seen, even in the city. They seemed to be condominiums, some with balconies hung with drying laundry.

Kikutani stared at the mass of buildings. The subway line had transformed this area into a bedroom community, triggering enormous development that seemed to be far from finished. He thought of the years he had spent in prison. Though the fixtures in the cellblock had been changed from time to time, the building itself had been untouched; while out here, during those same years, an unimaginable wave of development had swept from the city. In the midst of this torrent, the prison remained an isolated island where time had stopped. Oblivious to the world outside, the inmates were still stitching shoes by hand in the workshop, printing fliers and posters on their antique press.

The sandbar and the reeds were gone. The river alone flowed on. Kikutani looked down at the ebb tide carrying its froth of garbage and dead fish out to sea. A motorboat filled with young men and women skirted the dike and headed upstream toward the train bridge, leaving small waves lapping at the bank.

8

Kikutani did not mention his trip to Urayasu to Takebayashi. Though Takebayashi had been opposed to his going home to Sakura, Kikutani doubted that he would have objected to his visiting a place like Urayasu that was full of fond memories. Still, to report on something as insignificant as a day trip made him uncomfortable, as if he were being suffocated.

The flies had returned to the farm, so the henhouse had to be cleaned out even more frequently. Kikutani spent his days spraying liquid disinfectant or scattering pesticide on the droppings. The egg market showed no signs of improving, so toward the end of August Akiyama told Koinuma to begin removing mature birds from the house on a shorter rotation, as the government office had advised. Kikutani and Koinuma were busy at the annex vaccinating the young hens that would replace the older ones and clipping their beaks. As soon as they finished, the men from the company that disposed of the old birds arrived at the henhouse with truck-loads of empty baskets. Koinuma stopped to watch them loading the birds, but Kikutani went back to scattering poison for the maggots. Finally, when the old birds were all removed, Kikutani and Koinuma began the job of stocking the quiet cages with a noisy batch of new hens. By the end of the day, incessant clucking again filled the building. They increased the flow on the automatic feeder, and the line of eggs started moving along the conveyor belt toward the packing room.

In the midst of this work, Kikutani returned to his apartment one day to find a brown envelope in his mailbox. He thought it might be a letter from his brother informing him of his niece's death, but the handwriting was crude, and there was no return address. He had no idea who would send him a letter, but as he stood looking at the envelope, he was struck with the suspicion that it was another anonymous message like the one about his wife's affair. Finally he tore open the letter and unfolded it. As he skimmed down the page, he knew immediately, from the way it was written, that it was from an ex-convict. The man said he had been in the same facility as Kikutani, though they had not been friends, since the man had not got close to the "indefinite-sentence" men. But he did know him by sight. He went on to explain that after he got out, the halfway house found him work with a company that specialized in transporting and slaughtering chickens, and that he'd been shocked to see Kikutani during a recent job. He panicked and fled, but now he was terrified that Kikutani might have told someone about his past. The people who ran the company knew, of course, but he was worried about the men he worked with and couldn't sleep at night wondering what Kikutani might have said. The letter ended with a plea to keep his secret, out of charity and a sense of loyalty to their shared fate, and it was signed Jiro Takasaki.

Kikutani stood holding the paper as he tried to recall the day when the truck came to take the old hens. A dozen or so men had carried piles of baskets into the henhouse and almost brutally stuffed them full of birds. The author of the letter said that Kikutani had glanced his way several times, but Kikutani couldn't remember noticing any of the men in particular. He had been preoccupied with spreading the pesticide and had only a vague memory of the men in their company uniforms and caps carrying baskets of chickens from the henhouse to their truck. The man must have been a short-timer, Kikutani concluded. They typically knew all about the men with long or indefinite sentences, even what they'd done to deserve their punishment; so this man could be familiar with Kikutani though Kikutani had no idea who he was. As he sat on the floor in his room, a chill went through him. It gave him a sick feeling, that while he had been busy at work, someone who knew about him was watching him on the sly.

The man said he was afraid of people finding out about his past, but Kikutani was equally afraid. The idea terrified him that someone who knew what he had done and what his sentence had been was working for a company that had such close ties with the chicken farm. He looked at the letter again. He heard that there were men who got to know each other in prison and then met up after they were out to continue a life of crime. But most ex-convicts did everything they could to hide their past and lived in fear of discovery.

This Takasaki knew, of course, that Kikutani would be as frightened as he was, but his only thought was for his own secret. The shaky handwriting and mistaken characters suggested an almost ludicrous sincerity. But how had he learned Kikutani's address? If the man had gone to his parole officer to express his fears, he might have found a sympathetic ear, but Kikutani doubted they would reveal the address of another prisoner. More than likely, in his desperation, the man had followed him home from work. At this thought, Kikutani glanced around the room, feeling nervous and unsettled.

The next morning, he left his apartment unusually self-conscious. Until today, he had made his commute almost automatically, paying little attention to his surroundings. But now he thought he noticed people casting glances in his direction, and he found himself tensing as if for a fight. He studied the eyes of the men and women he passed as he made his way to the station, and he was sure he caught one of the drivers stuck in traffic staring at him. Waiting for the train on the platform, he stole looks at the faces of the other commuters. There were plenty of people throughout the city who knew about his crime, because they came from Sakura or had been in the same prison. Though he was aware of that danger, he had conducted himself carelessly. And now this letter from Takasaki had come to show him just how dangerous his lack of vigilance could be. The whole set of circumstances was ominous: Takasaki, imagining that Kikutani saw him, had written out of fear. But his letter frightened Kikutani with its revelation that Kikutani had been seen in turn. It was his first such encounter since his release, but he sensed that it was only the beginning. In the year and a half since he got out of prison, in all his wanderings about the city, how many people had recognized him and recalled what he'd done? Once he boarded the train, he found a place where few people would look at him and stared resolutely at his lap. He did not calm down until he got to the henhouse and submerged himself in the reassuring clucking. The lack of human eyes was a comfort in this sea of chicken heads bobbing for grain.

In the afternoon, Koinuma pulled two hens who had stopped eating from their cages and wrung their necks on the spot. It was up to Kikutani to dispose of the bodies behind the henhouse. He dug a deep hole, dropped the chickens in, and shoveled dirt over them. When he was finished, he went to the washroom and carefully scrubbed his hands. The warmth of the small bodies seemed to linger on his palms, and he grimaced as he recalled how the tongues had hung from their beaks.

As he left the washroom, he saw Akiyama at the bottom of the henhouse stairs. Catching sight of Kikutani, Akiyama came walking over. Kikutani removed his cap and bowed. He could tell that Akiyama had something to say to him.

"Did you get a letter from a man named Takasaki?" he asked. Though Kikutani had been in a constant state of agitation since receiving the letter and had thought of little else, the question still caught him off guard, and he blanched. How would Akiyama know about this? he thought. But Akiyama knew all about his past, and he had taken it on himself to act as Kikutani's protector. There was no need to fear him; Kikutani should answer honestly. "It was waiting at my apartment when I got home yesterday," he said, studying Akiyama's expression.

"I see," said Akiyama, nodding. He explained that Takasaki had left prison a year earlier and found work with a plumbing contractor. But he learned that a woman who kept a shop near his office was from his hometown, and he quit the company out of fear of discovery. After that, the parole board helped Takasaki find the job disposing of chickens, and he seemed to have settled into the work, enjoying the protection of his new employer. But when he spotted Kikutani at the farm, he became unhinged. His boss couldn't help but notice, and he called him in quietly and got him to confess the whole story. Takasaki was afraid Kikutani would reveal that he was an ex-convict and wanted to send a letter begging him to keep quiet. The boss assured Takasaki that Kikutani was in the same position and wasn't likely to say anything, but Takasaki seemed skeptical and even hinted that he might quit. His boss called Akiyama, asking for Kikutani's address, and gave the address to Takasaki. "So this man actually sent you a letter. Seems he's worried about what you're thinking. I just had another call from his boss asking me to quiz you about this whole business. But I don't see you telling anybody. Am I right?" Akiyama fixed him with an intent look.

"Of course," said Kikutani. "First of all, I don't even know this man. In his letter he said that I looked at him, but I never did. I have no recollection of ever meeting him. If I had seen someone from my old prison, I would have been the one to panic, but I would never have told anyone else about it." Kikutani said exactly what he felt.

Akiyama nodded. "I see. You didn't even notice him. He blew it all out of proportion in his head. I'll call them right away and tell them not to worry," he said, his face softening into a smile as he went back to the office. Kikutani climbed the henhouse stairs.

On the train home, he thought about this ex-convict he did not even know. Takasaki would be relieved when he got Akiyama's message through his boss, but Kikutani doubted this would set his mind completely at ease. The man seemed to be the nervous type, probably bothered by the least thing. He'd quit his first job because he'd been frightened, and he would probably take only slight comfort from Kikutani's reassurances. Takasaki might even imagine the worst and quit his new job as well. But it wouldn't be easy to find yet another boss so understanding, and he might spend a long time unemployed, essentially ruining himself. Kikutani decided to write back to the man. If he set his thoughts down in writing, Takasaki would know that there was absolutely no reason to be worried, and perhaps he would be able to regain his peace of mind.

Getting off at his station, he went straight to a public phone near the shops across the way. He dialed the number for Akiyama's house, which was next to the farm office. He decided against going to the office the next day and asking for the address of Takasaki's company: that would arouse the secretary's curiosity. It would be safer to ask now by phone. Akiyama's wife answered and put her husband on.

"What can I do for you?" Akiyama asked, caution in his voice at being called at home by Kikutani. When he heard that it concerned Takasaki, he said that he had already relayed the message. Kikutani thanked him and explained that he wanted to write back to put Takasaki's mind at ease. Akiyama agreed that that was a good idea, and after a brief pause he read him the address of Takasaki's employer.

Kikutani stopped on the way to his apartment to buy some cold beer and a light supper. After he finished his meal, he spread a piece of writing paper on the low table and found a pen. He wrote that he had not noticed anyone from his prison among the men who came to collect the old hens; that he was as worried as Takasaki that his past would be revealed and so would never say anything; and that they would probably meet again at work but should pretend not to know each other. He closed by saying that he lived alone, so there was no chance Takasaki's letters would be seen by anyone else, and that Takasaki should write him again if he ever wanted to talk over his troubles. He reread the letter, made a few corrections, and slid it into an envelope. On the front he wrote the address of Takasaki's employer, and then he left the apartment to find a mailbox.

An answer came five days later. Like the previous letter, this one began with a cursory greeting, after which Takasaki wrote that he received Kikutani's message through his boss, and then the letter had come to further reassure him. He had actually been able to sleep at night after that. The letter continued with an awkward account of his crime. Takasaki had married into a family that owned a liquor store in a small provincial city. After the first few months, his mother-in-law took a dislike to him, and as time passed, his wife sided with her mother. They had a child together, but eventually he was banished from his own bedroom and forced to sleep on the floor in the shop. His mother-in-law abused him at every turn, and he stopped eating with the family, taking his meals from the leftovers in the kitchen. He put up with this treatment for a long time, but finally the mother-in-law announced she was kicking him out of the family, and he flew into a rage and beat her to death. He also wounded his wife when she tried to stop him. He was sentenced to seven years. Released last fall, he was still in his probationary period. The letter went on to say that he had noticed the tall, intelligent-looking Kikutani working in the prison print shop and wondered what sort of crime he could have committed. He was shocked to see him again at the chicken farm and had thought that his own past would come out but Kikutani's kind letter had put his fears to rest. In conclusion he wrote, "I am seeking to rehabilitate myself and am grateful for your help and support."

Kikutani set the paper on the table and poured some beer into his glass. Takasaki's letter, with its frank confession, left him feeling indulgent both toward himself and this fellow sufferer. Perhaps because they were so alone, each felt the need to talk to someone who shared his secret. Kikutani found comfort in the knowledge that other men on parole felt as he did. The letter left him with tremendous sympathy for Takasaki and the wish to know him better.

Summer finally loosened its grip, and the days grew cooler. Kikutani waited two weeks before answering Takasaki's letter, but the reply came by return mail. Takasaki said he had carried Kikutani's first letter around with him, reading it again and again as he waited anxiously for the next one. He wrote that he was grateful to his boss and his parole officer for taking such good care of him. He said that he had started out in the slaughterhouse, but the constant stream of dismembered wings and heads and legs had reminded him of his past difficulties, and so he was assigned instead the job of picking up the chickens from henhouses and then delivering the meat to packing companies. He closed by asking Kikutani to write back, saying that he pictured his face as he fell asleep at night and it reassured him.

From years of proofreading, Kikutani found himself noticing the mistaken characters and orthographic errors, but at the same time the awkward way Takasaki expressed himself allowed his feelings to come through. He had no one else to write to, and these letters to Kikutani were his one source of comfort. Kikutani was beginning to feel the same way. They were two old dogs licking their wounds in private. The correspondence continued, with Takasaki complaining of this and that and Kikutani offering what advice he could. Takasaki wrote that he was born in Iwate prefecture and that his father died while he was still young, leaving the family quite poor. After finishing middle school, Takasaki went to Tokyo to work for a soft-drink company that gave him a place to live and allowed him to continue his education part-time. He continued making deliveries for the company after graduating from high school, until the owner of a liquor store he visited on his rounds picked him out to be his daughter's husband and the adopted heir of the family. Things were going quite well until the old man died, leaving Takasaki's mother-in-law in charge. Takasaki had never liked her, and things went from bad to worse until the final tragedy.

While he was in prison, he received divorce papers from his wife, which he signed and sealed without objection, thereby severing all ties with that family. He heard rumors later that she remarried. For his wife he felt no regret whatsoever, only hatred; but for his daughter, who would be in elementary school by now, he felt a strong attachment. He wanted to see her again, and often thought of hiding along her route to school to catch a glimpse of her. But he never carried out the plan, terrified of being seen in his old neighborhood.

His mother and his sister still lived in their hometown. His mother's letters to him were filled with anger, but he could tell that she still loved him. The letters blamed him for the fact that his sister had not received a marriage proposal, and when he wrote to say he was getting out of prison, he got a letter saying it would cause trouble if he came home. Since his release, he had not gone near the place.

On his day off at the end of September, Kikutani left his apartment and headed for Takebayashi's house. He had kept quiet about his trip home and to Urayasu, but he thought he would tell Takebayashi about his correspondence with Takasaki. It seemed to him that for Takasaki the chance to open up in his letters had helped him to gain a certain stability and peace of mind; and for Kikutani, too, this communication with a man whose face he didn't know was one of his few pleasures, a way to relieve the loneliness. As his parole officer, the person most concerned with his rehabilitation, Takebayashi would surely give his blessing to this exchange of letters, especially when Kikutani explained that it had been encouraged by both their employers.

Kikutani took his place across from Takebayashi in the living room. As was his usual practice, he began his report by talking about developments at the chicken farm. The extraordinary collapse of the egg market continued, he said, and there were beginning to be signs that some of the producers would go bankrupt. But Akiyama appeared calm in the midst of it all. Takebayashi said that eggs were selling cheap in his son's supermarket, but the volume didn't seem to be going up. After a brief silence Kikutani changed the subject, launching into the story of his correspondence with Takasaki.

"So I've been hearing," said Takebayashi when he'd finished his account.

"You've known about this all along?" said Kikutani, surprised.

Takebayashi nodded and looked out at the garden. "I've been wondering when you were going to mention it, but it seemed you didn't think it was particularly important. I'm glad you told me, though. I'd like you to tell me everything that happens to you, no matter how insignificant it might seem." His voice was almost a whisper.

"I will, then," Kikutani answered meekly.

"I'm told that Jiro Takasaki had a good prison record. He seems like an honest sort, but like most men just out of prison, he's bothered by a lot of little things. He has apparently decided that the best way to cope with his troubles is to tell you about them. I think this correspondence between the two of you is a splendid thing; I'd like you to continue."

Kikutani had the uncomfortable feeling that Takebayashi somehow knew not only that he and Takasaki were writing each other but also what they said in their letters. He had thought the correspondence was a secret, and it made him uneasy to think that Takebayashi had known about it all along. As he made his way home, he pondered how Takebayashi could have come by this knowledge. The only other people who knew about the letters were Takasaki's boss and Akiyama, who had helped them make contact. Perhaps Akiyama, out of a sense of duty as the employer of a parolee, had reported to Kiyoura, who had passed the information on to Takebayashi. But it seemed impossible that Akiyama, with his keen business sense and his calm personality, was secretly gossiping like this to Kiyoura. That left Takasaki; something must have leaked from his side. Kikutani had simply told Takebayashi about their letters in the course of reporting on his daily life, but Takasaki must have mentioned the correspondence to his parole officer at a much earlier point. Takasaki's officer would have included it in his report to the parole board, which would have relayed this information to Takebayashi as a matter of course. Kikutani suddenly had the feeling that a net had been tightly strung around him, and that his slightest movement was being carefully watched.

Autumn was coming on. From the train window, day after day, Kikutani could see the brown outline of the distant mountains, sharp and clear in the fall air. The flies disappeared once again from the henhouse, replaced by a swarm of red dragonflies. Some of the trees in the forest surrounding the farm were beginning to turn.

A letter came from Takasaki, but Kikutani hesitated to answer it. Their correspondence, for him, had been something akin to a secret affair, with all the joy of lovers nestling together for warmth in the darkness. But now he suspected that Takebayashi knew everything that they wrote to each other. It depressed him to think that the routine inspection of letters that he had endured in prison was continuing now that he was out. As time passed, he became obsessed about finding out exactly how Takebayashi had learned about the letters. He was certain that the leak came from Takasaki, but in order to get a better idea how the parole board kept watch on him, Kikutani would have to send another letter asking who knew about the correspondence and when. He laid out the stationery. He wrote that he had been surprised that his parole officer knew about the letters, and he suspected Takasaki had told someone. What really happened? Had Takasaki shown his letters to someone? As Kikutani wrote, he fell naturally into the style of a cross-examiner.

A few days later, reading Takasaki's reply to his letter, he realized that everything he had imagined about their correspondence had been true, and more. Almost as soon as Takasaki had spotted Kikutani at the chicken farm, written the letter, and got his answer, he reported the whole thing to his parole officer. After that, at each of his scheduled interviews, he gave an account of the latest letters. Though he never actually showed Kikutani's letters to anyone, he outlined their contents. What surprised Kikutani most was that Takasaki apparently felt he had done nothing wrong, despite the accusatory tone of Kikutani's letter. He had taken it as a matter of course that they reported all their activities to the parole officer, and in that context he discussed the letters; he seemed to have no sense that for Kikutani this had been a betrayal. Kikutani was confronted once again with Takasaki's almost comic seriousness and utter devotion to the rules, and reminded how thoroughly Takasaki had given himself over to the care of the parole officer.

Now that he thought about it, Kikutani realized he was offended that his correspondence with Takasaki should be so closely watched. At the same time, knowing the details of the process gave him a certain peace of mind. He would simply go on reporting his letters to Takebayashi, just as Takasaki had done to his parole officer, and the whole thing would be a matter of public record, so to speak. In any case, the two parole officers evidently took a benign view of the whole thing. So, though he found himself completely surrounded by the limits set by the parole board, as he had in prison, Kikutani might be able to find a kind of peace and stability born of those limits.

The days grew cold, and Kikutani began to wear a coat when he left for work in the morning. Descending from the bus at the stop near the farm, he would shove his hands in his pockets and set off down the road. The leaves had fallen in the forest, and slivers of ice in the branches shone like crystal. The heating system in the henhouse sent blasts of warm air through the vents as he made his way slowly past the rows of cages.

In the evening, when he returned to his apartment, the air was still, as if frozen in place. Not removing his coat, he would switch on the electric heater and squat before it, warming his hands. Then he would open the stopcock on the gas line and cook his supper. During his first winter out of prison, he had thought the idea of a heater slightly frivolous, and often forgot to turn it on even after it was in his apartment. But he was amazed how completely his body had lost its resistance to the cold in just a year's time. Even when he went to the public bath for a hot soak, he would hurry home, fearful of catching a chill.

The people who lived in the building still seemed to work at night, and when Kikutani left for the farm in the morning and returned in the evening, all was quiet. Even when he stayed in on his day off, it wasn't until the afternoon that he began to hear voices or the faint sound of music. But toward evening there was a flurry of closing doors and footsteps on the stairs, then silence. Kikutani rarely woke during the night, but on the rare occasions that he did, he found the whole apartment building alive with activity. Sometimes he would hear a man and a woman, apparently drunk, fighting at the bottom of the stairs. A few months earlier, he began hearing the woman in the next apartment moaning, usually just before dawn or in the late afternoon when he was off from work. The sound was faint, but he could hear a broken sobbing that would gradually build to a frantic, gasping scream. When it was over, there would be a pause, followed by a man's voice talking quietly with the woman. Kikutani knew that the renter next door had changed; he had run into a heavyset man with close-cropped hair on the stairs. The man was leaving for work in the early evening, perhaps as a cook in a restaurant, Kikutani guessed. He seemed to live alone, but brought women home from time to time.

When Kikutani heard the voices, he would sit quietly in the middle of his room, remembering how it felt to be with a woman. But those thoughts soon drifted into the memory of the knife in his hand as he crept into his house through the kitchen. A confused image of his wife floated up before his eyes, and unable to stand the moaning anymore, he would press his hands over his ears. The woman's voice became a torment, and he took to staying away from his room on his afternoons off. In December, the noises next door stopped. There were no more piles of take-out dishes left for pickup by the door, and Kikutani never heard the door opening or closing. The man had apparently moved out, leaving the room empty.

The correspondence with Takasaki continued at the rate of about two letters a month. Takasaki wrote that the collapse of the egg market meant that they were calling on bankrupt breeders and collecting for slaughter not only the mature chickens but also younger, productive hens and even chicks. He also said that he had asked his parole officer for permission to visit his mother-in-law's grave to make his apologies, but he'd been turned down. So he made a tablet with her name on it like the ones that go on graves and said his prayers to that. Kikutani's replies were noncommittal now, avoiding anything that might reveal his feelings. Takasaki's first letter of the New Year was slightly different in tone. He wrote, in his faltering way, that for a long time he had been wanting to ask whether Kikutani would agree to meet him for a talk. Kikutani, he said, was the only person other than his parole officer he could open his heart to, and if Kikutani could find the time, Takasaki wanted to get together. "Open my heart" was the sort of phrase prisoners were encouraged to use, and when Kikutani saw it on the page, he felt that Takasaki was still living his life as if in jail, though he'd been out for more than a year. He could feel himself pulling back in response to Takasaki's growing sentimentality. Nevertheless he felt a duty to try to connect with this man who had offered him a source of comfort. In fact, Kikutani himself had been thinking that he'd like to meet Takasaki. The past they hid from everyone else had become a bond between them, and it was natural that they should go beyond the letters and meet to cement their friendship.

He ought to welcome Takasaki's proposal. He wrote back quickly, agreeing to the idea, and there was a gust of letters after that to make the arrangements.

Kikutani's day off was Wednesday. Takasaki got his boss's permission to be absent on a Wednesday, and they planned to meet in the afternoon. Kikutani chose the roof of the department store in Shinjuku as a meeting place, and Takasaki wrote that he would go early and be waiting for him. During his visit with Takebayashi, Kikutani described these arrangements. "That sounds fine," Takebayashi muttered, his speech slurring a little.

The evening before the meeting, Kikutani drank sake in his apartment and stared at the TV screen, but he had trouble following the plot of the drama. This was his first meeting with another man from his prison since Igarashi, and he was nervous, almost bashful. What would they talk about? He was sure it would be awkward at first, and they would have trouble making conversation, but they would manage somehow. He tried to picture the mysterious Takasaki, imagining him as a short man with broad shoulders. Or, judging from the overly expressive letters, he might be slender, with glasses perhaps. Kikutani could feel the sake beginning to take effect, and he settled into the pleasant haze.

The next morning after breakfast, he washed his underwear, as he always did on his day off, and hung it on a line outside the door to his apartment. A sliver of leaden sky was visible between his building and the next one. He sat near the heater watching TV until lunchtime, when he made a porridge from some leftover rice. Then he shaved and put on his suit with a shirt and tie. Turning off the heater and the gas line to the stove, he left his apartment and went downstairs. He had enough time to walk to Shinjuku, but decided to take the train. Since they were meeting at three o'clock, they would probably eat dinner together, perhaps at one of the restaurants in the department store. They could also have a drink or two together. Kikutani thought that since he was older and had served a longer sentence, he should be the one to pay the bill.

As he stepped onto the platform at Shinjuku Station, he saw that he still had more than half an hour, so he went to a kiosk, bought some cigarettes, and sat down on a bench. Takasaki had asked to arrive first and wait, and Kikutani wanted to respect that wish. He would go at exactly the appointed time. Lighting a cigarette, he watched the crowds of people getting on and off the trains. He checked the platform clock every few minutes, and finally got up and headed for the gate. As he walked through the underground passage to the basement of the department store, it occurred to him that his heart had not beat with this kind of excitement since he dated his wife before they were married. He skirted the food section of the store and stopped in front of the bank of elevators. Takasaki might be among the people waiting there. Kikutani half expected someone to tap him on the shoulder, but the doors opened and he stepped inside. With each stop, the elevator car grew emptier, and when it reached the roof, he was the only one to get out.

Birds were chirping in the pet shop to the right, and on the left was a line of tanks filled with tropical fish. The woman tending the shop sat on a tiny chair looking bored. Kikutani pushed open the door that led to the roof garden, feeling the cool air wash over him. He walked toward the line of potted bushes in front of the concession stand where they had agreed to meet. During the summer and on into autumn, the roof had been crowded with families intent on the exhibitions of exotic insects or the tanks of goldfish to be scooped up with paper nets, but now it was almost deserted. The children's rides off in one corner, a small train and some rocket ships, stood motionless with no sign of their attendants. Kikutani stopped at the appointed spot and stared at the plant store. Two men moved among the pots, pausing now and then to look at a plant, but both of them seemed older than Kikutani. Struck suddenly with the feeling that Takasaki had arrived, he spun around and scanned the area, but there was no likely man in sight. Kikutani looked over at the clock on the wall by the pet store and saw that there were still five minutes until the time they had set, so he took a seat along the edge of the garden.

He had sent Takasaki a map showing the way to the store, but remembering that Takasaki had said he would come early, Kikutani began to worry that he was lost. Perhaps this was his first time in a department store since getting out of prison; perhaps he was wandering the aisles in the basement, terrified of the escalators and elevators. He might eventually find his way up the stairs. Kikutani cupped his hand around his lighter as he lit a cigarette. Fifteen minutes passed. Then he noticed a man a few yards away looking into a tank filled with brightly colored carp. He was short and thin, about forty years old, with a red scar stretching from one cheek around to his neck, perhaps from a burn. The man left the tank and walked toward Kikutani, who was convinced he would stop and speak, but the man passed without looking at him. Thirty minutes passed, and Kikutani was now staring at the entrance to the roof garden. He thought a number of the men emerging from the door might be Takasaki, but they would invariably walk off in another direction or turn immediately and go back inside, apparently unwilling to brave the cold. He grew impatient. He wondered if Takasaki had mistaken the date or time, but that seemed unlikely, since they had confirmed their appointment in several letters. Perhaps something had happened to him on the way here and he couldn't come.

Finally, it occurred to Kikutani that Takasaki could be waiting in some other corner of the roof garden, so he stood to make a quick tour. The cafe that had been open through the fall was shut up tight, and the video-game center was dark with a CLOSED sign hung from the chain across the entrance. In the middle of his circuit he suddenly had the feeling that Takasaki had arrived at the appointed spot while he was gone, but hurrying back, he found no one. A foreign couple was wandering through the garden shop, examining potted plants, stone lanterns, and miniature waterwheels, but otherwise the area was deserted. He sat down again. Takasaki was now a full hour late. Even if he had been terribly lost, he would have been here by now. His letters had repeated how much he was looking forward to the meeting, how much he had to tell Kikutani. The fact that he hadn't shown up could only mean that something unexpected had happened. Kikutani knew he should go home, but he was reluctant to leave. It was still possible that Takasaki would appear any minute, flustered and apologetic. Kikutani settled in to watch the door. Takasaki had been the one to propose this meeting, but the longer Kikutani waited, the more intent he became; if there was still any chance they would find each other, he would wait.

The air grew colder. The cluster of office towers darkened, and lights began to come on in the windows. Kikutani dropped his cigarette into a butt can and rose from the bench. As he walked through the garden, he could see that he was the last person on the roof. Pushing open the door, he rang for the elevator, which came immediately, and he got in.

The next day, he began habitually checking the mailbox when he got home from work. There should have been a letter from Takasaki explaining why he had missed the meeting, but none came. Kikutani imagined that Takasaki had fallen ill or been injured in an accident. On the third day after the failed meeting, he wrote to Takasaki. There was no answer.

On his day off, he went for his interview. Takebayashi was in bed with a cold, but when Kikutani arrived, he came out to the living room dressed in a heavy padded robe. He was pale, and his face was covered with a stubbly beard, and to Kikutani he seemed to have aged a great deal. Concerned for his health, Kikutani rose from his chair, saying that he would come again next week, but Takebayashi said that the fever had subsided and he would be fine. He sat with his legs warming under the electric brazier as Kikutani went through the motions of his report. Then he told Takebayashi that Takasaki had not shown up for their meeting.

"He said he went," said Takebayashi flatly. Kikutani looked at him in disbelief. "Takasaki's parole officer is a man named Hagino," Takebayashi added, adjusting the collar of his robe. "A former elementary school principal. He called me twice about all this." He reached for the teacup his wife had set on the table. Kikutani sat listening, rigid with anticipation. According to Hagino, Takasaki had gone to the appointed spot on the department-store roof and waited a few yards off. When Kikutani appeared, Takasaki was about to approach him, but he was stricken with fear and simply watched Kikutani from behind a pillar. For nearly three hours he stayed hidden, watching Kikutani wait and feeling awful, but he was unable to overcome his fear. As Kikutani left the darkened roof, Takasaki apologized silently to his retreating figure. "Hagino asked him why he hid from you when he'd been so anxious for the meeting, but he just muttered something about his legs freezing. It seems that the moment he saw someone who knew about his past, he couldn't go through with it. Hagino said he still couldn't understand the psychology of men on parole, after all these years." Takebayashi frowned as he finished speaking. Kikutani watched his face in profile and said nothing.

"If that were the end of it, there would be no problem," Takebayashi continued, "but I'm told Takasaki has quit his job. You sent him a letter, but the letter came back to Hagino from Takasaki's boss."

"If he's quit, what is he doing?" Kikutani was stunned.

"From what I'm told, he's become a day laborer. He goes out early looking for work, but often he doesn't find anything." Takebayashi's expression was gloomy as he took a sip of tea.

"But why would he…?" Kikutani whispered.

"Why indeed?" Takebayashi echoed, cocking his head to

one side. Just then, his wife entered the room with a pot of tea. "It's started to snow," she said, sitting down next to the brazier. Through the glass doors they could see flecks of white tumbling into the garden. Kikutani stared silently at the pond.

Toward evening the snow began to fall in earnest, and during the night it became quite heavy. The confused din of Tokyo was muffled, as if sucked up by the falling snow, and a profound peace spread across the city, interrupted only by the faintest wail of a distant siren. Kikutani sat with a vacant expression, reaching from time to time for his cup of sake. He wondered where Takasaki could have hidden himself on the rooftop that day. He had searched the area repeatedly but never saw anyone likely. Perhaps Takasaki had been in the greenhouse by the plant store, or behind the little shed near the carp tanks. He had probably passed right by Kikutani when Kikutani made his walk around the roof. But why hadn't he said anything? Kikutani wasn't sure, but he thought he could understand how Takasaki felt. Takasaki's first letter had been spurred by the fear that his coworkers would find out that he had been in prison. His biggest concern was to conceal his past. But once they started exchanging letters, he wrote in great detail about his childhood, the circumstances of his crime, his most private feelings. Moreover, he was the one to propose they go beyond the letters and meet face-to-face, and he actually came to the department store. But when he saw Kikutani standing there, perhaps he recalled all those intimate details he had set down in his long, chatty letters—at the time it had been like sending them off to a perfect stranger, little different from tossing them into a black abyss. So the sight of this person who knew all about him waiting quietly in his chair made Takasaki hesitate. Perhaps he was shaken by the realization that Kikutani was his double, a man who had robbed another human being of life. Something like this must have gone through his head as he shrank back into the shadows.

Kikutani could not be angry with Takasaki for not showing himself; it only struck him as a little ghoulish to have been watched in secret for so long. But now Takasaki had quit his job, vanishing into a darkness where Kikutani could no longer reach him. The bond that had joined them was severed, and it was doubtful that there would be more letters. Kikutani had imagined a number of things he would ask Takasaki when they met, and now it saddened him to think that he would never have the chance to ask those questions. Takasaki had written that he wanted to visit his mother-in-law's grave but was not permitted to by his parole officer, so had prayed to a funerary tablet instead. Kikutani wanted to know whether this was an act of penitence, but to ask this he would first have had to tell about his own experience slipping off to Sakura and standing before the grave of Mochizuki's mother. He even brought incense to burn at the grave, but when he got there, all his hatred for Mochizuki came flooding back, overwhelming any desire to repent, and he turned and walked away, deciding the old woman's death was part of the inevitable course of events. What Kikutani wanted to know was whether Takasaki was sincere when he prayed to his little altar, or whether he did it just to curry favor with his parole officer.

I want the truth, he imagined saying to Takasaki. I know that murder is the most hideous and shameful act that one human being can commit against another, but in my case I can't feel any regret for what I did to my wife, strange as that may seem. The whole thing was like fate. The old woman's death was not something I looked for or wanted, but that's what becomes of a woman who has a man like that for a son. But what about you? Did the hatred you felt for your mother-in-law vanish without a trace, despite the fact that she denied your very existence as a person? Do you really regret having killed her? Kikutani wondered how Takasaki would have answered.

He remembered the final clause of the finding the judge read in court the day of his sentencing: "The defendant has duly reflected on his several crimes and expressed his remorse, having openly acknowledged his guilt before this court, and he actively hopes for the eternal rest of his wife, Emiko, and Teru Mochizuki...." This assertion had been one of the mitigating circumstances that moved them to commute his sentence to an indefinite term of imprisonment; and at that moment, as he sat listening in the prisoner's box, the words seemed to express his true sentiments. But as the days began piling up in prison, he reconsidered. He still felt guilty about the death of Mochizuki's mother, but his guilt about Emiko faded and finally disappeared altogether. He lost his sense of remorse, even the recognition that what he had done was a crime, until by the time he was let out of prison, only his rage at Emiko and Mochizuki remained.

What, exactly, had his sixteen years in prison meant? During the first few years he would often wake from vivid dreams about that horrible night, and realizing he had done something utterly irrevocable, he would feel remorse. But as the years passed, the dreams became less frequent and finally grew quite rare. It seemed that the long weeks and months in prison served mainly to wear away one's sense of guilt. Takasaki had probably heard the same sort of statement about penitence during his trial, but that he had written to Kikutani in such detail about each little slight from his mother-in-law suggested that his hatred for her was something he still carried around with him. And if, no matter how timidly, Takasaki should confess that he felt the same as Kikutani, then Kikutani had another question to ask: he wanted to know what they had in common that led them both to kill. From there perhaps he could reexamine what they had done.

Needless to say, until the night of the incident Kikutani had never once associated himself with the act of murder. The court found that even though he lied about his health and returned unexpectedly from the fishing trip, he had not premeditated the killings—and that was the truth. Rather, as the finding put it, "the defendant flew into a momentary frenzy" at the sight of his wife and Mochizuki in bed having sexual intercourse, and "in the heat of the moment" he became "homicidal." Kikutani listened quietly to this part of the explanation, but in his heart he was skeptical. And afterward, as he turned these words over and over in his mind during the long, vacant hours in prison, he came to the realization that they were untrue. He had not flown into a frenzy, nor had he become homicidal in the heat of the moment. Rather, from the instant he peered in the window and saw Mochizuki's hips between his wife's thighs, he grew utterly calm, as if he had been doused with cold, clear water. There was no question of a homicidal frenzy; he simply walked into the house, grasped the handle of the knife, and plunged it first into Mochizuki and then into his wife—over and over and over. His memory of the whole sequence of events was extraordinarily vivid, but it was as though he had completely lost his will, as if he had been guided by some unseen force. One might almost say that he felt no hatred or anger, no emotion of any kind. The court concluded that there was a reasonable psychological progression that led Kikutani to the murders, but there was an enormous distance between the truth and their conventional description of the events after he peered in through the gap in the curtains.

But what about Takasaki? Perhaps *he* had flown into a frenzy and become homicidal in the heat of the moment. Perhaps he had not passed those dreadful minutes drained of all feeling. But now Kikutani would never know, since Takasaki had fled beyond his reach, beyond his questions. And in all likelihood Kikutani would never again find someone he could ask about these things. He felt keenly that he had missed his only chance. The deepening snow was visible in the ring of light outside the window. He glanced at it from time to time as he sipped at his sake.

9

The days were empty. In the evenings, when Kikutani returned home from work, he would look in the mailbox on the chance that there was a letter, but after a month he gave up this practice. His body felt heavy, as if sapped of energy, and twice he caught a cold. He came to understand the healthy stimulus to him that the correspondence with Takasaki had provided, and now that it had ended, he felt as though a gaping hole had opened in his chest.

The cold weather was coming to an end, and from time to time there were days that were quite springlike. One evening, on his way home from work, he stopped at a store in the shopping district near the station. Among all the modern storefronts, this one seemed faded and untouched. In peeling paint, the sign read TROPICAL FISH, and lining the sidewalk on either side of the entrance were tanks of fish and various sorts of seaweed. Next to them was a wooden tub crawling with turtles whose shells seemed to have been painted a lurid green. Normally, he didn't go in, intimidated by the old shopkeeper who sat at the back of the store keeping watch on the street; but today the shopkeeper was occupied with a woman who was selecting some fish food from the display rack on the right side of the store, so Kikutani entered along the row of tanks to the left. The lights shining down into the water illuminated little schools of exotic fish—telescope fish, Japanese goldfish, calicoes, spotted carp—all swimming among rising bubbles. There were bitterlings as well, but less well fed than the ones he had caught in the river, and lethargic. On the floor beneath the tanks was a tub filled with scarlet killifish. When the shopkeeper, finished at last with his customer, turned to look at Kikutani, Kikutani simply strolled as casually as he could back down the row of tanks and out of the store.

As he continued down the street, he suddenly remembered the fly that kept him company in his cell for a time. The memory, both funny and pathetic, put a twisted smile on his face. It had started about six months after he arrived at the prison. During the day, he kept busy at the print shop, but in the evening, when he returned to his cell and finished dinner, there were still the long, empty hours until lights-out. The prison was quiet at night, but he could sense the men in the cells around him. From time to time a toilet would flush. A guard's footsteps could be heard coming down the corridor; as the guard passed, he would glance in at Kikutani. But being in a building with hundreds of other men was little comfort against the crushing loneliness of being the only living thing in his cell.

Kikutani had heard that a prisoner on death row asked

to keep a bird and permission was granted. He thought he could understand how the man felt. Death-row prisoners were not allowed to go out to the workshops; they spent their days alone in their cells waiting for the sentence to be carried out. The prisoner must have thought that a little bird would keep him company while he waited. When the bird arrived, the man tended it carefully, feeding it each day and seeing that its water bottle was filled. But after he was executed, the guards found the bird on the floor of its cage, strangled. Perhaps the man had been jealous of the bird, not wanting it to live on after he was dead.

But the man had been given the bird only because he was under a death sentence; no ordinary prisoner could expect that kind of privilege. Kikutani stretched out on the mat in his cell and stared at his thumb bending up and down and circling around his other fingers; he studied it as if it were another living thing. At that moment, a large housefly that had somehow found its way into the prison slipped through the bars of his cell, buzzed around for a moment, and came to rest on the edge of the shelf. Kikutani's eyes fixed on the fly—the first living thing he had seen in the cell since his arrival at the prison. As it left the shelf, Kikutani was afraid it would disappear through the bars, but it landed again where the two mats that served as his bed came together. Flexing its jointed legs, it stroked its wings and then sat perfectly still. Kikutani froze, then slowly drew his legs to his chest and began inching backward until he could reach his work cap, which was lying on his uniform. As the fly started to stroke its wings again, he darted forward and nimbly slipped the cap over it. It struck him as nearly miraculous that he had caught something so clever and quick.

He sat back and flattened the hat, turning it carefully until the fly's wings emerged from the tiny crack between the cap and the mat. He pondered the situation a moment and decided that the only way he could prevent his prisoner from escaping was to cut its wings. Pinning the fly with the edge of the hat, he gently pinched off half of each wing; then he slowly lifted the hat and picked up the fly. He was still afraid the fly would disappear if he let it go; so he picked a thread out of his towel and tried looping it beneath the fly's wings. This proved more difficult than he'd expected, but at last he managed to secure a knot around the fly's abdomen, wrapping the other end around a pencil. The fly flapped what was left of its wings, but it simply rolled around on the mat, unable to take off.

Kikutani brought the fly up close to his eyes. At the end of its legs it had a clawlike hook, and just above its eyes were delicate antennae. The stripes that ran from its back down along its abdomen were covered with fine hairs. The next morning, he was relieved to find the fly walking about on the mat. He watched it as he ate his breakfast, realizing that it would probably be dead by the time he got back from work; but when he reached his cell in the evening, it was still alive, busily scratching its legs on the mat. He used his chopsticks to brush a drop of vegetable broth from his dinner on the fly's head, and after a moment it began to work its mouth. He spent that evening again watching the fly, but the next morning he found it lying on its back, dead. The legs were tightly curled, and the half wings were limp. He waited almost a week before he got rid of the little body; there was no outward change in its appearance, but he sensed that it had become dry and brittle.

Why had seeing the fish made Kikutani remember the fly? He thought about life in his apartment now: when he came home at night and opened the door, the air seemed cold and stagnant; to drive away the gloom, he would turn on the TV and light the fire under the kettle. After preparing his simple supper, he would eat, then sit in front of the TV drinking sake. He had grown used to this routine, but after the letters from Takasaki stopped coming, these long evening hours seemed wearisome. He would trim his fingernails and toenails, or pluck white hairs from his head with the help of a small hand mirror. But most often he simply lay on his back on the tatami and stared at the ceiling. He wanted something living in the room, he thought. Just as the sight of the fly crawling around his cell had eased his loneliness even for a few days, a living thing in the apartment, waiting for him to return from work, would make the place bearable. His urge to look around the tropical fish store no doubt came from this lack.

Kikutani opened the door to his apartment and sat down on the tatami without even taking off his coat. His lease strictly prohibited keeping a cat or a dog, so he was left with fish or birds. Since he was surrounded by thousands of chickens at work, the idea of more wings and beaks at home seemed depressing. Fish, then, he decided. He could almost see the gently waving tail fins of the tropical fish in their brightly lighted tanks. He didn't need anything exotic or expensive; plain goldfish would be enough. During his childhood and right through his married days, he had tried a number of times to keep fish, but he always managed to kill them. Once, the water went suddenly cloudy, and he found all his fish floating belly-up on the surface of the tank. On another occasion one fish developed an odd fuzz on its scales, which it passed on to the rest, and they died one after the other. He followed the advice of friends who had more success with their fish, carefully changing the water or adjusting the amount of food, but the results were always the same, until finally he lost all interest. The thought of returning home to a tank of dead fish was not pleasant.

Then he remembered the tiny killifish in the tub under the tanks. They were much easier to raise than goldfish, he remembered; they needed little food and infrequent changes of water. They were perhaps too small to qualify as pets, but if he got several, he might enjoy watching them swim around their tank. When he finished dinner, he left the apartment and went back to the shops. His expenditures up to this point had been exclusively for daily necessities, so it felt extravagant to be spending money on something that might be considered a hobby. He entered the store and went over to look in the tub. Floating on the surface was a small piece of wood on which the words 400 YEN FOR TEN had been written in black ink. Kikutani looked up as the shopkeeper approached.

"I'd like ten of these, please," he said. Nodding, the shopkeeper disappeared into the back of the store, reappearing after a moment with a small, squarish fishbowl made of clear plastic. Without a word he scooped up some killifish with a net and dropped them into a plastic bag filled with water. Kikutani paid for the fish and left with the bag and the bowl.

When he was once again seated on the tatami in his room, he gently poured the contents of the bag into the tank. The fish seemed momentarily disoriented by the motion of the water, but as soon as the bowl settled, they began swimming about and pressing their heads up against the plastic wall. Kikutani lowered himself to the level of the bowl and peered in. He had thought the fish were all the same size and shape, but on closer examination he saw that some were sleek while others were a little chubby—probably the difference between males and females, though he had no idea which was which. Their tiny eyes were jet-black, but when the light struck their transparent bodies, they shone with a sort of luminous glow. He had thought he was buying perfectly ordinary freshwater fish, but swimming before him, as lively as could be, were these wonderful diaphanous creatures. He sipped at his sake and followed the paths they traced around the tank. As the drink began to have its effect, a tranquil light shone in his eyes.

The plum blossoms had scattered, and buds were swelling on the cherry trees. The hens at the farm reached their annual peak for laying, and the flies appeared again as if out of nowhere. Akiyama continued his shrewd management, watching the price of imported feed and buying with cash when he could get the feed cheap, or judiciously delaying replacement hires when a position became vacant. The larger producers with modern equipment had been making adjustments in supply, but small farmers who kept chickens to supplement their income continued to overproduce, prolonging the slump in prices. To remedy this, the large cooperatives, with the support of the agricultural advisory office, began to move some ten million eggs into cold storage. The situation was made worse by the fact that demand was sluggish for mayonnaise, ice cream, and confections, which consumed some forty percent of the total egg production, and it was unlikely that help would come from that quarter. It was no wonder, then, that Koinuma was anxious. "The boss is a tough customer," he would say, half to himself. "He'll stick it out, and the market's got to change sometime." But the newspapers were full of articles about the slump, and Kikutani found himself studying Akiyama's face for clues to their fate. Akiyama, however, showed no signs of panic, and he could often be seen laughing in the office with the young salesman from the feed company or other visitors.

Arriving home from work, Kikutani would set the fishbowl on the low table under the light and take his supper while watching the killifish. He invariably had a cup or two of sake as well. He had devised a means of changing the water in the tank without disturbing the fish. He would fill a bowl with tap water and let it stand; then once a week he would add the water slowly to the tank. This way, it stayed clear, and the fish seemed happy. When he took a pinch of their food—a powder made of water fleas—and sprinkled it over the surface of the tank, the fish swam up and sucked it in. They were fattening up and deepening in color. Kikutani bought some seaweed to add to the tank.

In his mind the fish were linked with the tethered fly from his past, and he was afraid he would come home one day to find them dead, as had happened with the fly. But the killifish were more reliable. Only a few hours of sun came into his apartment each day through the narrow window, but before he went off to work, he left the tank where it would get the most exposure, and when he came home, he would find all ten swimming merrily about. He felt a certain admiration for these little fish who could survive day after day in the empty apartment.

One evening, while watching the tank, he noticed another minute creature besides the killifish. Looking closer, he saw there were in fact several of them floating among the clumps of seaweed. They were almost completely transparent except for faint dots toward the front, which appeared to be eyes. At last Kikutani realized that he was looking at tiny fry. He was moved by the thought that his pets had gone about the business of life in their bowl, giving birth to these baby fish despite the meager diet he fed them and their cramped quarters. He knew now that there must be females among his little school, and he gazed into the tank with renewed interest. There had always been plumper fish among the ten, and it was these that he examined, finding some with transparent, pearl-like eggs affixed to their abdomens and others trailing sticky strings of eggs, like rosary beads floating behind them.

The eggs had been fertilized and hatched all in this little bowl, he realized. But he recalled something that one of his fellow fishermen from Sakura had told him long before. The man, who managed a grocery store, had a concrete pool in back of his house where he kept some of the roach he caught on their fishing trips. At spawning time, the man said, the females would lay the eggs, but if you left the eggs in the pool, the other fish would eat them along with any fry that had hatched. Kikutani watched the slow, deliberate motion of his killifish and thought how different they were from the frenetic roach. Perhaps they didn't practice this sort of cannibalism. The adults seemed to ignore the fry even when they swam quite close by. Still, fish were fish and instincts were instincts, and there was a good chance the killifish too would eat their offspring. This thought upset Kikutani, and he worried that he would see the fish begin swallowing the babies at any moment. He remembered the owner of the shop: a taciturn, gruff type, but he must know a lot about fish. It would be embarrassing to ask about the reproductive habits of his killifish, but Kikutani had the feeling that the man would give him an honest answer. He left the apartment.

The store had no customers. The owner, sitting on a stool in back before an ancient desk, rose as Kikutani came in. Kikutani explained about his hatchlings and said that he had heard that the adults might eat the young if they were left together. He wanted to know whether this was true.

"Of course it is," the man replied curtly. Kikutani asked if there was any way to avoid this happening. "Well, you could get another tank and transfer the eggs once they're attached to the seaweed, but it's probably easier just to move the fish. The eggs and the fry are sensitive to water temperature and other things, and you'd probably have your best luck leaving them in the same tank." Kikutani thanked him, bought another small tank, and left the store.

Back in his room, he filled the new tank and, using the palm of his hand, scooped up the fish to transfer them. Remembering that the shopkeeper had said the eggs were attached to the plants, he gently lifted a strand or two. On the underside of the stalks and spreading onto the branches and leaves were an amazing number of tiny, transparent eggs that shimmered as the light struck them. He lowered the plant back into the water.

In the days that followed, he looked forward to getting home for his first glimpse of progress in the tanks. The eggs hatched in rapid succession, and each time he looked, there were more young fish. Right after they were born, the fry tended to hide in the seaweed, but as they grew, they began to venture out. Their movement was hypnotic, a brief spurt forward, and pause, and another spurt. The tiny eyes darkened and became much easier to see. After about a week, all the fish were big enough to leave the shelter of the grass and move around the tank. When Kikutani sprinkled food over the surface of the water, they gathered in a little school to poke at it.

He pulled the grasses from the tank again and found that the remaining eggs, apparently unfertilized, had grown whitish, as if covered with mold. Deciding that the hatching was finished, he washed off the grasses and returned them to the tank where the adult killifish were swimming. He could see that tiny pearls were still being pushed from the swollen bellies of the females, and when he checked the grasses the next day, they were covered with new eggs. Two days later, he moved the grasses back to the incubator tank, and the day after that, he discovered tiny fry once again swimming among the fronds. On the day of his regular visit to Takebayashi, he mentioned that he had succeeded in hatching several dozen killifish.

"Fascinating," said Takebayashi. He smiled as he told of a time when he raised carp fry. A spawning female had been pursued around the pond by several frenzied males, who nearly pushed her out onto the bank. Finally she began rubbing up against a hemp palm he had planted in the water and laid her eggs on its stalk. Almost immediately there was a great spray, and the males leaped over her, releasing showers of sperm that turned the water a frothy white. Takebayashi transplanted the palm to another tank, and the eggs hatched, but every last one of the fish had a deformity of the dorsal fin or the tail fin, so he gave them all away to the neighborhood children. "I doubt you'll have such problems with your killifish. If you can nurse them through the winter, you'll have a third generation by spring. You could go into business," Takebayashi said, drawing a laugh from Kikutani.

The old man seemed in good spirits, pleased to see Kikutani so satisfied with his fish, compared to the last visit, when Kikutani had been devastated by the end of his correspondence with Takasaki. They went out into the garden and squatted at the edge of the pond to sprinkle fish food. The carp formed a seething mass of color and spray as they battled for the food, some coming up to suck audibly at the finger that Takebayashi held just above the surface. Kikutani marveled that these ferocious creatures could be related to the tranquil fish he watched each day, and he felt that his pets were better suited to him.

By the time the rainy season set in, the young fish were noticeably bigger. A few of them had died for no apparent reason, turning white and sinking to the bottom of the tank. Each time this happened, Kikutani retrieved the fish with a pair of chopsticks. The hatchlings were no longer limited to their jerky, forward motion but could swim freely about the tank, changing direction with a flick of their tails. On his visits to Takebayashi's house, Kikutani would describe the growth of his fish in great detail. About thirty of the fry had survived and were beginning to take on the coloring of adult killifish. During their talk in late July, Takebayashi took a sip of tea and unexpectedly changed the subject.

"I've been wondering...do you have any interest in getting married again?" Kikutani gaped at him, his own teacup suspended in his hand. He wasn't sure he had heard correctly, the words having sailed past his ears like a light breeze. "It seems to me that you've completely adjusted to your new life and that you have your feet on the ground. Why shouldn't you start thinking about it? To tell the truth, I met with Kiyoura the other day, and we discussed the possibility. He liked the idea and said he would check with Akiyama. He called back after that to say that your boss is very enthusiastic and would like nothing better." A smile crept over Takebayashi's face as he finished speaking.

Kikutani had not stopped staring at him. Why, he wondered, had this idea occurred to Takebayashi? Takebayashi had probably heard from Akiyama that Kikutani was a serious, reliable worker who never missed a day or was even late. His salary was enough now to cover all his expenses. And he had a flawless record with the parole board, which kept track of his psychological well-being. They had probably added up all the factors—Kikutani's fish, the hatching, emotional stability, established livelihood—and come up with this: marriage. He felt grateful once again that these men were all so concerned about his future. On the other hand, the fact that Takebayashi had consulted with Kiyoura and Akiyama reminded Kikutani that he existed within the limits they set for him and could never hope to move beyond.

"Of course, it's completely up to you. But we just wanted to let you know that you've reached a point where you could consider it," Takebayashi added, turning to look at him.

"It never occurred to me," Kikutani muttered hurriedly as he set his cup on the table.

"That's what I thought you'd say. But give yourself some time to think it over. As Kiyoura always says, before a man can completely readjust and live a normal life again, he must have a home and a family. That goes for you too," said Take-bayashi, still grinning.

Kikutani felt irritated. Takebayashi's prescription might be right for most men, but in Kikutani's case it simply did not apply. For one thing, barring a full pardon, he would be under the supervision of the parole board for the rest of his life. But more important, what sort of woman would want to marry a man whose past held the murder of two women? The whole idea was unthinkable, and that Takebayashi, who knew this as well as anyone, should have gone so far as to ask Kiyoura and Akiyama seemed to ignore the reality of the situation. Kikutani frowned and looked away.

"As a matter of fact," said Takebayashi, picking up his teacup, "I have someone who might be right for you." At this, Kikutani's eyes shot back. He was astonished: Take-bayashi had not been speaking in the abstract but raised the topic with an actual woman in mind. "It's the lady who brought us tea a few minutes ago: Toyoko Orihara. She works in my son's market." Kikutani knew her: not only had she brought them tea, she was the one who, under orders from Takebayashi's wife, had put together a bag of coffee and canned goods from the store to give him as he left. Still, he had only the vaguest impression of her, a small, pale woman coming and going in the room. "She's had a hard life," Take-bayashi continued almost gingerly, "but you'd never know it to look at her. She's modest and serious. My wife, too, thinks she's right for you."

"I appreciate all this," said Kikutani, trying to keep his emotions under control, "but I really don't want to get married. I'm satisfied with my life as it is." He was upset that

Takebayashi had taken it on himself to decide not only that Kikutani should marry but whom. He could accept the idea that he had to take orders from his parole officer, but he still had some rights as a human being, and it galled him to think that they were being overlooked.

"This is all sudden, and it's natural for you to be a little confused. I just want to add one thing: I've mentioned this to Toyoko, and she says that she's more than willing if you are...." There was a soft light in Takebayashi's eyes, but Kikutani wanted suddenly to be alone. Takebayashi spoke as if he were suggesting a second marriage to a man under ordinary circumstances; but no matter how much he went on about Kikutani's readjustment to society, Kikutani still lived every day in mortal fear of having the secret of his past discovered. His was a meager existence, a matter of simply surviving to see the next day, like a wild animal in a cave hiding itself from prying eyes.

"I'm not someone who can get married," he said. "I think you know that as well as I do, and I'm not sure why you insist on this." He was dismayed by the whole conversation and on the verge of tears.

"Well, I guess I should tell you that I've already explained your situation to Ms. Orihara, and she says it makes no difference."

Kikutani could feel himself go pale. "I can't believe you did that," he stammered. "I thought your first duty as a parole officer was to keep our secret. What gave you the right to tell a perfect stranger?"

"Sometimes it's our first duty. But when we think it's in your best interests, and when someone like Kiyoura, who has enormous experience in these matters, agrees, then there are times when we tell. Of course, I made her swear that she would never tell anyone else." Takebayashi seemed completely unruffled. Kikutani looked away, staring out at the garden. "But it's not as though we're insisting. Kiyoura and I simply thought that it was time to consider your future, and that means a family. It was just a coincidence that there happened to be someone we thought might be suitable. You don't have to decide now; just think it over at your own pace. Lots of men on parole get married, some to much younger women. They even have children. I know of several cases myself, and that's why I brought this up." The smile had disappeared from Takebayashi's face.

"Very well," said Kikutani after a moment. "I'll come again." He rose from his seat and bowed.

Takebayashi followed him to the door and watched as Kikutani put on his shoes. "It's all very well to be dedicated to that job of yours," Takebayashi said. "But don't overdo things when you're not feeling well. You're getting older, just like the rest of us, and your health is important." Kikutani bowed once more and stepped out into the street.

10

At the farm, the schedule for removing and slaughtering the older chickens was pushed up again to decrease production, and the henhouse was filled with the clucking of young birds. Feed consumption increased as well. Summer bonuses were distributed, but they were so small, they brought only gloomy looks.

Kikutani's anger at Takebayashi subsided as time passed; he was still upset that Takebayashi had told the woman about Kikutani's prison record, but as Takebayashi had said, there were perhaps times when it made sense to tell. Kikutani had got the job at the farm because Kiyoura told the whole story to Akiyama; perhaps there was no difference between that and Takebayashi's telling this woman who he thought would make a good marriage prospect. There must be men who got out of prison and married without telling their wives the truth. But in Kikutani's case, since he would be under the supervision of the parole board for the rest of his life, there was no way to hide his past. If he married, it would have to be to a woman who knew everything and was still willing to be with him. But what sort of woman would marry a man who had killed his wife and burned an old woman to death in her house? Takebayashi had said that Mrs. Orihara had lived a hard life, but how could it compare to his? And a hard life couldn't explain why she was willing to marry him. The next time he went for his interview, there was no more talk of marriage from Takebayashi, who limited himself instead to the unusually hot weather and how hard it was on his health. The woman was nowhere to be seen, and Takebayashi's wife brought the tea.

At the beginning of August, Akiyama made a rare appearance in the cafeteria during their break time for a simple announcement: the wholesale egg market had taken another sharp downturn and was approaching total collapse. A number of large, nationwide producers had closed down, and the industry was in complete turmoil. "Things are bad for us, too," he said, "but we're doing everything we can to get through this. Not that we should be rejoicing in the misfortunes of others, but the fact that these big companies are going under may mean that supply will be getting back in line with demand, which could give the market a boost. I realize your bonuses were pitifully small and I'm sorry, but please bear with me a while longer." Akiyama's face was grim and set as he turned to leave.

"I think we're seeing the light at the end of the tunnel," stated Koinuma when he had gone. "And when things get better, you can bet he'll make it up to us. This is just what he was waiting for all along," he said, lighting a cigarette.

Less than two weeks later, a long article appeared in the newspaper backing up what Akiyama reported. Under the headline "Cheap Eggs Bring a String of Bankruptcies," the story told of a large company that folded after industry-record losses exceeding two billion yen and the subsequent failures of a number of related companies. The price for a kilogram of eggs had fallen from three hundred and twenty yen the year before last to one hundred and forty yen today; some supermarkets were virtually giving away ten medium-sized eggs for fifty yen. And mayonnaise makers had taken advantage of the cheap eggs to roll back prices seven percent. A smaller headline, "Bankruptcies Have Ripple Effect," described the tribulations of three breeder farms that were stuck with three million chickens when their client farms went out of business. But if each chicken laid, on average, 0.8 egg per day, the daily market would have roughly 2,400,000 fewer eggs. Temporary shutdowns and bankruptcies would certainly continue for some time, further reducing production capacity, a factor that should eventually allow the market to recover, the article concluded.

Signs of autumn were appearing. Kikutani made his visit to Takebayashi's house, fully expecting the subject of marriage to resurface, but it didn't come up again, almost as if Takebayashi had forgotten all about it. Paradoxically, Kikutani began to daydream about this marriage as he sat drinking in the evening. The woman would make him breakfast in the morning and prepare a lunch box for him to take to the farm. She would continue to work at the supermarket, but Takebayashi would probably see to it that she got home early enough to have Kikutani's dinner ready when he got back from the farm. They would sit down together to eat, and afterward he would watch TV and drink just as he did now. Perhaps she would watch with him. Then they would lay out the futon, and he would take her in his arms. Emiko was the only woman he had known; he wondered if he would find this new body desirable.

He had always tried to put the years before the incident out of his mind, as if they had never happened. The fact that he was once married to Emiko had no meaning for him anymore; he had to live now as a completely different person. This new woman looked to be over forty, so she wasn't likely to get pregnant. It would be just the two of them, but that was surely less lonely than his life now. Still, there would always be his past, his crime, to come between them like a looming wall, even if she knew all about it and said she didn't care. Would she be able to stand being touched by hands stained with another woman's blood? He was sure that marriage was not for him, and the next time Takebayashi brought it up, he would make that clear.

Fall clothes began appearing in the shops along the way to the station, and winter coats were hung out in display windows. Kikutani turned on his heater in the morning before leaving for work and again at night. One evening in late October, he found a folded piece of paper in his mailbox when he arrived home from work. For one second he imagined that Takasaki had changed his mind and come to see him while he was out, but the note was an urgent request from Kiyoura: Kikutani should come immediately to the halfway house. As he stared at the hastily scribbled words, he had a bad feeling. Perhaps his parole had been suddenly revoked—but as far as he knew, he had done nothing to deserve such severe punishment. That Takebayashi had introduced the subject of marriage suggested that Kikutani was thought of as a more or less model parolee. Unable to solve this puzzle, he decided it was best simply to go see Kiyoura. Setting his lunch box on the floor inside the door, he went back down the stairs.

He hurried out to the street lined with shops, crossed to the other side, and entered the alley leading to the halfway house. In a moment, he was pushing open the door. He called through the receptionist's window, and a young man on Kiyoura's staff appeared from the door to the meeting room to say that Kiyoura was with a visitor. The glass door opened again, and the sound of slippers padding across the floor preceded Kiyoura's appearance.

"Takebayashi has died," he said hurriedly. Kikutani shuddered as he peered into Kiyoura's face. "He went to the bathroom about midnight last night and collapsed in the hall. An ambulance got him to the hospital, but he died soon after. It was a massive heart attack." Kikutani was lost. How could this man be gone? He had seen him only the week before, and they had talked about the trip Takebayashi had just taken with his wife to a hot spring, about the beauty of the fall leaves, about their happiness at being able to travel for the first time in a long while. Now he was no longer in this world.

"The day after tomorrow is an unlucky date for funerals," Kiyoura continued, "so the wake is set for tonight. I'm going now with the rest of the staff here. The funeral is tomorrow at one o'clock. What do you want to do?" He waited a moment for Kikutani to answer. "Don't feel you have to go," he said at last, explaining that it was quite normal, when a parole officer died, for his charges to miss the funeral. It was, in fact, rare for them to go, since it was generally known when a man had been acting as a parole officer, and if unfamiliar people appeared at the funeral, they would be assumed to be ex-convicts. Because of this danger, it had become customary to go the next day, to pay respects in private. Kikutani was still too stunned by the news of Takebayashi's death to think what he should do.

"I know that Takebayashi liked you and had taken a special interest in your case; that's why I sent someone over with the note. But it might be better to skip the wake tonight—it will be mostly close friends. And tomorrow you have work. Why don't you go visit the house after the seventh-day services are over? I'll tell Mrs. Takebayashi that's what you're planning." Kikutani nodded in agreement as Kiyoura said goodbye and disappeared into the reception room.

He headed back to his apartment, his head empty of all thought. The neon lights from the shops seemed to stab at his eyes. Once home, he turned on the light and sat on the tatami, recalling the white stubble on Takebayashi's face the day he visited him after Takebayashi's cold. He had always seemed so healthy, but in fact he had been an old man with an old man's body. Picturing him standing on the bank of the pond sprinkling food for the carp, Kikutani was overcome with sadness. His visits to Takebayashi had been mandatory, but they had also become something to which he looked forward with pleasure. Takebayashi would always be waiting for him at the appointed time, and he and his wife would make him feel welcome. He would nod as Kikutani went through his report, watching him with his gentle, calm eyes. Kikutani relied on the support of Kiyoura and Akiyama as well, but for Takebayashi he felt a deep affection and gratitude for the way Takebayashi had enfolded him in the warmth of his family.

He went into the kitchen and turned on the faucet at the sink. As he began splashing water on his face, he wept aloud. Back on the tatami, he sat perfectly still, looking down at his lap. The siren of a patrol car could be heard out by the shops. He sat for half an hour, then rose and left the apartment. Winding through the rows of houses, he turned a corner. Up ahead to the left was a string of lights above a mass of wreaths. A tent had been set up before the house, and beneath it was a knot of people. The familiar place that Kikutani was accustomed to visiting had been utterly transformed.

He stopped at the end of the street. Even without Kiyoura's cautions, he was reluctant to enter the circle of light. It was enough simply to see the house in the midst of funeral preparations to confirm for himself that Takebayashi was dead. Tears streamed down Kikutani's cheeks. Takebayashi's cold body was lying inside, those peaceful eyes closed, never to open again. Finally, realizing that it would look strange if he continued standing there, Kikutani retreated down the street. But he had no desire to go home and soon found himself turning yet again, back toward Takebayashi's house.

As he approached, he could hear the chanting of sutras. Several women entered the tent, followed by a white-haired man who had just got out of a car. Kikutani stopped in front of the house and made a deep, formal bow before walking on. On his back he could feel the eyes of the men in the tent, but he was happy he had done that much.

The next morning, Kikutani arrived early at the farm and went to the door of Akiyama's house behind the office. Akiyama's wife appeared, followed by her husband dressed in a sweater rather than his work clothes. Since it was the first time that Kikutani had visited his home and the hour was early, Akiyama looked ill-at-ease. "What's up?" he asked. Kikutani told him that Takebayashi had died and that he would like to be allowed to leave work early to attend the funeral.

"I know how much he's done for you," Akiyama said. "Of course you should go to the funeral. Unfortunately, I have a co-op meeting today, so I can't go with you, but would you mind taking something from us? It'll be ready for you to pick up at the office when you leave."

Kikutani bowed and shut the door behind him. When Koinuma arrived, Kikutani told him that a man who had been like a father to him had died, and he would like to leave early. Koinuma agreed, and a few minutes after eleven o'clock, Kikutani left the henhouse. He stopped in at the office to collect Akiyama's incense offering, then went out the gate.

Faint streams of cloud floated like ripples in an otherwise clear sky. On the way from the station, Kikutani stopped to buy a cheap black tie and an envelope for his incense money. He finished dressing back in his room, slipped some bills into the envelope, and left the apartment. It was frightening to be going to a place where people would know what he was, but when he thought of all the kindness that Takebayashi had shown him, he knew he had to go. Judging from what he'd seen of the wake from out in the street, he was sure that there would be many people at the funeral; perhaps no one would notice him in such a large crowd.

A number of men and women stood along the street by the house, probably remaining to talk after they paid their respects. As Kikutani had expected, there was a crush of people around the entrance, but he tried not to think about all the eyes on him and fell in behind two men in black suits who were waiting to go inside. Following the men into the tent, he signed his name in the register and handed someone his envelope and the one from Akiyama. Then he joined the line for lighting incense, leaving enough space for a deep bow when he reached the altar. The line, which snaked out through the garden, inched forward slowly toward the veranda, where the incense was to be offered. Three monks were seated before the altar, which had been set up in the living room, and on either side was a row of relatives who bowed to the guests as they approached. Kikutani looked up at Takebayashi's wife seated on the right as he made his own bow, and when he saw her look his way and nod, his eyes flooded with tears and he lost his composure. His shoulders heaved and his hand trembled as it lit the incense. Placing his palms together for a moment, he hurried away from the altar. Certain that this show of grief had attracted attention, he made his way to the back of the garden and stood by the pond wiping his tears. A line of people passed on their way out after finishing at the altar, but he preferred this to the crowd in the street.

After a time, the crowd began to thin out, and the monks stopped chanting. At this point a group of men in dark jackets, apparently from the funeral home, appeared in the garden and climbed onto the veranda or stood by the incense stand. In the living room the chanting started again, signaling the final departure. The coffin was taken down from the altar, and the family gathered around, some of them weeping audibly while the lid was hammered into place. Takebayashi's widow emerged from this family group to stand on the edge of the veranda. She looked around the garden until she spotted Kikutani and beckoned to him.

"Thank you for coming," she said. "Would you help carry my husband's coffin?" Her eyes were red and bloodshot, and her hands were wringing a handkerchief. The coffin was carried from the living room and passed down to the men standing in the garden. Kikutani hurried to join the group, reaching out to support the bottom of the heavy coffin. As he touched it, he could feel a sob welling in his throat. Struggling to keep his knees from shaking, he helped carry the coffin through the garden and out into the street, where they pushed it into the back of the hearse. As soon as he finished his part, he moved away and blended into the crowd of mourners, wiping his face with his handkerchief.

A man in his sixties with thinning hair, who looked a great deal like Takebayashi, made the formal greeting to the guests, and the family and friends who were going to the crematorium climbed into a line of cars. Among them were the son and Mrs. Takebayashi, who was clutching the funeral portrait and the tablet that would go on Takebayashi's grave. The cars moved off, following the hearse. Kikutani and the others still waiting in the street bowed their heads. A van that was bringing up the rear disappeared around the corner, and the crowd began to disperse. Kikutani walked a while in the direction the cars had taken.

That evening, when he had finished supper, he went out and wandered toward the halfway house. Takebayashi's death meant that he was without a parole officer, and he needed to ask Kiyoura's advice about how to proceed. Luckily, Kiyoura had just returned, and he led Kikutani into the reception room.

"So, you showed up at the funeral," said Kiyoura, dropping into a chair. "I was surprised to see you carrying the coffin. I looked for you afterward, but before I could find you, I had to go to the cremation. Mrs. Takebayashi was especially glad you came."

"Mr. Akiyama was kind enough to let me leave work early. I brought an incense offering from him as well."

"I see." Kiyoura nodded, fishing a cigarette from his pocket.

"I've come to ask who will be looking after my case now that Mr. Takebayashi is gone," Kikutani said quietly.

"Well, I've just been on the phone with the parole board discussing that. They asked me if I would fill in, and I agreed. It seems that everyone else in this district has his hands full at the moment. Someone should have room before too long, but in the meantime I'll be handling it. You're pretty much on your own, anyway, so it doesn't amount to much. Just stop in for a visit a couple of times a month, and that should do it." Kiyoura took a sip of the tea that one of the young staff members had brought.

This was more than Kikutani could have hoped for; he had been anxious about who would take over for Takebayashi, but he was relieved and glad that once again he would be able to rely on Kiyoura, who had been so understanding even before Kikutani got out of prison. "Thank you," he said, smiling and bowing to Kiyoura.

"That's settled then," Kiyoura continued. "What you need to do now is go thank Mrs. Takebayashi for everything they've done for you. When the seventh-day ceremonies are over, I'm going myself, so we can go together." Kiyoura leaned back in his chair. They set a date that fell on Kikutani's day off, ten days later.

The day of the visit was cold. Kikutani put on his coat and walked to the halfway house. Kiyoura had sent someone to buy flowers, and Kikutani asked to be allowed to pay half. Then they left for Takebayashi's in Kiyoura's car. A desk covered with a white cloth had been placed in front of the family altar in the living room. On it rested a box containing the urn and the tablet that would eventually go on Takebayashi's grave. Kiyoura waited until Kikutani had finished lighting incense before handing the flowers to Mrs. Takebayashi. Exhaustion was visible on her face.

"I was so glad when I saw you at the funeral," she said to Kikutani. "Most men on parole don't make it to their parole officer's funeral—or so my husband used to say. It really was good of you. And I know he would have been so pleased." There was a gentle light in her eyes. Takebayashi must have had responsibility for a number of men, but only Kikutani had appeared at the service. No doubt this was why she had asked him to help carry the coffin, as if he were an old friend of the family. Kikutani sat silently, staring down at his hands.

"My husband worried a lot about you," she continued after a moment. "He wanted you to settle down and have a home life. I think Mr. Kiyoura has mentioned this to you as well, but there is a wonderful woman who works in my son's store, and my husband would always say that when the time was right, he hoped you two would get together." She turned to look directly at Kikutani. "I'm told that you had no interest in any of this, and my husband thought that was reasonable enough, but I thought I could ask again. Don't you think it's about time you forgot about the past?" She was scolding Kikutani ever so gently.

"I second that," Kiyoura chimed in. "They say you committed a crime, but one could almost say instead that the crime happened to you. The law is a system of rules meant to protect our way of life; and it was these rules that sent you to prison for all those years. But when your parole was granted, that was society's way of saying that you had paid your debt, that you should live the rest of your life like any other man. It makes no sense that you should go on being punished forever for something you did in one tragic moment. That's what Takebayashi thought, and that's why he suggested you get married when he found a likely person." Kikutani listened to all this without looking up. Mrs. Takebayashi poured some water from the kettle into the teapot and offered them tea.

"Anyway, it's something to think over," Kiyoura said, taking a sip of tea. Mrs. Takebayashi said that she planned to hold the hundred-day service in Shinshu and place the ashes in the family grave at a temple there called Bodaiji. Kiyoura told her that the parole board was applying to have a posthumous award given to Takebayashi, and that he had agreed to take over as Kikutani's parole officer for the time being.

Then Kikutani told her how grateful he was for all their kindness.

"I want you to think of this as your home," she said, "and come to see me when you can. I'm afraid I'll be a bit lonely now, and I know I'll be glad of the company." On the verge of tears, she rose, as if suddenly remembering something, and went into the next room. In a moment she returned with a neatly folded kimono. "Please take this as a memento of my husband. I know people don't wear Japanese clothes much anymore, and you may not have any use for it, but I want you to have it…." Wrapping the kimono in a cloth, she set it in front of Kikutani, who took it carefully in his hands and bowed. After pausing once more before the altar to pray, he followed Kiyoura from the room.

"Please make sure you come," Mrs. Takebayashi called as he climbed into the car. Kikutani nodded, and they drove away.

"She's a fine woman," Kiyoura said quietly as he navigated the narrow streets. "I'm told that in the old days Takebayashi was quite a lady's man and got into a good bit of trouble, but she always knew how to handle it. She has so much sympathy for other people because she's suffered herself." Kikutani sat in silence, the kimono resting on his knees.

The first snow fell in mid-December. It was Kikutani's day off, so he went to the halfway house for his meeting with Kiyoura. They sat in the reception room, and he went through his usual report. When he finished, Kiyoura changed the subject.

"I had a call from Mrs. Takebayashi the other day. She wanted me to ask you whether you have any interest in marriage these days. It was something her husband had wanted to see happen, she said. I don't suppose you've given it much thought."

Kikutani looked down and was quiet for a moment. Then he looked at Kiyoura. "Do you think I should be getting married?" he asked.

"That's really something you have to decide. I don't know what to tell you." Kiyoura leaned back in his chair and crossed his legs.

"To be honest, the idea frightens me. I've lived by myself for so long that I can't imagine what it would be like to have someone else around," said Kikutani. Since that evening in Sakura, he had been alone; his time in prison had been spent in a one-man cell, and now that he was out, nothing had changed. It made him uneasy to think of days—and nights—in a confined space with another person.

"I hear you're keeping fish." Kikutani looked up, startled by Kiyoura's voice. "It was when you told Takebayashi about your pets that he began thinking you should have a real home. When you're on your own, you can do as you like, but it can get lonely sometimes, too. And it only gets worse as you get older. The fish are a sign that you want someone to be with—at least that's what Takebayashi thought." Kiyoura's tone was casual. "A woman for a bunch of killifish—not a bad trade," he added. Kikutani chuckled softly, and Kiyoura began laughing as well. During cold weather, his killifish would nearly stop eating, ignoring the powdered water fleas he sprinkled in the tank and hiding, almost motionless, among the stalks of seaweed. After a while, Kikutani looked up at Kiyoura.

"He said that this woman didn't seem to care about my past, but I find that hard to believe. Why wouldn't she?"

Kiyoura thought for a moment. "For one thing, she's been married before. Her husband was an alcoholic, and he gambled. He lost everything they made, and he even pawned what little she had that was worth anything. When she complained, he became violent, and it seems she even lost a baby once when he kicked her in the stomach. Still she put up with him for a long time. One night he was wandering around drunk, and a car hit him. Since then she's lived alone. She's suffered herself, so when she heard about you from Takebayashi, she evidently thought things might work out. But I guess the real reason is she saw you at their house and she liked you."

The woman's story was sad, but not so uncommon. And it did not explain why she should want to be Kikutani's wife. "I imagine she feels sorry for me."

"That's probably part of it. They say she does talk about how much you've been through." Kiyoura's eyes followed his cigarette smoke as it snaked toward the ceiling.

"Well, if she really thinks I'd make a suitable husband..." The words slipped from Kikutani's mouth, but once they were out, he didn't regret them. If the Takebayashis and Kiyoura were so eager for this to happen, then what was he to do but go along with them? It was about time he got started with this new life, he told himself.

"Fine," said Kiyoura, a kind light in his eyes. "But if that's the case, I guess I'd better meet the lady in question myself." Kikutani thanked him and rose to leave. The snow had changed to sleet. Kikutani turned up his collar and walked in the direction of the shops.

Three days later, a letter from Kiyoura was waiting in Kikutani's mailbox saying that Kiyoura had had a long talk with the woman and that she struck him as honest and sincere, just as the Takebayashis said. She did indeed know all about Kikutani's past and had no objection to marrying him. Furthermore, Mrs. Takebayashi and her son were willing to vouch for her. At this point, Kiyoura wrote, he had realized it was necessary to sound out the parole board about the idea, so he contacted them and received the go-ahead. Kiyoura ended by suggesting that Kikutani meet the woman—Toyoko Orihara—on his next day off, not for a formal matchmaker's introduction but simply for a talk.

Kikutani set the letter on the low table and ate his dinner. He tried to recall the day the woman had brought them tea at Takebayashi's, but he had not even seen her face. He thought perhaps he remembered her bowing slightly as she set the teacup in front of him, but nothing more than that. He smiled to himself, recalling Kiyoura's comment: a woman for a bunch of fish. Staring into the tank, he mused on the strange course that had led from these fish to his meeting with Toyoko Orihara.

Two days later, he put on a new shirt, knotted his tie, and left his apartment. The day was cold and overcast. Unlike on past visits to the Takebayashis, he found himself hesitating at the entrance, calling out to announce his arrival. Almost immediately he heard footsteps in the hall, and Mrs. Takebayashi appeared.

"We've been waiting for you," she said cheerfully, urging

him to come in. He followed her to the living room, where he sat before the table that held the urn to burn incense and offer a brief prayer. Then Mrs. Takebayashi guided him to a cushion next to the low table and left the room—probably to call the woman, he thought as he settled stiffly on his knees in a formal posture. In a moment he heard them in the hall, the paper doors slid back, and Mrs. Takebayashi entered with a woman carrying a tray of tea and sweets. When Mrs. Takebayashi had taken her place across from Kikutani, the woman served the tea. He bowed silently.

"This is Toyoko Orihara," said Mrs. Takebayashi. The woman knelt and placed her hands neatly on the tatami as she bowed to Kikutani. As he returned the greeting, he could feel his body beginning to sweat in the overheated room. "I'll leave you two alone," Mrs. Takebayashi said. "Have a nice chat." And with that she closed the sliding doors behind her and retreated down the hall.

Kikutani reached nervously for his teacup, painfully aware of the woman who was still kneeling beside him. When she spoke, he turned to look at her, but her face, hovering just behind his shoulder, was vague, as if in a haze. He looked back at the table and began to answer her questions about his work at the farm, his commuting schedule, and what he did in the kitchen. He could feel her studying his profile as he talked, but when he turned again, he was still unable to get a good look at her. They sat silently for a moment.

"I'm told you keep fish," she said at last.

"Yes," he nodded, embarrassed.

"They must be cute."

"I suppose you could say that. They don't do much except swim around in their tank," he said, almost inaudibly.
She laughed quietly, and he could feel the tension ease a little. She had found his answer funny. He smiled as he turned
once more to look at her.

Her face was small, lightly made-up with pale-red lip-
stick. He could see fine wrinkles at the corners of her eyes
and a few strands of gray around her temples; she was clearly
no longer young, a discovery he found reassuring. Glancing
around at her from time to time, he began to talk about
Takebayashi. She told him how kind Mrs. Takebayashi, her
son, and her son's wife had been to her, going so far as to pay
part of her rent. After half an hour there were footsteps
again in the hall, and the doors slid open.

"Are you two finding lots to talk about?" asked Mrs.
Takebayashi as she sat down across from them. Kikutani
and Toyoko nodded. "Wonderful! Then perhaps we should
move on to the business at hand?" she said, looking at
Toyoko.

"As I've been saying, it's really up to Mr. Kikutani...."
Toyoko looked down demurely, but her tone was precise.

"And Mr. Kikutani?" said Mrs. Takebayashi, a smile
playing around her eyes, as if she were certain of his response.

"Well," said Kikutani, becoming flustered, "there is
something I'd like to ask first...."

"And what would that be?" said Mrs. Takebayashi with a
slight frown.

Kikutani squirmed in his seat. "I was wondering exactly
what Mr. Takebayashi told Mrs. Orihara about me," he

stuttered. "I want her to understand that my background is not like that of other men."

"Yes, of course she knows. She's been told that you had to spend a long time in prison, and why."

"I see," said Kikutani, feeling himself blush.

"So, what do you say?" said Mrs. Takebayashi, fixing her eyes on Kikutani.

"I say yes," said Kikutani, wiping the sweat from his brow with his palm. "That is, if it's really all right with Mrs. Orihara..." He wasn't attracted to Toyoko as a woman, but he felt a deep gratitude to her for her willing-ness to marry him despite his past. And how could he resist going along with something that was urged on him so earnestly?

"I'm so glad! And my husband would be too," Mrs. Take-bayashi said, glancing toward the family altar. Toyoko made fresh tea. "Then this is the end of my role. It's up to the two of you to discuss how you should proceed from here. I'll tell Kiyoura-san what you've decided, if you don't mind. I'm happy for you. I truly am," she said, sitting back to sip her tea with a relieved look. Toyoko stood and left the room for a moment, returning with a pen and a notepad. She wrote down her address and phone number and handed the page to Kikutani.

"I should be getting back to work," she said.

"Heavens, no," said Mrs. Takebayashi. "You should take the day off. Why don't you and Mr. Kikutani go somewhere together?" She looked reprovingly at Toyoko.

"I have to be going myself," said Kikutani, struggling up from the pillow.

"Really?" said Mrs. Takebayashi. "Well, then you two

get in touch soon." He sat again for a moment in front of the altar, palms together. Then he said goodbye to Mrs. Takebayashi and went out into the hall. The two women followed him to the entranceway, bowing as he left the house and walked stiffly down the street.

11

As the year drew to a close with preparations for the New Year celebration, Mrs. Takebayashi and Kiyoura made sure that the marriage discussions continued. Then one night in late December, there was a simple banquet in a room at Kiyoura's favorite Chinese restaurant. Kiyoura, Mrs. Takebayashi, and her son were the only guests besides the couple. The banquet was to serve as both wedding ceremony and reception, and Kikutani was deeply grateful to Kiyoura for sparing him the formal procedures. Toyoko, too, seemed delighted with the arrangements.

During the party, talk turned naturally to the couple's plans after the wedding: it was decided that Toyoko would move into Kikutani's apartment, and since he had almost nothing that could be called furniture, she would bring what she had with her. She would continue working for Takebayashi's son at the store, but he would see to it that she got home in time to prepare Kikutani's dinner. Since they would have both their salaries now, they could begin saving toward the day when they could afford to move to a bigger place. Everyone at the party seemed happy and relaxed, and Kikutani smiled as he watched them.

At last it was over, and they rose to leave. Kikutani waited by the door while Kiyoura and Takebayashi's son paid the bill. Toyoko, who had been standing next to Mrs. Takebayashi, came to his side. "I'll wait for you tomorrow after work," she whispered. "I'd like to see the apartment." Kikutani nodded automatically, watching her as she walked back to Mrs. Takebayashi.

That night, he dissolved some detergent in a bucket of water and set to cleaning the apartment. He wiped down the kitchen shelves, the walls, and the door. Then he scrubbed the tatami. Finally he cleaned the heater and the television, his only furnishings. The next morning, when he had finished breakfast, he doused the entranceway and washed it out before leaving for work.

Kikutani's nerves were on edge even after he fell into his routine at the henhouse. He had never imagined himself remarrying; but now it seemed that events were moving along by themselves, as if he had been tossed in a stream that was carrying him away. If Toyoko was coming to look at the apartment, it could only mean that she would be moving in soon. His head was filled with expectation and anxiety over the life they would live together. On the train home, he felt something close to dread. How should he treat her when she came to live in his room? The banquet meant that they were married now; he tried envisioning Toyoko acting like his wife. If she did, he would have to respond in kind, and he didn't think he was ready; he wanted a bit more time to adjust.

The train pulled into his station. The stores were bustling with year-end shoppers, and the sidewalks were crowded. As he turned the corner, he could see someone waiting by the alley that led to his apartment. His heart beat faster as he approached. Toyoko, dressed in a dark-blue coat, bowed as she recognized him.

"Good evening," he said, his voice cracking. "It's this way." He led her down the alley. Climbing the stairs, he opened the door and followed her into the apartment. He went to the kitchen and set his lunch box on the sink. He lit the heater in the one tiny room. Toyoko, who had been standing in the entrance, finally removed her shoes and stepped up into the apartment. She folded her coat and set it down with her bag in one corner.

"I'm afraid it's awfully small…," Kikutani offered, shrinking away from her. She pretended not to hear, disappearing quietly into the kitchen to check the sink, his kettle, and the few dishes and utensils. She seemed embarrassed at the utter lack of amenities.

"Have you eaten yet?" she asked, turning back to look at him.

"I usually make something when I get here," he said.

"That's what I thought. I brought some rice I steamed at home, and some beef. I'll make us sukiyaki." She retrieved her bag from the room and went to the kitchen again. Taking a pot and some vegetables from the bag, she turned on the faucet and began chopping the onions. Kikutani sat by the low table and studied her back as she worked.

Toyoko lit the burner on the stove and wiped the table in front of Kikutani. She laid out the utensils and a hot plate. Kikutani noticed that the chopsticks and teacups were not his own but new ones she must have brought with her. The teacups were a matched set in husband-and-wife sizes. The smell of cooking filled the room as she carried the pot of soup from the kitchen. Setting it on the hot plate, she sat down across from Kikutani and removed the plastic wrap from the rice, spooning some into his bowl. Kikutani picked up his rice bowl and dipped his chopsticks into the soup.

"How is it?" she asked.

"Delicious," he answered. Since getting out of prison, he had tasted beef a few times at a chain restaurant that served one-bowl meals, but this was his first sukiyaki. The onion and the tofu had taken on the rich, sweet flavor of the meat, and the rice was perfect.

"I'm sorry I didn't bring more rice," she said, serving him a second bowl. Then she poured boiling water from the kettle into the teapot.

Finally Kikutani set his chopsticks on the table. "Thank you. That was wonderful," he said, nodding.

Toyoko giggled. "It must have been difficult for you, making your own dinner every evening. I never want to cook for myself when I get home from the store; and it's no fun eating alone anyway. I enjoyed this meal more than any I've had in long time," she said, reaching for her teacup.

Kikutani had relaxed somewhat during dinner, but as they sat facing each other over tea, he could feel himself tensing again. Acutely conscious of being alone in the room with Toyoko, he looked around at everything but her. When he tried to help clean up, she told him to sit down. She quickly cleared and washed the dishes. Nervous, he turned on the television and sat staring at it with the sound low. At last Toyoko emerged from the kitchen and sat beside the low table, looking around at the room.

"I was wondering when I should move," she said. "Mr. Takebayashi said that he would arrange for us to use their car tomorrow, if that suits you." Kikutani was stunned by this announcement, but he heard himself saying that it would be fine. "Really?" she asked cheerfully. "In that case I'll plan to bring my things tomorrow afternoon. Could you ask the superintendent to open the door for me?"

"That won't be necessary," said Kikutani, hopping up. "I have another key you can take with you." He opened the closet door, fished the spare key from the bottom of a cardboard box, and set it on the table. Pocketing the key, Toyoko gathered up her coat and slipped into her shoes.

"Well, then, I'll have dinner waiting for you tomorrow," she said. Her eyes sparkled as she backed out the door, smiling. It was the first time all evening she looked womanly, Kikutani thought as he nodded to her. She closed the door behind her, and he could hear her putting on her coat on the landing. He stood in the entrance listening to her footsteps on the stairs.

Arriving home from work the next day, he hesitated as he opened the door. He noticed immediately that the cold air that usually greeted him was warm and smelled of dinner. On the floor in the entrance was a line of women's shoes and sandals. Almost before he was in the door, Toyoko appeared from the kitchen wearing an apron.

"Welcome home. You must be chilled," she said, taking

his lunch box as she disappeared again. Kikutani stepped out of his shoes and looked around the transformed room. The walls, which had been bare, were concealed now behind a chest of drawers and a tea cupboard. In the corner next to the window was a makeup stand, and where the low table had stood was a new table, set for dinner and draped with a quilt that covered the electric leg-warmer beneath. The window had been hung with curtains made of material with a broad red stripe, and the whole effect, to Kikutani's eyes, was bright and gaudy, as if someone had changed the bulbs in all the lights.

Toyoko appeared carrying bowls and plates, and when he was seated, she filled his glass with beer. Taking a sip, Kikutani picked up his chopsticks and considered the feast: vegetable stew, simmered tofu, and herring poached in soy sauce. As he ate, she explained that she had brought only the necessities, disposing of her old television, radio, heater, and other items. Kikutani nodded, glancing around at the furniture. When dinner was over, he turned on the TV, but after a moment Toyoko appeared and suggested he go to the public bath. When he was first paroled, he had continued the prison rule of bathing just twice a week, but at some point he had begun to go every other day. He rose and left the apartment.

The bathhouse seemed more cheerful and better lit than usual, and he took a long soak in the steaming water, pondering the sudden change in his fortunes and his comfortable new life. When he was warmed through, he got out of the tub to wash himself, taking greater care than usual, and then settled into the water again. Before long, however, he was back in the apartment staring at his futon laid out next to

Toyoko's. She had changed into her pajamas and was sitting on the edge of her mattress watching TV. The overhead light had been turned off, but a small lamp stood by the end of the beds. Kikutani put his soap and towel in the kitchen and began brushing his teeth. When he finished, she brought him his nightclothes and waited while he changed.

"We have to be up early tomorrow," she said. "Are you ready for bed?" Nodding, he lay down on his back. Toyoko turned off the television and the heater and settled down on her own futon. "Should we leave the lamp on?" she asked, turning to look at him.

"Whichever you like," he answered, continuing to stare at the ceiling.

"Well, I always turn it off," she said, reaching over to do so. Kikutani closed his eyes. There was a trace of perfume in the air. He was overwhelmed with the realization that lying next to him was a living, breathing human being, and a woman at that. It occurred to him that this was, in fact, their real wedding night, and custom dictated that they should be consummating the marriage. But how was he to broach the subject? With Emiko, it had all happened rather naturally; but the woman next to him still felt like a stranger, and he hesitated to reach out for her. There was part of him, too, that preferred simply to go to sleep now and wait until their life together made them more comfortable with the idea of sex. The room was quiet, but he was sure that Toyoko was still awake. He opened his eyes slightly and shut them again.

"Aren't you cold?" she said at last. Kikutani could sense her face turned toward him in the dark.

"No, I'm fine," he muttered, his voice hoarse.

"Would you like to get in with me?" she whispered. Her

tone was almost coquettish. As he pushed himself up on his elbow, she slid back and raised her quilt. Kikutani moved over to her futon. Pressed against her side, his face almost touching hers, he could feel the warmth of her body through her pajamas. His heart began to race, and his throat was dry. Taking her head in his hands, he pulled her toward him until he could feel her chest heaving. Gently, hesitantly, he kissed her as she moaned quietly and pressed against him. Slowly, he unbuttoned her pajamas and let his hand run over the soft mounds of her breasts; then he moved down and gingerly touched her nipples with his tongue. Her body stiffened and began to writhe as her groaning grew louder. Emiko's breasts had been much larger, her body longer and more slender. By comparison, Toyoko was compact and solid, and the arm that was wrapped around his shoulder was surprisingly strong. He could just make out her face, eyes closed tight, by the faint light coming through the curtains. She was gasping now, as he carefully slid his hand lower.

Waking the next morning to the sound of running water, he saw that the heater had been lit and Toyoko's futon was already folded away. He rose and went to the bathroom, where he found her scrubbing the floor. She glanced around at him.

"Good morning," she said quietly. She left him and went back to the tatami room. When he followed her a few moments later, she had put his futon in the closet as well and was working in the kitchen. Slipping out of his pajamas and into his pants, he sat down at the table for breakfast. Seated across from him, Toyoko seemed slightly embarrassed; she would glance at him every so often and look quickly away.

Kikutani sat silently working his chopsticks. He was conscious of her eyes on him as she handed him his lunch box. "See you this evening," he said, leaving, closing the door. His new life had begun.

On New Year's Eve, she made traditional soba noodles, and on January 1, they ate soup with mochi cakes. On January 2, they called on Kiyoura and Mrs. Takebayashi to pay their respects and then went to a nearby shrine to offer a prayer and buy a good-luck charm: a tiny bow and arrow. Later in the day, Toyoko went to work in the store. Kikutani started back at the farm on January 4. At some point during the holidays, she began calling him "dear."

Akiyama was delighted to learn of the marriage and gave Kikutani an envelope with money for the couple to buy themselves a wedding present. Kikutani realized he should tell Koinuma as well. "I thought you looked pretty happy lately," Koinuma said, his eyes smiling. "That explains it."

Toyoko proved to be a diligent housekeeper, cleaning the apartment daily and doing the laundry and airing the futons on her day off. The refrigerator she had brought with her she kept stocked with beer and the foods she found on sale. Kikutani, for his part, discovered an appreciation for the pleasures of married life. When he got home from work, the apartment was already warm and dinner was on the stove. In the morning, he could stay an hour longer in his futon and still arrive at work on time; and when he opened his lunch box, there was always something different and tasty. At night, Toyoko proved to be rather adventurous in bed. Sometimes she would reach out and grab his arm, pulling him to her, and other nights she would simply crawl over into his futon. As he moved above her, she would cling to him with amazing strength, moaning and sighing until it was over, and when he rolled back on his own bed, she would turn over and bury her face contentedly in her pillow, falling asleep a few moments later.

He went for his regular appointments with Kiyoura, who invariably asked how he was finding life with Toyoko. In as few words as possible, Kikutani indicated that he was satisfied.

About the time that the cold weather was easing its grip, the egg market finally reached bottom and began showing signs of recovery. Bankruptcies continued among the large-scale producers, and the advisory office's policy of voluntary production quotas was having a real effect, meaning that supply and demand were at last stabilizing. In addition, the season was approaching for increased production of food products, including those with eggs, that would be used for the summer gift-giving season, so the market rose further on these expectations. "It seems it's finally over," said Koinuma cheerfully. "The boss must be relieved."

The days passed peacefully now. The baby killifish had grown to the point that they were nearly indistinguishable from the adults. By March, they had left the clump of sea grass and were swimming busily throughout the tank. Toyoko took over the job of feeding them, and he showed her how to change their water. In the evenings, he would watch TV while drinking sake; she would watch with him or work on a crossword puzzle in one of her magazines. She wore a thin gold chain around her neck; it held a magnetic stone that was said to be good for backache.

One evening toward the end of March, Toyoko spoke up as they were watching TV. "Would you be willing to come home with me sometime soon to meet my family?" she asked. Her mother lived with her older brother and his wife in Tochigi prefecture, in the town where Toyoko grew up. She said that she usually went to spend New Year's with them but had sent her brother a message that she would not be coming home because she was marrying Kikutani. Her brother wrote back saying they wanted to see her and that she should come with her new husband. Kikutani had heard from Mrs. Takebayashi that Toyoko had a family, but he was reluctant to meet them. "I'm not opposed to going," he muttered, "but what have you told them about me?"

"Of course I didn't tell them you were in prison. I just said you worked at a large poultry farm," she answered without hesitating. It was the first time she had said the word *prison* in front of him, and he could feel himself flinch. He had imagined that she would conceal his past from her relatives, but it seemed cold and calculated when he heard it put into words. On the other hand, he thought, perhaps he was being too sensitive. He had no reason to be unhappy with her; they had built a life of sorts in full knowledge of his past, and it was unfair of him to make trouble over minor details. It was natural that her brother would expect his little sister to bring her new husband to meet the family, and no doubt Toyoko wanted to reassure her mother as well. And as her husband, Kikutani had a duty to pay his respects to her relations.

"Would we need to stay overnight if we went?" he asked, studying her reaction. He had never missed a day of work at the farm; more to the point, he was still under the travel restrictions imposed by the terms of his parole.

"We couldn't possibly get there and back in one day," she said. "If you can't get two days off, we'll have to leave after work. We could get there late at night and come back the next evening." There was a hint of dissatisfaction in her voice. He realized that she assumed the problem was with his job; since the situation was likely to come up again, he knew he had to explain about the parole board. Avoiding her eyes, he quietly described the system that required him to report overnight trips. Her look told him that this was unexpected news, and he shifted his gaze uncomfortably back to the TV.

"They keep you tied down like that even after you're out of prison?" she asked, clearly shocked.

"I'm not exactly tied down. I just have to get Mr. Kiyoura's permission before we go. If we leave in the evening and are back the next night, I'm sure he won't mind." He blinked weakly at her.

"Fine, then ask him, please."

Kikutani nodded silently at her annoyed request. The next evening, he went to the halfway house and explained the situation to Kiyoura.

"It sounds like a good idea to me. By all means, go," Kiyoura agreed immediately.

Three days later, the evening before his day off, he hurried home and met Toyoko on the station platform. They changed trains for Kitasenju, where they boarded an express. It was his first time on a train other than the commuter lines, and he looked out the window with great interest as they passed station after station. They arrived shortly after eleven, and her brother was waiting for them with his car. His wife and Toyoko's mother, still up when they arrived at the house, greeted them warmly. The mother, who was in her late seventies, bowed to Kikutani and tearfully asked him to look after her daughter.

Kikutani and Toyoko spent the night in a cottage behind the house, and the next day, the brother drove them to a cemetery on the edge of town to visit the family grave, after which they called on all the other relatives, one by one, for the formal introductions. The village was surrounded by fields, and Kikutani could see that the business of the region was agriculture. The brother and his wife made their living by farming and doing odd jobs on the side, and they were able to make enough to support Toyoko's mother as well. Everyone was so friendly to Kikutani that he at last began to relax and lower his defenses. When the sake was brought out to go with their early dinner, he drank his happily.

The brother drove them to the station, and they caught the train back to Tokyo. Though it had been short, Kikutani had enjoyed this brief escape from the city; he had no place of his own to go, but now he had his wife's hometown. And as long as she kept his secret, her relatives would be happy to see him, and he would be happy to go whenever she got the urge. One thing bothered him, however, and that was Toyoko's gloomy look when they were alone. She had hardly spoken on the train, but sat quietly lost in her thoughts. Perhaps she felt the whole thing was too hurried and the excitement of the trip had worn her out, he thought, settling back in his seat and savoring the warmth of the sake. The train was nearly empty.

"Dear," she said suddenly. Kikutani opened his eyes. "I understand that you can't go off traveling whenever you want, but are there other things you can't do?" Seeing the grim look on her face, he sat up in his seat. He realized now that her dark mood had to do with the travel restrictions.

"Not many," he answered almost inaudibly. "I can't vote. That's about all."

"Vote?" she muttered and fell silent, as if she had forgotten what she wanted to say. They sat quietly for moment. He could feel her eyes on him.

"There are some restrictions, but nothing that's going to bother us. The only thing I really have to do is go for my interview twice a month with my parole officer." He looked sheepishly at her.

"So you were visiting old Mr. Takebayashi because you had to? I was told you just dropped in from time to time." She looked skeptical.

"It's called an interview, but there's nothing formal about it," he said, looking straight ahead. "You just show up, and that's it."

"But why do you have to go at all, now that you're out of prison?" He was finding it difficult to answer her, but it was clear that Takebayashi had never explained to her what it meant to be on parole.

"Because those are the rules," he said, looking out the window. He was wide awake and sober now. She said nothing for a moment.

"And how long do you have to follow these rules?" she asked at last. He glanced at her, then back out the window.

"As long as I live," he said. In the dark he thought he could make out empty fields stretching away from the tracks and the lights of farmhouses in the distance. A light closer by must be the headlights of a car. Kikutani leaned back in his seat and closed his eyes.

12

There was a change in Toyoko's attitude. She hardly spoke now during dinner, and her eyes seemed hollow as she watched television with him afterward. He thought she knew the whole situation before they were married, but it was clear that she had been told nothing except the fact that he committed a crime in the past. She'd had no idea that he was still closely supervised, and he guessed that she was probably sorry that she had married him. Perhaps she was even thinking about leaving. Before the wedding, he worried that he would never be able to love any woman except Emiko; but now, less than three months later, he saw how wrong he had been. Toyoko might not be as beautiful as Emiko, but she had a certain spirit; and though she was ten years younger than Kikutani, they were comfortable together. Her sexual instincts were keen, and she seemed almost ecstatic when he was with her. He had come to love her violent response to his caresses. Her small, warm body satisfied him, and he had begun to seek it out more and more often. Now he feared the thought of life without Toyoko, recalling the dreary days he had spent alone. He could never go back to that existence, and he wanted her to understand his situation and stay with him forever.

Each evening when he got home, he opened the door, fighting the fear that she would be gone and the place empty. It was only after he heard her in the kitchen that he could relax. When she turned out the lamp by her pillow a few hours later, he would make love to her, hoping to tie her to him through their sex.

One night in the middle of April, he came home to find that the vacant look had vanished and her eyes were sparkling. When she finished cleaning up after dinner, she came back and sat next to him. "There's something I want to tell you," she said. Kikutani, who had been smoking a cigarette and watching the TV, was certain from her serious expression that she would announce she was leaving him. She watched him as he turned off the TV and settled back onto the floor. "I went to have a word with Mr. Kiyoura today," she said, fixing her eyes on him. She must have gone to tell Kiyoura about the divorce beforehand, he thought; but it was cruel of her to have gone without even discussing it with him. "I wanted to find out all about your situation. He told me that men like you with indefinite sentences get out on parole but are always under supervision.... So now I see that you'll have these rules to follow as long as you live." Kikutani sat quietly, staring at the wall. "But there is something called a general pardon. Mr. Kiyoura said you'd know about it. If you get pardoned, then your sentence is over; no more rules at all. You could travel wherever you wanted, vote in the elections. There would be no more interviews with a parole officer. That's what he told me."

"That's true," he murmured, "but…"

"So I asked Mr. Kiyoura what you had to do to get a pardon, and he explained all the conditions: they have to be sure you won't commit another crime, that you're a good citizen, things like that. He said he thought you would probably qualify. You become eligible after five years on parole; it's been three years since you were released, so it's only two more years until you can apply."

Kikutani was relieved that she hadn't wanted to talk to him about divorce, but he was unsure why she was so interested in the subject of a pardon. "They do occasionally grant pardons, but I hear it's very difficult to actually get one," he said indifferently. The procedure was, in fact, arduous. The original request had to come from the parole officer; then the chairman of the local parole board had to apply to the central committee on corrections and parole through the pardons division of the Justice Ministry. At this point, the applicant was thoroughly investigated and his case carefully documented. If everything came back absolutely clean, then the pardon would be considered.

"But if they have the law, then someone must be getting pardons. Mr. Kiyoura said that the most important thing is that the person be truly sorry for what he's done. I know how sorry you are, so all we have to do now is find a way to make that obvious. You're so serious, it's hard for you to express your feelings; but you've got to try. They have to be able to see how much you want to make up for what you've done." Her voice was tense, almost shrill, and Kikutani was moved to tears. She wanted nothing but to put an end to years of punishment, to let him live as a free man. Most likely she had considered divorce as well, but now that she had discovered the possibility of a pardon, it was like a beacon to her. In her desire to make their life together complete, she had become obsessed with this one thought. He remembered that Takebayashi had said she was right for him, and now he was sure of it. He nodded but said nothing.

On his next day off, he went to the halfway house for his interview. Kiyoura mentioned that Toyoko had been to see him. "She's quite a woman," he said, laughter in his eyes. Kikutani bowed his head in confusion and gratitude, and by way of apology for his wife. Kiyoura reached for a cigarette, turning suddenly serious. "I explained to her about the procedure for obtaining a pardon; she seemed excited, but you know how difficult it is. You shouldn't have any problem as far as your current situation goes, but the key is how much penitence you've shown toward your victims— your wife and her relatives, and the old woman and hers. In theory, this means that you write letters to the survivors and go often to visit the graves. But the problem is whether or not you can actually do these things. When you asked about going to the graves, I told you that you needed to wait, and I still think so. You have to consider the feelings of the families; and I doubt they'd appreciate a visit from you, even now." Kiyoura folded his arms and looked at Kikutani, whose head was still bowed. "I'm not saying this to crush her hopes, but of all the cases of men with indefinite sentences I've handled, only one has actually been pardoned—it's that hard."

To Kikutani this seemed natural enough. Under the heavy weight of an indefinite sentence, he felt extremely grateful simply to have been released on parole; it was a bit too much to ask that the sentence itself be completely forgotten. All the more so if only one man in all Kiyoura's experience had been granted a pardon; the odds weren't very good. Toyoko seemed to have fixed her hopes on this unlikely idea of a pardon. But perhaps, even if it was nothing more than an illusion, the possibility of parole would be enough to keep them together. "What you need now is patience," said Kiyoura. "You've got a good wife and a steady job. Just keep on the way you're going; it may take ten or even fifteen years, but somewhere down the line you may qualify. When the time comes, I'll do my best to see that it happens; and in the meantime you shouldn't give up hope."

Kikutani left the halfway house and walked toward Shinjuku. "Indefinite sentence" meant just that: spending the rest of your life in prison. He had deprived two human beings of their lives, and still he had been paroled under the appropriate provisions of the penal code. Perhaps he couldn't go off on long trips, but he could walk the streets freely, eat what he liked, sleep when he wanted. How could he presume to want more liberty than this? His interviews with Kiyoura twice a month? They were something he looked forward to. In fact, he was more than satisfied with things the way they were.

Shinjuku was filled with people who seemed to have come out to enjoy the smell of spring in the air. Feeling suddenly at ease, Kikutani walked along the street until he came to a tobacco shop selling dozens of brands of cigarettes. He studied the contents of the display case, thinking that he might treat himself to foreign cigarettes from time to time.

He arrived home in the late afternoon. As he usually did on his day off when Toyoko was still at work, he rinsed the rice and started the electric steamer. Then he brought out the low table and set the rice bowls and teacups on it. When he was finished with these chores, he spread the newspaper on the tatami and read until the rice was done. He heard the switch on the rice cooker click off and glanced at the clock. Toyoko was late. She came in a moment later, as he was switching on the TV.

"I'm home," she said, slipping out of her shoes and hurrying into the kitchen. She pulled some fried pork cutlets from a bag, set them on a plate, and came into the tatami room for dinner. Kikutani watched the news while they ate. When they were finished, they sat at the table drinking tea.

"There's something I want to ask you," Toyoko said.

"What's that?" he answered, eyes still on the TV.

"Do you know what burial names they gave to your wife and the old woman who died in the house?" Kikutani looked over at her, startled by the question. "I left work early today and stopped in to see Mr. Kiyoura on my way home. He said you were there today for your interview. We talked about your pardon, and I told him that as a first step we wanted to visit the graves of the two women. I asked him if he would give you permission to travel. He told me what he told you: that we have to think about the feelings of their relatives and shouldn't be going right now. He said we had to be patient." She paused a moment and then went on. "So I asked him what we could do in the meantime, and he said we should set up an altar at home and show remorse that way. I said I didn't see what good it would do if the families couldn't see how sorry you are, and he said that we should wait until the time was right to go visit the graves. Until then, the home altar would help. And I told him that's what we'd do. That's why I asked about their burial names—we need them to make the funeral tablets for the altar."

Toyoko was consumed with her new project, but Kikutani simply stared at her in silence, feeling vaguely terrified of this relentless storm that had come blowing into his life, disturbing his hard-won peace. It seemed she was determined to dig up and thrust under his nose the one thing that he most wanted to forget. He told himself he had to stay calm, but he could feel the blood draining from his face. If he didn't say something, she would realize how upset he was; he had to answer her as casually as possible.

"I don't know," he managed at last.

"You don't?" she said. "Mr. Kiyoura said you probably wouldn't. In that case, we can just use their regular names. Your wife was Emiko; what was the old woman's name?"

How had she learned Emiko's name? Kiyoura would know, but he wouldn't have revealed any of the details of Kikutani's case. Perhaps she had gone to look up the records in the family register. The name of Mochizuki's mother had come up constantly during the investigation and trial, burning its way into Kikutani's memory. He wished more than anything to forget this name; he could never bring himself to actually say it. Trying to control himself, he shook his head to indicate that he didn't know and looked away. He felt abused, wounded; he wanted to scream, to tell her not to do this.

"I see," she said. "Well, then, we'll just have to make do."

Kikutani took out a cigarette and lit it. He had begun to tremble in little spasms, and his mind had gone blank. Toyoko rose and cleared the table, taking the dishes into the kitchen. A suffocating feeling came over him, and he wanted to run from the room, but his body would not move, as if it had been chained to the spot. Toyoko, however, was oblivious to his emotions. Having failed to learn the burial names, or even the old woman's real name, she apparently gave up on the idea of making funeral tablets for the altar. But he had to be on the alert for her next scheme and find a way to distract her from this whole topic.

He had ten years left, twenty at the outside, and he wanted to live them in peace. Looking back at the TV, he lit another cigarette, noticing that his fingers were still shaking. Toyoko finished the dishes and came to join him, flipping through the pages of the magazine she had spread out on the tatami. Kikutani noticed with relief that she seemed to have forgotten her plan for the moment.

"Do you want a drink?" she asked suddenly, as if she just remembered to offer. He nodded, and she disappeared into the kitchen.

13

At the farm the next day, they started applying the powder for the maggots for the first time that year. When the flies suddenly began multiplying about ten days earlier, the pesticide had been ordered. The egg market was improving steadily, and Kikutani heard through Koinuma that Akiyama planned to hire another man in the near future to help them in the henhouse. The white trucks were busy coming and going with their loads of eggs. But even as he was spreading the pesticide on the chicken droppings under the henhouse, Kikutani remembered Toyoko's incessant questions. He struggled for breath, recalling her burning eyes and her insatiable curiosity about burial names. Kiyoura had told her to be patient, but Kikutani knew he would have to ask Kiyoura to dissuade her altogether. Kiyoura could tell her again that a pardon was extremely rare, that it was fine to dream but she shouldn't be running around trying to make it happen. Kikutani was sure that Kiyoura believed in his penitence just as much as Toyoko did, which is why Kiyoura had suggested the home altar, and Kikutani was afraid that they would both discover the truth—that he was not the least bit sorry for what he had done. The sun shone in a blue sky for the first time in days, making tiny rainbows in the mist of pesticide.

In the evening, he headed home. Getting off at his station, he stopped in at the tropical fish shop to replenish his supply of fish food. Now that he had so many grown fish, they emptied the bottle much faster. Climbing the stairs to the apartment, he found himself enveloped in an unfamiliar smell. He stood in the doorway until he recognized the odor: incense mixed with burning candles.

"Hello, dear," said Toyoko, coming out of the kitchen for his lunch box. Kikutani removed his shoes as he studied what had been set up on top of the tea cabinet. A small candle stand with pencil-thin tapers had been placed on a white cloth next to a tiny urn, out of which incense smoke coiled toward the ceiling. On this makeshift altar were two funeral tablets, one inscribed with the characters for EMIKO in gold ink. Kikutani stood rooted to his spot in the doorway, grimacing at these thin strips of white wood as Toyoko returned from the kitchen.

"I've been to the altar store," she said, going up to the tea cabinet. "Since we don't know both names, I had them write *old woman* on one of the tablets. I suppose we need a little altar as well, but I thought this would do for now." She reached out to smooth a crease in the cloth. Kikutani's body went rigid, as if frozen. As he stared at the candles, the flames seemed to flare up, shining with a strange brilliance. The characters on the tablets pierced his eyes.

"We'll pray here together," Toyoko was saying, "starting today. Once in the morning and once when you get home. We can light incense and say a few words. If we're really regular about it, the people who grant these pardons will understand how you feel. Why don't we start now? Here's some incense." Kikutani felt as though he were floating away, borne on the stench of the smoke. His gaze was riveted on the tablet that said EMIKO as his hand relived the instant that the knife struck the bone in her chest. Before his eyes, Mochizuki's house crumbled once again, sending spectacular clouds of sparks into the night sky. "Why don't you sit here in front of the tablets?" Toyoko said, taking him by the arm. His blood seemed to come suddenly to a boil, seething into his head, and he glared at her as he brushed aside her hand.

"What's the matter?" Toyoko stuttered, surprised at his response. Kikutani opened his mouth, but nothing emerged, though he could feel his lips crawl on his face like living things. "What's the matter?" Toyoko repeated. "Mr. Kiyoura said we should do this in place of going out to the graves, that it would show the right attitude...." He wanted to scream that he wasn't sorry, that he still despised Emiko for betraying him, that he'd been to the grave of Mochizuki's mother but had been unable to pray there, that he'd thrown away the incense. They said he needed to write letters apologizing to the bereaved families, but how could he apologize when all he felt for Mochizuki was contempt and resentment? She told him he had to pray to these tablets in order to be pardoned, but he couldn't, he couldn't even pretend to..."Here we go, then," Toyoko whispered, peering into his face. A crimson blur began to cover the room—this room that was no longer his but had somehow been filled with tablets and incense. His heart crystallized into a mass of irrepressible rage: he could not allow anyone to come in and upset his world. Shaking feverishly, he took a step toward Toyoko.

"Get out!" he commanded, but his tongue stuck in his mouth, and the words ended in a shrill wail. Toyoko backed away, eyeing him nervously. As the red color darkened, he realized it was the same one he'd seen that night. It terrified him, and he told himself he must not move, but the more he tried to banish the horrible redness, the more he realized there was nothing he could do. The sound of countless bubbles popping filled his head, and his hand shot out, thrusting against her shoulder. She staggered back, stumbling down into the entranceway, as he moved menacingly toward her, screaming inside that this was *his* room, that she had to leave. Horror spreading over her face, she reached behind to open the door. "Out! Out!" he croaked, following her onto the porch and shoving her with all his might. Toyoko's mouth opened in a silent scream as she fell backward into space. Her body tumbled down the steps, a mass of skirt and thighs, landing with a dull thud on the concrete below. Her eyes stared up at him.

The crimson splash grew brighter, dyeing the dark metal staircase. She must go, he told himself over and over, she shouldn't have brought those things into my house. Then, as he looked down at her from the top of the stairs, the red began to fade. He became aware of a man and a woman, dimly visible under the streetlight at the end of the alley. Were they just passing by, or had they heard the noise and come out to investigate? In either case, they bothered him; he wanted to chase them off, tell them this was none of their business, that it concerned Toyoko and him and no one else. He didn't like the fact that she lay exposed before them, and he hurried barefoot down the stairs. Standing over her, he gazed into her eyes. Her mouth was slack and hung slightly open. "It's your fault," he muttered. "You brought all this stuff here and made me angry. You should have known my nerves couldn't stand it." Conscious of the watching eyes of the people down the alley, he slipped one hand under her neck and the other under her thighs and tried to lift her in his arms. She was surprisingly heavy, however, despite her small size, and after several attempts he gave up. He turned around and dragged her onto his back, and then made his way carefully up the stairs, clutching at the rail. Struggling through the door, he lay her body on the tatami and stood panting as his anger abated and his body cooled.

He sat down and lit a cigarette, his hands shaking violently. From time to time he glanced over at her as he tried to calm himself and slow his breathing. Her bare legs seemed to jerk slightly for a moment and then were still. On her left kneecap a dark red mark had appeared, apparently where it struck the stairs. It was impossible from the beginning, he thought: he could not live with Toyoko in this place where he hid himself from the world. She would never understand—no one could. Either she had to go, or he would leave himself; one way or the other, he would be alone again. He was lighting another cigarette as he caught sight of something red. Blood bubbled out of Toyoko's ear and was trickling from her earlobe onto the tatami. He puffed at his cigarette as he watched the red pool spread to where her necklace dangled on the floor. He felt uneasy. Stubbing out his cigarette, he walked over and knelt beside her. He brought his cheek close to her nose, and then he was certain: she wasn't breathing. Panicking, he pressed his ear against her chest, but there was no heartbeat. His face contracted with terror as he grabbed her by the shoulders and shook her, but the only result was a fresh spurt of blood from her ear. He felt for her hand, which was already growing cold, and studied her for a moment.

Why had this happened? he asked himself. Was it the red color that made his body move by itself? And why, he wondered bitterly, was life so terribly fragile? Had her skull shattered? It occurred to him that he had committed another crime—that she had fallen down the stairs because he pushed her—but his body had been in the grip of that indescribable force. He reached out and touched the cold skin of her face, overcome with the realization that she was dead.

He wept as the words of the court finding came back to him: "a momentary homicidal frenzy." It had been momentary, but he had not wanted to kill her. His hand had shot out, knocking her down the stairs. It was simply fate, something over which he had no control. He rose, eyes blank and staring, and stumbled back down the stairs without bothering to put on his shoes. The alley was empty. The lights from the street were blurred by his tears. If he had stayed in prison, passing his days between his cell and the print shop, none of this would have happened. In prison he was hidden from prying eyes, alone in his own world; but here there were too many people, too much to worry about. It had been wrong to let him out.

Kikutani walked toward the halfway house, to see Kiyoura. Kiyoura had worked so hard to get him out of prison and back on his feet, and now Kikutani had betrayed that trust. Kikutani had turned a living human being into an unmoving mass—and he wanted to ask Kiyoura why this should have happened. He entered the alley and stopped in front of the building, tears running down his face. Pushing open the door, he peered through the receptionist's window. Kikutani bowed sheepishly as Kiyoura looked up from his desk.

Reading Group Guide

1. In what ways is *On Parole* an investigation of the burdens of freedom and the risks of commitment? How does Yoshimura present those burdens and risks, in relation to Kikutani and others?

2. In what ways do uncertainty, bewilderment, and confusion continue in Kikutani's life after his years in prison? Why is he unable to overcome these impediments to a normal life? Does this inability derive primarily from his years in prison or from his character, or from a combination of the two?

3. What experiences and details of modern life that we take for granted are completely new to Kikutani? How do his reactions prompt us to see details of everyday life in new ways? Why does Yoshimura single out these details?

4. Why is Kikutani unable to feel remorse for his two murders? Why is he, nevertheless, compelled to remember them in such tormenting detail? Standing at Mochizuki's mother's grave, why does he feel only a "sense of satisfaction…at having destroyed Mochizuki's house"?

5. To what extent does Kikutani's state of indefinite parole represent every person's predicament in living and functioning adequately—and with a full sense of self-worth—within society? To what extent do society's rules, by their very nature, preclude Kikutani's—or anyone's—ability to comply with them? How do we deal with the demands and constrictions of society?

6. One reviewer has noted that Kikutani's three primary emotions are rage, fear, and numbness. What does he fear, and why? What, in terms of both the past and the present, prompts his rage, and why does it persist? How does he deal with his fears and his rage? What causes the numbness?

7. In what ways—and why—does Kikutani model his life outside of prison on his life within prison? Why does he have such difficulty in adapting to a life of freedom? In what ways does the chicken farm reflect the conditions of life in prison?

8. Afer his first nervous conversation with Koinuma, Kikutani feels that his past is "still coiled tightly about his heart,…waiting to destroy him." What indications are we given from this point on that his past may destroy him? What decisions and actions on his part shape his "inevitable" fate? What might he have done differently?

9. Even more than three months after being paroled, Kikutani sees the outside world as an "emptiness" and quails before the "vast, borderless expanse known as society." Does he ever lose this sense of emptiness and this view of society? How can society be a "vast, borderless expanse" and, at the same time, a restrictive, rigidly ruled setting for one's life and work?

10. After seeing the "hotel woman" on his way back from the department store, Kikutani decides that "he needed to face squarely what he had done, what his crime meant." What efforts does he make to do so? Does he succeed or fail, and why?

11. Why does Kikutani return to his village and to the graves of his victims? What other meanings of laying his past to rest are open to him?

12. As he sits alone in the village shrine after his detailed recollection of the murders, Kikutani feels "a sudden resolve, a determination to stop hesitating and do things." How is this resolve related to the memory of the murders just narrated? In what ways, since his parole, has he been hesitating and not doing things? What are the results of this sudden resolve?

13. We are told that Kikutani's childhood aversion to pain, suffering, and violence persisted into his adult years. "But if he hated blood and suffering so much, why had he been so calm and collected as he stabbed his wife to death?" How would you answer that question? What was the "unknown element" that "seemed to lurk inside him" and "manifested itself in the red haze"?

14. When he returns to the drastically transformed fishing village of Urayasu, Kikutani has "the unsettling feeling that he had come to some foreign territory." To what extent is his sense of entering a foreign territory the consequence of external changes and to what extent is it the consequence of his crime, of his separating himself from everyday, normal life?

15. What correspondence does Yoshimura show, explicitly or implicitly, among prison life, life as a parolee, and normal everyday life?

16. What role does loneliness play in Kikutani's life, from his childhood through the present?

17. Why does Yoshimura provide so much information about the wholesale egg industry?

18. "They say you committed a crime," Kiyoura says to Kikutani, "but one could almost say instead that the crime happened to you." He then presents his theory of the law and societal rules. To what extent do you agree or disagree with Kiyoura's view of crime, the law, imprisonment, and parole and his attitude toward Kikutani and other parolees? Does Kikutani, as a man who committed two murders and feels no remorse for those murders, deserve the opportunity to become a member of society again?

19. As Toyoko persists in her plans for Kikutani's expression of remorse and his redemption, "he wanted to scream, to tell her not to do this." Why doesn't he tell her not to do it? Why doesn't he tell her how he feels and what he thinks? Is this failure linked back in any way to his relationship with Emiko and her murder?

20. After killing Toyoko, Kikutani weeps "as the words of the court finding came back to him: 'a momentary homicidal frenzy.'…It was simply fate, something over which he had no control." To what extent is this true? What does Yoshimura seem to be saying about the role of fate and personal choices in individual lives?

Written by Hal Hager & Associates, Somerville, New Jersey